THE DEVIL
INCARNATE

JILL BRADEN

WAYZGOOSE PRESS

THE DEVIL INCARNATE
Copyright © 2013 by Jill Braden

Published in the United States by Wayzgoose Press.
Edited by Dorothy E. Zemach.
Maps by Will Mitchell.
Cover design by DJ Rogers.

Printed in the United States

ISBN-10: 1938757084
ISBN-13: 978-1-938757-08-2

TABLE OF CONTENTS

THE SEA OF ERYKOLI

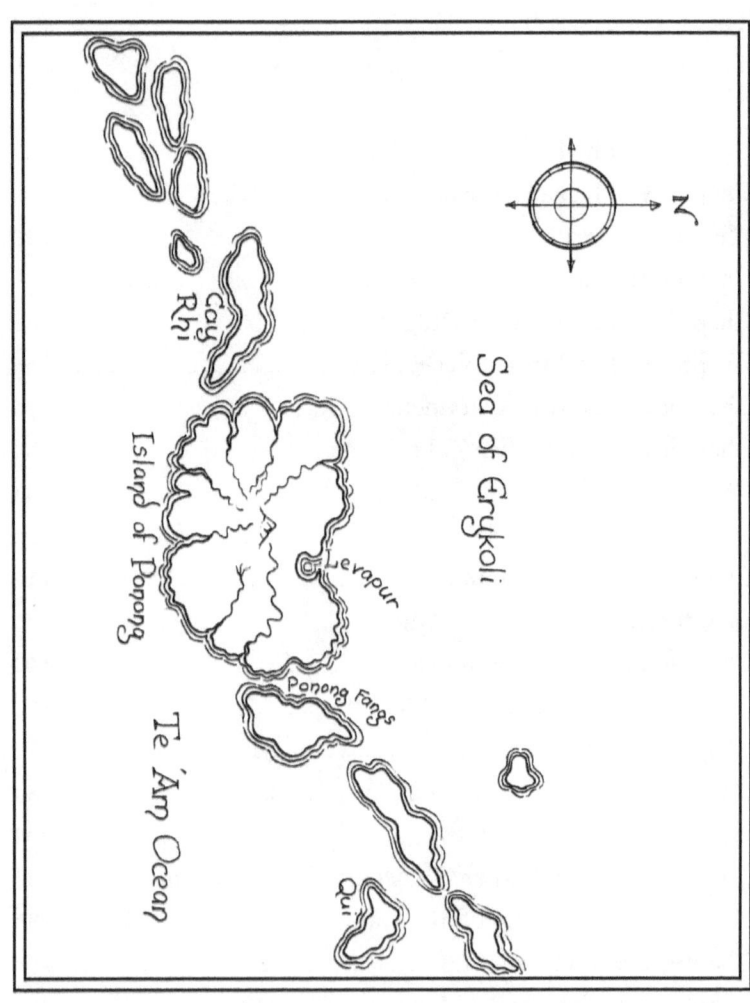

THE ISLAND OF PONONG

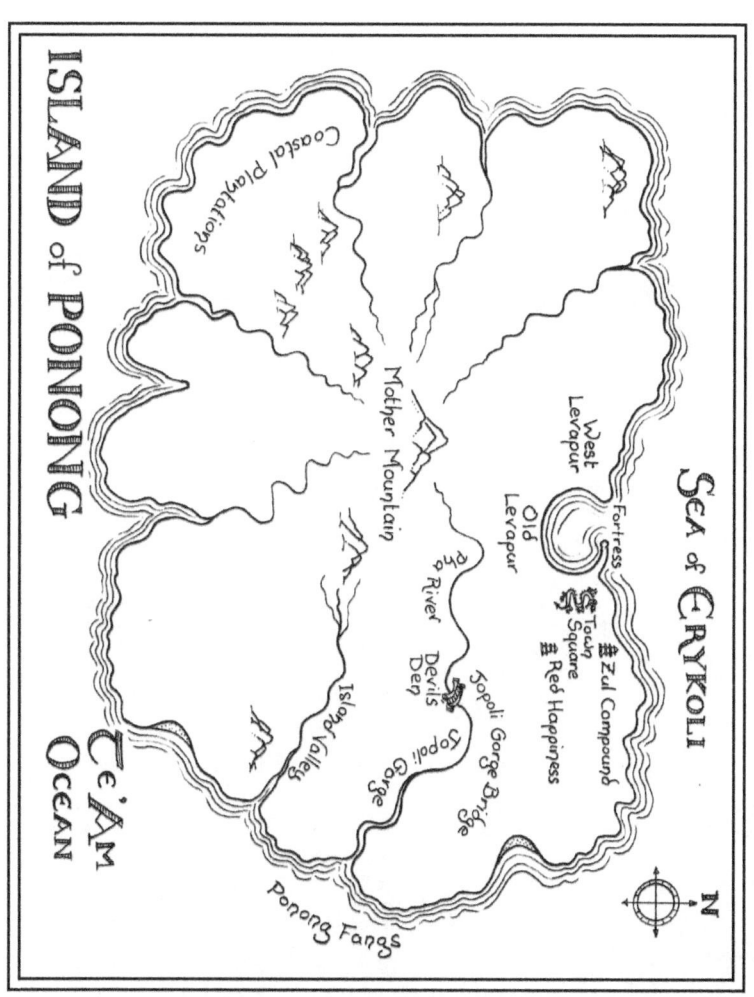

Chapter I : The Plan

The morning QuiTai awoke completely sane, she knew Petrof was dead.

He'd killed her family. He'd eaten her daughter. And he'd tried to kill her too. Three days wasn't nearly long enough for him to suffer, but it would have to do.

Her arms, legs, stomach, and face were raw where she'd scratched at imaginary ants that crawled over her skin on millions of tiny, prickling feet. She hadn't been taught how to shield her mind from the empathic connection with Petrof through her venom. Some would call it sacrilege to try. The goddess Hunt decreed that the Ponongese should feel their prey's suffering, so they'd deliver a quick, merciful death, but QuiTai had enjoyed sharing every moment of Petrof's horror and descent into madness as the jungle consumed him.

Now that her mind was free of him, she had business to attend to. The first step was to get out of bed. Her thick, wavy black hair had come undone from its traditional braid, and every wrinkle in her sarong reminded her of how sour her skin was, but the steady drum of monsoon rain against the shack's tin roof made her want to pull the sheet over her head and drift back into sleep.

The inland shack she'd withdrawn to was smaller than Kyam Zul's apartment, too small to divide into rooms. The shack's only bed was a low, wide cot of woven leather strips. The thin bedroll she'd put on top of it hadn't done much to smooth out the lumps. Days before, she'd told Kyam that her bed had countless pillows, each as comfortable as a lover's lap. There was a bed like that waiting for her, but not on Ponong. She'd have to travel through the mouth of the underworld to reach her hidden estate on the tiny island of Quinong to reach it. The vision of soft sheets tempted her, but she knew there was far too much for her to do in Levapur to run away now.

She forced herself to sit up. Her first step on the bare dirt floor made her wince. The infected werewolf bite on her ankle oozed pus. If she'd been in her right mind the past few days, she would have gathered herbs and cleaned the wound properly. Now it was going to be much harder to heal. Although the weather was soul-sappingly hot, she suspected the dull ache in her bones was the start of a fever.

Each step sent sharp pains up her leg as she hobbled across the room. Three low stools sat around the cooking pit, but she forced herself to stand as she lifted the small iron teapot onto the hook and swung it over the remains of the fire. The fire looked as if it had died, but as she stirred it, bright orange embers glowed in the downy white ashes. She added a small log and a handful of dry leaves. The kindling flamed too quickly to light the log, but the embers she'd banked against it would eventually catch.

There were signs around the shack that hunters had used the remote shelter despite the green symbols painted around the doorway. They hadn't touched her emergency food and water, though. Taboos against violating the trust of communal shelters were stronger inland than they were near Levapur.

While she waited for the water to heat, she went to the doorway and leaned against the threshold. There were no wood screens over the windows. Rain blown inside by gusts of wind turned the dirt floor to mud in places. She combed through her hair knee-length hair and braided it, even though she planned to hobble to the nearby stream and bathe as soon as she had the strength. She didn't consider herself a beautiful woman – not even particularly alluring, despite the many lovers who spouted such nonsense words during their love-making – but she had her vanities. She'd never risk being seen with her hair down as if she were a child, even in this remote place. And she most certainly wouldn't let anyone see her in a wrinkled, filthy sarong.

The shack sat on the north face of Ponong's mother mountain. According to legend, at night the bioluminescent jellyfish floating in mountain's caldera lake cast green light to the stars, but she'd never seen it.

Curious birds with orange heads and bright green breasts watched her from nearby trees, their heads swiveling constantly. From the tracks in the mud and piles of little round black droppings, she guessed a herd of the diminutive island goats had passed this way only a few days before. Perhaps the hunters had been after them, but there was no sign of a kill.

Through a break in the trees, QuiTai looked down into the valley. The wide, shallow river winding between the steep mountain slopes was as gray as the sky. Sheets of rain pocked the surface of the water. She'd seen children play in the river before and knew of two small villages along its banks, but there wasn't a human to be seen there this morning.

Her gaze moved to the smaller mountain across the valley. Agricultural terraces like bands of malachite carved laboriously into the mountain's rock face reached all the way to the peak. The villagers working in the rice paddies would have blended into the scenery if it hadn't been for the pale yellow of their woven hats.

It was a good thing the Thampurians rarely set foot across the Jupoli Gorge Bridge, although they claimed to control the entire Ponong Archipelago. Some day, when they grew brave – or greedier – they might dare to explore the island and discover these and many other forbidden farms. If they thought Levapur was hot and humid, they'd melt in the interior valleys, but the Ponongese couldn't rely on that to keep the Thampurians from stealing the food from their mouths.

She wished nature had provided other deep water routes through the archipelago besides the Ponong Fangs, which separated the island of Ponong from a much smaller island. Or maybe if there hadn't been a natural harbor on the sheltered side of the island, the Thampurians would have left the Ponongese alone. She'd often heard her grandmother ask their gods, "Why us? Why not some other people?"

Gifts from the gods always came with a price.

The whistle of the tea kettle roused her from her thoughts. Although she knew she should drink tiuhon tea to help fight the fever rising in her blood, she chose pale leaves that smelled like fresh grass and sunlight. While it steeped, she went back to the doorway.

Could she be content now that Petrof was dead? Vengeance had robbed her of too much time already. It had made her do unforgivable things. She wanted to let it go, to find peace and move on with her life, but she knew she couldn't. Once people figured out that Petrof was dead and she was still alive, the men who'd hired him to kill her might seek another assassin. She would be foolish to give them the chance. Despite how weary she was of killing, it came down to them or her, and she definitely chose herself.

Taking inventory of her situation, she put into the negative column an ankle that had to be tended to and a colonial militia that would gladly hang her on sight. On the plus side, she was the Devil now. Better than that, she was QuiTai. If there was one thing she excelled at, it was gathering information and digging for the truth. The men who'd hired Petrof didn't stand a chance against her.

She blew a gentle breath over the surface of her tea. Before she tasted it, she glanced at the tin in which it had been stored.

"Maybe the people who stayed here were hunters. Maybe they were hunting me."

To her ears, her voice seemed to crack uncontrollably, like

a teenage boy's.

With a flick of her wrist, the tea flew out of the cup and onto the ground outside the shelter. Several of the tiny birds flew down to see if she'd scattered food, then flew back to their perches and scolded her for fooling them.

"How should I find the men who paid Petrof to kill me?" she asked the birds. "Tell me that, and I'll give you crumbs."

Their trust, once lost, seemingly couldn't be restored. If they knew, they kept the answer to themselves. What she needed was some sage advice. A vision. She slumped against the doorway.

Across the valley, mist swirled over the higher mountain peaks like curls of smoke.

Or vapor.

The corners of her mouth curved.

A plan unfolded in her mind.

CHAPTER 2: THE ZUL COUSINS

Every year at the first sign of monsoon, Thampurians in Levapur stayed home and vowed to wait out the rains. After the third week, tired of staring at their walls and perhaps deciding getting wet was better than throttling their families, they returned to the brothels and gambling dens in the Quarter of Delights.

At the Red Happiness, three people behind the bar filled drinks as fast as they could, and the sex workers rarely spent more than half an hour in the long, narrow room before heading upstairs with a different customer. Even though the rain fell heavily, so many people were on the veranda that wrapped around the first floor of the brothel that most stood in clusters around the wicker chairs. Everyone was in the mood for a party, especially Kyam Zul.

Kyam wore his finest Shewani jacket and trousers. Everything else he owned was packed. Finally, after over a year in exile, he could go home, his dishonor forgiven. He smacked the mosquito that landed on his knuckles, and then smeared the blood and insect away. How he hated this damned island.

He shared a small table with his cousin Hadre. They were tall, broad shouldered, well-educated gentlemen, scions of the most powerful of Thampur's thirteen families. Hadre always looked the part; Kyam didn't usually bother. Hadre wasn't much older than Kyam, but years at sea had etched lines around his eyes and his straight black hair was turning gray at the temples. Kyam's hair had finally been cut properly, although his bangs still fell into his dark eyes, and for the first time in months, he hadn't missed a patch while shaving.

"Business is good," Hadre said. He glanced around the bar with his glass still pressed to his bottom lip.

Kyam wasn't sure how he felt about that. It depended on who profited – the Devil or QuiTai. She'd been right about the records in the government office: They were in such disarray that he hadn't been able to find the deed to the Red Happiness in his short search. Not that it mattered now. If she chose to stay with the Devil, it was no longer his business. Had never been his business. She had certainly made that clear.

He wasn't going to miss the Red Happiness, but he wanted one last look at it before he moved on. No brothel on the continent was so self-indulgently tawdry, but it struck a perfect balance between Thampurian furnishings and colonial decadence. Lewd figurines gleamed under the white-light jellylantern chandeliers that must have cost a fortune. Nowhere else in Levapur, not even the Governor's compound, was that well lit.

A new Ingosolian Madam stood at Jezereet's post on the sweeping staircase that led up to the rooms. That was the only change Kyam could see from before his adventure with QuiTai. But he couldn't help trying to detect something different about it, something he'd missed those many nights and afternoons he'd sat in the bar, painting, drinking, and occasionally going upstairs with one of the workers. As he glanced around, he realized that he was searching for some hint of QuiTai's presence; but the flocked wallpaper and Thampurian furnishings didn't reflect her personality, except that both were meticulously maintained façades.

Kyam tried to think of QuiTai as the aloof, cruel, inscrutable Devil's concubine he'd matched wits with from the first hour he'd set foot in Levapur, because that woman would be much easier to salute as a formidable foe when he left. But the memory he always returned to was of her sitting on the stoop of an apartment building, hugging her knees to her chest. She'd turned to him, offering a rare true smile. She'd said, "There's more. Want to hear it?"

She'd been talking about the crime scene they'd just left and the harbor master's mutilated body – hardly a topic to inspire such a delightfully unguarded moment – but in his dreams, she hinted at something he'd failed to grasp, even though it was probably right in front of him. He only had that one intriguing glimpse of her soul to go on. It wasn't nearly enough, no matter how many times he replayed it in his mind. His answer, then as now, would always be, "Yes. Amaze me."

If only he could find out what had happened after she fled Cay Rhi with some of the slaves. Had she escaped the militia? Was she back with the Devil? And was Petrof still trying to kill her? He at least deserved to say goodbye to her.

"Feeling your rum?" Hadre asked.

Kyam picked up his empty glass and shook his head. "Don't care if I am. I can sleep it off as I sail for home."

"You must be drunk if you've already forgotten what I told you."

Kyam leaned back in his chair and laughed. "You almost had me believing you. Almost."

"I wasn't joking, Kyam. I can't honor your articles of transport." Hadre grabbed his drink and swallowed half of it in one gulp. He made a face then drank the rest.

"But Governor Turyat and Chief Justice Cuulon both signed my papers. I assure you, those signatures are real." Kyam still grinned, but Hadre's grim expression added unwelcome uncertainty to his celebration.

Hadre couldn't even look at him. "There isn't a captain in the Zul fleet who will honor your papers, even if they were signed by the king."

Kyam started to say something, but the deeper meaning behind those words sank in and he closed his mouth. He tried to cling to his joy, but it was fading fast. "Grandfather."

Hadre nodded.

"Why does he always do things this way? He could have just told me himself."

"Because he's a cruel old man who treats his family like tiles to be played."

"Hadre! Respect."

Hadre grabbed his empty glass and lifted it as he turned to catch the bar keep's eye across the room. After his glass was filled, he turned back to Kyam. "And when will he respect you? You're a sea dragon! Grandfather might not have let you follow the sea, but you've been sailing since you were five years old. You know most ships in our fleet better than you know your house back in Surrayya. How can you sit there and accept being landlocked?"

"There must be a good reason." Kyam was growing angry, but not at his grandfather. Hadre had no place talking about the head of their family like that. Grandfather was difficult to please, but he had a right to high expectations of his family. Kyam could recall each time Grandfather had praised him, maybe because there had been so few, but he'd worked hard for those scraps of approval. "It's not our place to question him."

"Underneath all your dash and devil-may-care, you really are a traditional Thampurian at heart, Ky-Ky." Hadre's thick black brows drew together. "A landlocked sea dragon is no better than dirt. I told Grandfather that." Hadre's smile was grim. "Grabbed him by the shoulders and shook him."

Shock left Kyam speechless for a moment. Another thought interrupted before he scolded Hadre for assaulting their Grandfather. "Wait. You didn't have time to sail home and back here in two days. How could you have possibly – " Because he was here, Kyam. Didn't want anyone, even you, to know. Sailed out this morning."

Kyam couldn't believe it. Little of this conversation made sense, and he wasn't drunk enough to be that confused. "And he didn't see me?"

"He gave me a direct order not to tell you that he was here. He didn't have the balls to tell you the bad news to your face, so he ran away and left it to me."

Anger lashed out of Kyam's control. "Are you calling him a coward? How could you be so disrespectful? How could you attack him?"

Hadre tipped his glass back and forth, sending waves of rum close to over-spilling the rim. "Your argument is with Grandfather, not with me. Besides, Grandfather made sure I learned my lesson. He gave the *Golden Barracuda* to cousin Malk and sailed home on it. I'm presently the proud captain of the *Winged Dragon*."

Hadre lost the *Golden Barracuda*? The *Winged Dragon* was the oldest and smallest junk in the Zul fleet. It should have been scuttled decades ago. Being assigned to it was a disgrace almost as bad as exile. But then he remembered what Hadre had done. "Serves you right."

Hadre's temper, always much slower to burn than Kyam's, flared across his face. He leaned over the small table, grabbed Kyam's lapel, and yanked him forward. "You listen to me, cousin." He whispered urgently, but so quietly that Kyam had to strain to hear him over the festivities swirling around them. "I'll bet you never knew that your masters in Intelligence were willing to let you off with censure over the Oin Affair. Grandfather is the one who insisted on exile. And I beg you to remember that obeying Grandfather over your superiors in Intelligence is what got you into trouble with that little caper."

Kyam shook his head. "It wasn't like that – "

"The hell it wasn't. He wanted you in Levapur for a reason, so he set you up to be disgraced and exiled. Now that you've thwarted the Ravidian plot and regained your honor, everything is forgiven back in Surrayya. Intelligence gave you back your rank. But he's ignoring that and treating you as if you're still in disgrace." Hadre let go of Kyam. "He's warned the rest of the thirteen families not to allow you to board their ships either. Face it. He's marooned you here. He took the sea away from you."

Kyam's chair tipped over as he came to his feet. "I know my duty to my family. If he'd asked, I would have told him that I'd obey him and stay here to see his plan through."

"But he didn't ask, did he?"

The Home Port was the only Thampurian-owned tavern Kyam knew of in Levapur. If it hadn't been for the fans churning the stuffy air inside the dim room, it could have been on one of the wide streets bordering Suvat Park back in Surrayya. The authentic Thampurian dishes used imported spices and meat. Anyone who dared order rum would be served whiskey with a scowl. Normally Kyam avoided the place, but tonight he needed the touch of home.

He almost walked out when he saw Major Voorus and three other colonial militiamen at a table. He was their hero now, which was why he planned to sit with his back to them and hope they didn't notice him at the far end of the bar.

Kyam signaled the barkeep to bring him a drink.

He was still torn about Hadre. Maybe he'd visit him in the morning, and they could pretend they'd never had that conversation at the Red Happiness. No; Hadre would have to apologize, first to him, and then to Grandfather. Some things just couldn't be overlooked.

A hand clapped against his back.

"What the hell are you still doing here, Zul?" Voorus asked.

Although Voorus wasn't a member to the Zul clan, Kyam and Voorus looked more alike than even he and Hadre did. It wasn't just their height and build; the shape of their faces and even their noses suggested kinship. Many people had remarked on it.

Kyam wished Voorus would go back to the other soldiers. It wasn't that he disliked the man as a casual acquaintance. Voorus was likeable enough to drink with occasionally, and he'd been a damned good man to fight beside on Cay Rhi. But he'd also tried to execute QuiTai, taken over Kyam's raid of the Ravidian's secret base, and after they'd captured the Ravidians he'd secured the base... Kyam almost snorted. *Secured the base.* QuiTai foresaw that in her odd way of picking at words like a death bird stringing out the guts of carrion. He had no idea how she'd done it. One minute they were hacking their way through the jungle; the next, she was predicting they'd find that the natives of the key had been forced into slavery, and worse, that the colonial militia meant to keep those slaves captive. He hadn't wanted to believe her because it went against everything Thampurians believed in – but she'd been right.

"If I had signed articles of transport, I'd be out of here on the next ship. Hell, I'd shift and swim all the way back to Thampur," Voorus said.

Voorus' breath was sour with drink. His eyelids drooped.

The reality of Kyam's position was sinking in. He couldn't leave Ponong until his grandfather freed him. "I'm going to extend my stay." Kyam was careful not to sound bitter.

"On this filthy island? You're going to need more to drink than that!" Voorus snapped his fingers at the barkeep. "A whiskey for my friend."

"It isn't necessary."

"It is if you're going to stay in Levapur."

For a fleeting moment, Voorus looked sharply aware and focused. He glanced around the tavern. When he sat on the stool next to Kyam, he fidgeted.

One of the soldiers Voorus had been drinking with weaved over to the bar. "Hey Voorus! We're heading over to the Red Happiness. Coming along?" He leaned on the bar for support. "Well, if it isn't Colonel Zul. Finally able to show your face in here?"

Before Kyam could say anything, Voorus whipped around to face the soldier. "Except for the plantation owners, every Thampurian on this island was forced to come here because of some disgrace, Lieutenant. Don't pretend you're here for the weather."

Kyam couldn't see Voorus' face, but his tone made it easy to guess his expression. The young soldier's face mottled as if he choked back his anger. He stumbled away to join his friends.

"I thought you soldiers made it a point of honor to overlook the past," Kyam said when the room grew quiet.

Voorus leaned against the bar on his elbows and seemed to stew over the confrontation. Then he laughed, hollow and joyless, as he shook his head. "Honor." He made a dismissive sound. "What's that?"

An uneasy feeling crept over Kyam. Voorus had the look of a man caught in a moral dilemma, and he seemed drunk enough to want to talk about it. Kyam had heard one man's confession this evening and was in no mood for another.

He looked around the tavern. The other patrons acted with typical Thampurian tact and pretended they hadn't heard or seen anything unusual. Even though the other men didn't seem to be listening, he saw their glances. "Come on, Voorus. Let's take a walk."

If Voorus was drunk, at least he wasn't belligerent. Looking sad now, he nodded and rose. He didn't finish his drink.

Any illusion that they were in Surrayya disappeared as Kyam walked outside into a wall of suffocating heat and humidity. Everywhere he looked, the jungle encroached on Levapur, from ferns sprouting out of cracks in the turquoise stucco to the colony of bats huddled under the canopy of the mango tree to the vine cascading over the roof of the rice merchant's shop.

Voorus walked down the steps from the veranda with a loose, unsteady gait that for a moment made him seem all knees and elbows. Mud splashed on his boot when he stepped into a puddle. "Damn this infernal island," he said, without any anger.

The heat of loathing usually burned out after the first year in Levapur. It took too much energy to keep it going. The weather sapped a man's vigor like a mosquito feasting on his blood. After a while, defeat and drink seemed more practical. It was amazing that more Thampurians in Levapur didn't escape into vapor dream.

Raindrops that shredded umbrellas and stung like sea wasps had pelted the town all day. Now that it was only intermittent drizzle, people rushed to finish their errands before the shops closed. Kyam was glad to see so many people. Maybe the crowds would make Voorus think twice about talking about whatever it was that bothered him.

It didn't.

"It isn't right. I don't care about our orders. I was sworn in to defend the king and our way of life. Don't get me wrong, Zul. I hate these damn snakes. But we should be teaching them how to be civilized, and that means upholding our own laws."

Kyam gestured for Voorus to keep his voice down. They were in a Thampurian neighborhood, but there were plenty of Ponongese around, and they hated being called snakes. Not that they could do much about it, but the past few weeks, even before the Ravidian situation, he'd felt something different about the mood in Levapur and didn't think it was wise to provoke the Ponongese. He couldn't put it in words, but it was as if tension coiled under the surface of the sleepy town. So many times he'd tried to convince himself that it was his imagination, but QuiTai had admitted she sensed it too. He had reason to trust her ability to foresee trouble.

If only he could talk to her! Now that he knew he was stuck on Ponong for a bit longer, he couldn't dismiss his foreboding as someone else's problem. Somehow, he knew that he was going to get caught up in it. Maybe QuiTai, with all her cunning, could see a way to steer him through it unscathed. If he screwed up, he'd never be allowed to return to Thampur. Maybe this was why Grandfather wanted him here. The old man had a way of seeing ahead, just like QuiTai.

Kyam realized Voorus expected him to say something. "Levapur has always been lawless, Voorus. That's part of its charm."

"Charm." Voorus spat into the stream trickling down a rut in the middle of the street.

As they reached the next alleyway, Voorus grabbed Kyam's elbow and looked around them so dramatically that people naturally paid more attention to him. He yanked Kyam behind a staircase.

"My soldiers are back. You know which ones. The men who went missing," Voorus whispered.

Kyam's chest tightened.

Voorus would never have survived in Intelligence. He didn't understand the meaning of the word coy. It was obvious to Kyam that he meant the soldiers who'd chased QuiTai and the slaves when they'd escaped from Cay Rhi.

"Did they catch the people who ran?"

Voorus pulled away. "Can I trust you?"

Here was the moment he'd been dreading since Voorus sat next to him in the tavern. "Probably not." When Voorus scowled at him, he softened his answer with a slight smile. "You're military; I'm intelligence."

The little joke was a mistake. Voorus seemed even more determined to unload his thoughts on Kyam. He plucked at Kyam's sleeve like a child wanting attention while he whispered, "My men realized they were in enemy territory, so they gave up the search. It took them a couple days to find their way back to civilization – if you can call this town civilized." He took a deep breath. "Some of the militia think the snakes should be held captive, but some of us... It's wrong, Zul. Wrong."

Shocked, Kyam stared at Voorus. Fear seemed to have sobered the man. Could it be that Voorus had a sense of moral right and wrong after all? He was ashamed that he'd thought so poorly of him. "Have you told anyone what they did?"

Voorus looked at him as if he had gone insane. "They'd hang my men."

"Then why, for the love of deep water, did you tell me?"

"Because I think you knew what the Devil's whore planned to do, and you let her. I think you agree with me. I think you're a real patriot too."

Kyam searched Voorus' face for any hint of cunning. He realized that Voorus was looking at him for the same sign. Trust was an awful lot to ask. On Cay Rhi they'd had each other's backs, but that was against the Ravidians. Now it was

Thampurian against Thampurian.

Which was the real treason? Refusing to follow orders, or betraying the principles you'd sworn to uphold? Kyam saw that Voorus knew the right answer, but was he willing to put his life on the line for that principle? He obviously wanted to know the same thing about Kyam. As if he could spend all night waiting in the stinking alleyway for an answer, Voorus' pleading gaze never left Kyam's face.

One of them had to break the silence. Since Voorus was the one who wanted to talk, he did. "I know that you hate her, Zul, so the way I figure it, you feel the same way I do about the slaves. Otherwise, you would have let us take the Devil's whore captive on Cay Rhi."

Kyam had to be careful. As Voorus pointed out, theirs were treasonous acts, if only by failure to act. A man in trouble might turn over anyone to save his own neck.

"So she and the escaped slaves are somewhere on this island," Kyam said slowly to buy himself time to think. If Voorus was telling the truth, QuiTai had eluded the soldiers and gotten away. A burden lifted from his soul. He'd known he was worried about her fate, but he hadn't realized how tightly his nerves had been knotted as he'd awaited news. If only she'd sent him some sign. But where the slaves only had to dodge the soldiers, there was more danger lurking in the jungle for her. Maybe her luck ran out. She couldn't outsmart everyone forever.

"You know what worries me?" Voorus asked.

Dear Goddess of Mercy, there was more? Wasn't the threat of death enough? "What?"

"The Devil's whore has three days' head start on us."

Kyam had no idea where Voorus' thoughts were headed.

"Why hasn't she done anything?" Voorus asked.

Kyam's brow furrowed. "What do you expect her to do?"

Voorus shrugged. "You know her reputation as well as I do. She's capable of any brutality. We know she has separatist sympathies. And think about this – there are only about eighteen hundred Thampurians on this island, and that's if you count the plantation owners. There are thousands of Ponongese, and they hate us. You can see it in their eyes. They're just waiting for any excuse to slaughter us, and she has that excuse, Zul. We gave it to her! For all we know, she's touring the island with those escaped slaves and whipping the Ponongese in the remote villages and outer islands into an army. We know how bloodthirsty these savages are. They tore those werewolves apart with their bare hands on the steps of the government building for their part in the Full Moon massacre." He nodded sharply. "Think on that."

Kyam's stomach lurched. He hadn't been in Levapur when that had happened, but QuiTai's description of the carnage had been enough. And he knew how casually she reacted to death, how ruthless she could be, and how much she hated Thampurian rule of her home.

"You should have let me throw her into that cell with the werewolves when I had the chance," Voorus said.

He was surprised no one had demanded an explanation about that from him yet. At least he'd had time to work on a good excuse. "She alone knew where to find the Ravidians. I needed her alive."

Voorus nodded. "Well, obviously. I didn't think you'd let her go without a damned good reason."

Hopefully, if anyone else asked, they'd accept his explanation as easily as Voorus had.

Voorus grasped Kyam's sleeve tighter and pulled him back out onto the road. People picked their way across puddles in the street. The Ponongese boys toting their packages waded right through the muck.

Voorus seemed headed somewhere in particular, but if he wanted to go to the fortress, they'd turned the wrong way. "It would have been better if my men had killed them all – the slaves and her. Then we wouldn't be in this mess. The slaves aren't the problem. They let themselves be put in chains, after all. No leadership there. No spirit. Typical Ponongese. But her... She's dangerous. You can see that crafty native cunning in her shifty eyes. Thankfully, Petrof is still out there, waiting for his chance. Once he kills her, we're safe."

Now Kyam really wished he could talk to QuiTai, but

he wasn't helpless on his own. He was a spy, a colonel in the Intelligence community. Some people whispered that he'd risen to his rank through connection, but he knew how hard he'd worked to earn his position. He could figure this out without QuiTai. He was smart. He knew how to investigate. If only he were as quick to see the bigger picture as QuiTai was. He had a bad feeling that lag might be the difference between weathering the coming storm and falling victim to it.

His mouth was dry as he asked the terrible question that hovered over the moment. "What makes you think Petrof hasn't killed her already?"

"He would have collected his reward by now. They haven't said anything about that."

Someone paid Petrof to kill QuiTai? He realized he was just seeing the clouds when the typhoon was almost on them. "Who are 'they'?" Kyam asked.

Voorus stopped at a yellow apartment building on the edge of the Thampurian neighborhood. It was in much better repair than the one Kyam lived in. "Like I said, slavery is wrong, and no amount of justification from my superiors will make me betray the basic tenants of Thampurian law, but I'll be damned if I'll stand by and let these snakes slaughter every last Thampurian on this island. I guess it's a good thing that troop of soldiers came from Thampur on your grandfather's boat. We're going to need their numbers." He searched through his pockets. "If I were you, Zul, I'd sleep armed, and I'd move out of that apartment of yours. That place is crawling with snakes. Meanwhile, the Zul compound across town sits empty." He found his key in the breast pocket of his uniform jacket. "I never could figure your motive; unless you're collecting intelligence on them. But do you have to live among them to do that? Hell, I'd move back into the barracks if those new soldiers hadn't taken over every spare bed in the fortress. It might be damp and the cots are lumpy, but at least I'd have a couple feet of stone between me and the snakes when the slaughter begins."

CHAPTER 3: DREAMERS

QuiTai resisted licking her cracked lips as long as she could. When her skin didn't burn, chills wracked her body, but she didn't have time to be ill. There were no rumors yet that the soldiers who had chased her and the escaped slaves from Cay Rhi had returned to Levapur, but they could at any moment, and then the hunt for her and the slaves would begin again.

Earlier in the evening, she'd slipped into the Dragon Pearl's second-story vapor den. The Dragon Pearl's owner, Lizzriat, wouldn't allow a Ponongese past her front door, but QuiTai hadn't needed a front door, or stairs, to get inside. She'd climbed onto the veranda but stayed outside in the deeper shadows around the back of the building. It was unlikely that anyone would come outside, even though the veranda was covered. There was an apartment building across the way, but the carved wood shutters were closed tight against the rain, and from the darkness behind them she guessed the interior shutters were closed too.

The rain had been falling all day, but the drops now were

like lead fishing weights that pummeled the roof. The faint green light from the jellylanterns inside the den was no match for the fading twilight.

On the street below, people waded through the rising muddy water coursing downslope, their expressions shifting between resignation and impatience, while the addicts headed for the Dragon Pearl were seemingly oblivious to the deluge. They made no attempt to stay dry. They probably hadn't eaten dinner, because the need for vapor was always stronger than any other hunger. They would pass by the gambling tables on the first floor and walk up the stairs. Some would sprint.

QuiTai peered between the slats of the typhoon shutters to watch the shadowy outlines of customers enter the den. They took delicate pipes from velvet-lined cases and jostled for their turn to cook the black lotus over the small spirit lamps. As the tar melted, they climbed on the raised platform along the wall and sucked the vapor into their lungs. One by one, they slipped into dream. Some would be lost to the vapor for hours; the heavily addicted would rise for another pipe sooner.

QuiTai opened the shutters and crept into the den. The reek of black lotus hung in the stuffy air. Pipes cluttered the tables around the still burning oil lamps. Overhead, ceiling fans churned sluggishly in the heat as if they knew their efforts were wasted.

If they hadn't been so addicted, the dreamers probably would have grumbled about the lack of a mattress on the crowded communal bed against the wall. They didn't even have pillows. Thampurian sensibilities had no place here. They sprawled together in a tangle of limbs. Some mumbled. A few stared into the darkness, but if they saw her, they only knew her as part of their dreams.

QuiTai's eyelids drooped. She rubbed her face. The deep pink sea wasp scar on her hand was hotter than the rest of her palm. At least it didn't hurt anymore, but the rest of her body simply ached. She wanted to sleep more than she'd ever wanted anything.

QuiTai kicked empty vials out of her way. They rolled

across the scuffed floor.

She coaxed the nearest man into swallowing a few precious drops of her venom. The vision the Oracle brought her through him was useless. She didn't care that the man was embezzling money from the bank where he clerked. She needed the name of the person who had paid Petrof to kill her and her family.

The connection to the conduit would break when the small dose of her venom worked through his system, but with time so precious, she decided not to wait. She dosed a second dreamer while still connected to the first.

QuiTai had never tried to use two conduits in such a short span of time, and now she understood why it was a bad idea. The thoughts of both stumbled through her mind as she tried to focus on the Oracle. The dissonance of the dreamers' thoughts made her dizzy. She gripped the edge of the pallet and pulled deep breaths through her nose. Mind reeling, she waited for the Oracle to speak.

The second vision came, but it was as useless as the first.

Please, Goddess, if I offended you, forgive me. But I need this vision. I need an answer.

Maybe she was a masochist, but she had to try one more time before she gave up. With Petrof dead, she no longer had a conduit at hand. She had to make the most of this night and the den's supply of dreamers.

At least the connection to the first had grown weak enough that she could barely sense him. The second conduit was also fading a bit. It would be a couple hours before their minds completely separated from hers, but with each passing minute, her head and stomach felt better. Now if she could only cool the blistering heat under her skin.

All of the dreamers were Thampurian. With so many to chose from, and only one last chance to get it right, she searched through them for someone who might tempt the Oracle to say something useful. From their clothes, the dreamers in this room were merchants and low-level clerks. Perhaps that was her mistake. The few times she'd summoned the Oracle through a Thampurian, her chosen conduit to the goddess had been a member of the inner circle of the colonial government.

Except the harbor master's brother. He'd been dirt, the lowest a Thampurian sea dragon could get, yet the vision the Oracle had brought through him had been so strong.

She tugged at her bottom lip. Perhaps it was because he had been dying at the time. After all, a proper summoning of the Oracle always ended with the death of the conduit. She'd accidently discovered black lotus as a substitute for the poisonous red paste the Qui used in their ceremonies. While it wasn't harmless, at least black lotus didn't kill. At least not quickly. No. It took years.

A wave of grief overcame her.

Jezereet had known the danger. She'd chosen the vapor. QuiTai rubbed a tear into her cheek. She didn't have time for emotions. Sniffling slightly, she frowned at herself and bent over the dreamer with his head near the edge of the pallet. Her fangs sprang from behind her upper teeth. They felt much lighter now that she'd used so much of her venom.

This one's lips were deep red, and his clothes, while still in good repair, looked as if they belonged to a stouter man. Those were sure signs of a long-term user. Perhaps her mistake had been picking dreamers who weren't deeply addicted. The dirt Thampurian had been a heavy user. Yet Petrof, who had been her main conduit to the Oracle the past few years, had taken the vapors only occasionally.

She could mull this over later. When the Thampurian soldiers returned – if they returned – she'd have plenty of time to reflect while in hiding.

She took deep breaths and steeled herself for the trial to come. If only she could wait an hour; but by then the dreamers would be rousing, and she didn't want to wait for one to take a second pipe.

QuiTai pressed her mouth to the chosen dreamer's. Her tongue slipped between his lips and pried them open. His breath stank like a bloated corpse. She milked two drops of her venom from her fangs and let them slide onto his tongue. Any more than that could be dangerous, not that anyone would suspect venom if he died. Without puncture marks from her fangs, they'd think he was simply another black lotus addict lost forever to the vapor.

She pushed another dreamer onto his side to make space for her to sit on the edge of the pallet. He rolled back with a sigh. His arm flopped over her thighs. Glaring at him was useless; he didn't know she was there.

QuiTai turned her attention to her chosen conduit. He swallowed. She felt the bob in her throat. Exhaustion swept over her and her mind went blank for a moment, but she couldn't be sure if it was she or the dreamer causing the void.

Her thoughts jolted to a dream. She floated through a stylish continental casino. The black and white floor tilted so sharply she should have slipped, but she had no problem walking across it. She was sure she stood upright, but so did the woman in the skeletal hoop skirt who walked on the wall. The laugher of grotesquely distorted gamblers and prostitutes seemed to come from another room in muffled waves. A powdered face, green in the glow of a jellylantern, popped up inches from her. The lips were obscenely red. She reeled back.

Forcing herself to touch on reality, she put her hand to her chest, as if that would push down the tiny bubble of panic rising through her ribs. As she'd been taught, she reminded herself that it was his dream that she saw. Every Qui had her own mantra to ground her. QuiTai repeated hers with eyes shut tight. Her parched lips moved as she exhaled the words.

The conduit's dreams meandered like Kirith Diaal celebrants stumbling through a darkened maze. Now they were out of the casino. Her stomach lurched as they moved to the deck of a ship, but quickly whisked away to him frolicking in the sea with another sea dragon in their shifted forms. She felt the slide of a long, scaled body against hers. The intention was clear as its coils wrapped around her.

QuiTai was no prude, but she really didn't want to take part in his dream encounter. Sexual fantasies tended to jolt from scene to scene, sometimes replaying the smallest part many times. Besides, that slither of a muscular, scaled body against hers reminded her too much of Kyam Zul, and she couldn't be distracted by thoughts of him right now. She pushed past the conduit's dreams and into his memories.

She heard footsteps. Not sure if it was part of the memory she'd connected to, she opened her eyes.

In the real world, an Ingosolian slid open the den's door. Her eyes widened when she saw QuiTai, but she didn't make a sound. She slipped in and quietly slid the door closed behind her. She took her time drawing the latch before turning her head and watching QuiTai from the corner of her eye.

QuiTai didn't dare suck in the breath for which her lungs burned. She knew that this Ingosolian, Lizzriat, wasn't Jezereet. Jezereet was dead. Petrof had killed her when she'd stopped him from strangling QuiTai. Her body had been shipped back to Rantuum several days ago. She knew that Jezereet was dead. She'd closed her beloved's eyes. But Lizzriat's soft, pale blue cheek in profile, framed by rampant shoulder-length paprika curls, was like a glimpse of Jezereet ages ago, before she'd taken the vapor, back when she was the toast of the stage on the continent; and it hurt, how it hurt when a tiny sliver of hope and denial stabbed her heart.

Ingosolians outside Ingosol usually chose to shift to a conforming gender aspect for safety's sake. There was never a female as curvaceous or a male as broad-shouldered and firm-jawed as an Ingosolian living in another country. They found other cultures' obsession with gender absurd and loved to mock it. That mischievous streak was just one of the many things QuiTai adored about them. Lizzriat, however, chose an androgynous aspect, as if she were in Ingosol, where being any gender for an extended period was considered eccentric. Even thinking of Lizzriat in terms of gender was dangerously close to an insult. Since the workers at the Red Happiness almost always chose to shift feminine, QuiTai often referred to all Ingosoloians as female – but that was a limitation imposed by the Ponongese and Thampurian langauges. It was simply impossible to refer to someone as just a person, and only an ignorant, boorish fool would be low enough to refer to another person as 'it.' So even though Lizzriat's vest, white shirt, and trousers were cut in a masculine silhouette , QuiTai thought of Lizzriat as female. The effect of the foppish suit, to QuiTai's way of thinking, was far more enticing and sensual than a purely male or female form.

Everything about the Ingosolians was beautiful.

Jezereet had always claimed that black lotus made QuiTai amorous, even poetic. QuiTai remembered no such thing, but as long as she was connected to the conduits, she too was under the influence of the vapor. If Jezereet had been telling the truth, she had better keep tight control over her thoughts of Lizzriat.

Lizzriat turned slowly but kept her hand on the door. "I'm surprised to see you here, Lady QuiTai."

"I won't stay long." QuiTai bit the insides of her cheeks and pinched her arms to help her focus.

"Perhaps, if I knew what you wanted... " Her long fingers extended an invitation for QuiTai to speak.

"Right now, only that you don't summon the soldiers who are no doubt downstairs at your gaming tables. I realize that I'm asking for a huge favor, given our history."

"We've never been enemies," Lizzriat said.

"Nor are we friends."

Petrof had often commented that QuiTai was a consummate liar. That was true, but she also made it a habit to speak blunt truths because Thampurians loved to dance around a subject for hours. It always shocked them when she went straight to the heart of the matter. She enjoyed their dismay and embarrassment. Lizzriat's eyes shone though, as if she were enjoying a private joke. Jezereet had often reacted the same way to QuiTai's attempts to shock her.

QuiTai folded her hands on her lap. "If the soldiers knew a Ponongese was here and that you failed to report me, they'd close this place. Maybe arrest you. At the least, they'd levy a hefty fine before you could open your doors again. It would be unforgivable of me to hurt your profits like that."

That should be enough to warn her to keep her distance from me.

Lizzriat chuckled. "So it seems that all I have to gain by reporting you is harm to my business. I'm not that stupid."

"I'm still endangering you. I want you to know that I recognize the risk that I pose to you, and the debt implied."

Lizzriat inclined her head slightly, acknowledging the debt rather than denying it. She crossed the room and extinguished the oil lamps. "Let me worry about the soldiers, Lady QuiTai. I hold too many of their markers for them to get greedy about payoffs."

"All the more reason to hang you."

Lizzriat's faint smile drew into a serious line. In the green glow of the jellylanterns, her bluish skin appeared the color of a warm lagoon. "So stop endangering me. Tell me what you're looking for. I will help you, if only to get you out of here sooner."

QuiTai held up a finger. "I may have it in a moment."

While she didn't think Lizzriat would summon the soldiers, QuiTai was still glad that she'd already shared her venom with the dreamer. It wasn't a lack of trust in the Dragon Pearl's owner... QuiTai almost laughed out loud at her thoughts. Of course she didn't trust Lizzriat. There were very few people who'd earned that honor. Lizzriat probably didn't trust her either, with good cause. QuiTai owned the Red Happiness brothel, but most people assumed the Devil did. The thinking, QuiTai assumed, was that if the Devil were willing to muscle into a legal business like the brothels, surely he'd turn his interest to the gambling dens next. That would explain why the owners of the gambling dens flinched when QuiTai walked in.

Or maybe it didn't.

No, there was no love lost between her and Lizzriat, although they treated each other with careful respect. Still, baring her fangs to a Thampurian, even one lost to the vapor, was punishable by death. It was safer that Lizzriat didn't know what she'd done.

She lightly placed her hand on the dreamer's chest and leaned over his body. Thankfully, they still had a connection. QuiTai closed her eyes again. Her conduit's dreams had fractured and now floated on a vast void inside his mind. She'd been in that oblivion. Most people who used black lotus spoke of that place in hushed voices that betrayed their longing to return.

She loathed it. Her conduit wanted to sink further into it. She forced herself not to fight her way out since she might drag him to consciousness. While he drifted, she imagined a place where she could hold onto solid reality and bridge through him to the Oracle. She caught onto a memory and dragged herself out of his void.

She bit her rough lips. The temptation to ask the Oracle a question almost overwhelmed her.

"Never ask the goddess. She will bring you a vision of what she wants you to see," her mother and grandmother had lectured.

QuiTai exhaled slowly and opened herself to the vision.

Grief and anger rushed over her. She caught glimpses of a Thampurian woman. One moment the woman was young and happy, the next older and suspicious. The woman was sad and angry that her husband addicted himself to black lotus. He was angry with her for trying to stop him from taking the vapor, but he didn't have the strength to pour his fury out on her. Impotent in many ways, all he could do was let the rage, and black lotus, slowly eat his soul and body.

In a voice not his own, he said, "She will marry the rice merchant days after my funeral."

The Oracle had spoken.

QuiTai's shoulders slumped. She opened her eyes. Why would the Oracle want her to know that? All this trouble for another useless vision. She was so damn tired. The hot, stuffy room didn't help. She turned to Lizzriat. "I'm sorry to have endangered you for that." Her hand flicked toward the dreamer dismissively.

Lizzriat seemed puzzled. "For what?"

QuiTai cocked her head as she regarded Lizzriat. "Didn't you hear him speak?"

Lizzriat shook her head.

QuiTai wished she had enough venom left to use Lizzriat as a conduit. Maybe then she'd know if she lied. But what little she had left she might need to defend herself.

"Did his lips move?"

Lizzriat's paprika curls fell into her eyes as she shook her head.

There were times when QuiTai swore she could feel time slow. Her pulse boomed at half the speed of her normal heart beat. Or perhaps it was because her mind sped up and she could see things at an accelerated pace.

This was interesting beyond measure, if the Ingosolian told the truth. Could it be that the Oracle spoke directly into her mind? She tried to think back to when she'd been very young and she'd witnessed the Qui priestesses summon the Oracle. Had the conduit's mouth moved then? She couldn't remember. They'd taken a tiny drop of her venom and mixed it with theirs so that she'd been connected too.

She put on one of her resigned smiles with a tiny overtone of chagrin, so Lizzriat would think she was a little embarrassed. "That's the problem with vapor addicts. Sometimes they ramble. Other times, they say nothing."

"So you didn't find it?" Lizzriat frowned as she bowed her head as if deep in thought.

"No. But I will go anyway. May your rice bowl always be full, Lizzriat."

Lizzriat didn't seem relieved that she was leaving.

QuiTai set aside her musings over the Oracle and concentrated on the now. The Ingosolian seemed to be holding something back. "Is there a favor I could do for you in return, since you've been so accommodating?"

Lizzriat drew in a long breath. So there was something, but not a question that came easily. QuiTai waited for her to work up the courage.

"I was warned never to approach you, but the werewolves were hanged."

QuiTai suddenly had a clear understanding of the problem Lizzriat feared to speak about. "You're running out of black lotus."

The tension in Lizzriat's shoulders eased.

The regular black lotus distribution had ended when the werewolves were arrested and executed. How interesting that no one bought enough to last more than a few days; or maybe they couldn't resist smoking all they had once they'd taken the vapor.

QuiTai had run every facet of the Devil's organization except the black lotus trade. Petrof expressly forbade any dealer to allow her to buy it, and made an example of the one who'd dared break his rule. It had been his way of controlling Jezereet, and through Jezereet, hurting QuiTai. But now Petrof was dead, and QuiTai had reclaimed the criminal enterprise she'd built for him. There was no one left to stop her from controlling the black lotus trade.

"Could you tell the Devil — ask the Devil, if he could send someone? I'd be grateful." While her words were polite enough, QuiTai could hear what it cost Lizzriat's pride to speak like that.

QuiTai had no doubt that gratitude was grudging at best, but it explained Lizzriat's reluctance to summon the soldiers more than any supposed friendship between them. "No harm will come to you for mentioning the black lotus to me. Since his werewolves were arrested, the Devil has been rethinking some parts of his organization. I will remind his new dealers to bring you some."

"Tonight?"

QuiTai hated to disappoint a customer, even though it meant tracking down LiHoun and asking him to find someone, anyone, in the Devil's network who dealt black lotus.

What a surprise that there actually was one downside to Petrof's demise. It bothered her that she was uninformed, and that for nearly a week that segment of her business had been neglected. The profits on black lotus alone... Not to mention that at any sign of weakness in the Devil's organization, others would try to muscle in. She'd have to retaliate, of course, and regain control by any means necessary, but she preferred to avoid that. She had to figure out that end of the business, and she had to do it now.

"I will see what I can do." QuiTai never promised what she wasn't sure she could deliver.

Lizzriat nodded sharply. She clearly disliked being in QuiTai's debt.

QuiTai rose and crossed the room. Her limp was growing worse. A warm trickle oozed down her ankle into her sandal. She was hot and miserable and the sharp edge of her brain felt dulled, but she couldn't let that show. "I have a favor to ask of you in return."

"So many favors traded in one night. How will we keep score?"

QuiTai's fingertips barely brushed against Lizzriat's arm. It was so cool to the touch that she wanted to place her hands on it and absorb the sensation. Lizzriat didn't pull away as she expected. "Please be kind enough to check the hallway for me so I can slip down the back stairs."

Lizzriat slid the door open a few inches and peered out. She sucked in a breath as she quickly closed it. "Governor Turyat and Chief Justice Cuulon are in the hallway – looking for me, no doubt. They take a private room, but they might come in here if I don't go to them. You have to leave. Now!"

QuiTai reached past her and pushed the door open a fraction of an inch. She pressed her ear to the door jamb.

"She's still out there! She can ruin us!" the Chief Justice said. QuiTai knew his voice too well.

Lizzriat tried to tug the door closed. The silent but determined struggle made it almost impossible for QuiTai to concentrate on the Chief Justice's and the Governor's conversation. If only Lizzriat would stop fighting her, there would be no reason for their bodies to be pressed so close, with so much enticing squirming.

Focus. The Chief Justice and Governor.

Of all the corrupt officials in the colonial government, these two would be in the best position to know who had paid Petrof to kill her and her family. She should have waited to use them as conduits – after all, they were frequent customers of the Dragon Pearl's den. This fear was muddling her brain more than she cared to admit.

"If only Zul hadn't tricked us into taking slaves – "

That voice had to be Governor Turyat.

"Shut up!"

Zul tricked them into taking slaves? They couldn't mean Kyam Zul, could they? Hadre? No. A name clicked into her mind. Grandfather Zul. She could believe he was involved. From the little she knew through Kyam, his grandfather was a sneaky, conniving, manipulative master of intrigue.

She simply had to meet this man.

But what was this about tricking them into taking slaves? It had been their idea, hadn't it? She tried to remember the exact words of her conversation with Kyam on the deck of the *Golden Barracuda*, but couldn't recall it well enough. She forced herself to let it go, for now. Eventually it would come to her. Right now, she had more pressing problems.

The violent whispers continued. "This is no time to get lost in the vapor, Turyat. She's escaped, she has the slaves, and she could bring us down at any second. We have to find her!"

Lizzriat and QuiTai stared into each other's eyes as their silent fight for control over the door waged on. Lizzriat suddenly gripped the back of QuiTai's head and pulled her close for a kiss. The slide of her tongue over QuiTai's fangs sent strong, pleasant sensations through QuiTai's body.

Lizzriat wasn't the only one who knew a few lover's tricks. With her fingertips, QuiTai lightly stroked the inside of Lizzriat's wrist until she gasped and let go of QuiTai. She tugged hard on the door, but QuiTai didn't let go.

"That usually works for me," Lizzriat whispered.

QuiTai swore she could still feel Lizzriat's tongue. "I could say the same. But you're welcome to try again." Jezereet had never done anything like that.

"I think, instead... " Lizzriat's fingernails dug into the scar on QuiTai's palm.

Pain she hadn't felt in days burned through the welt.

"We're ruined. Ruined!" was the last thing QuiTai heard before Lizzriat won the battle over the door.

QuiTai gently rubbed the deep pink scar line, even though that didn't make it feel better. "Ooh. You fight dirty." Her gaze traveled down to Lizzriat's dapper half-boots and back up to her eyes. "I approve."

"Normally I wouldn't care, Lady QuiTai, but I'm glad you do, because you strike me as a vindictive sort."

"Such cruel words." QuiTai clasped her hands over her heart. "Alas, as you well know, it's time for me to go. But, um..." She flicked her tongue over her lips as her gaze made a rather pointed journey from the ruffles of Lizzriat's shirt to the last button of her waistcoat. The corners of her lips curved. "Mmm."

She'd let Lizzriat decide what that might have meant.

QuiTai limped past the stirring dreamers to the typhoon shutters. Rain fell so heavily that she could only see the outline of the building across the street. She gripped the veranda post and found a tenuous toe-hold in the intricate carving before climbing down.

By the time QuiTai dropped into the ankle-high muddy water that ran through the street, her clothes were soaked. She lifted the hem of her sarong above the torrent as she limped upslope toward PhaJut's brothel, where she hoped to find LiHoun.

CHAPTER 4: PHAJUT

QuiTai slipped through the back alley doorway into PhaJut's brothel in the Quarter of Delights. Like the Red Happiness, PhaJut's place catered mostly to foreigners, although his sex workers were all Ponongese.

The sour smell of the old building made her nose wrinkle. Stacks of broken furniture crowded the dark back hallway, as they had when she'd worked there. She ducked into the brothel's kitchen and handed the cook a few coins to fetch LiHoun, since she didn't dare let the customers see her. Then she crossed the hall to PhaJut's office to wait. If PhaJut objected to her visit, too bad. Her rapidly dwindling supply of tact had been nearly depleted in the Dragon Pearl.

Luckily, he wasn't in his office. It was a small, dimly lit room with a desk and only one chair – he'd always liked to make his visitors stand. There wasn't much on his desk, not because PhaJut was an orderly person, but because brothels, while legal, tended to be secretive businesses. Her desk at the Red Happiness was also bare.

She moved the desk chair close to the window before she

sat and faced the door. Just this one little piece of business and then she could rest. Her chin sank toward her chest. She jerked back her head and opened her eyes wide. Lethargy crept over her. She bit her lip and stretched her arms.

Quiet footsteps headed down the hallway. She rose and perched on the window sill in case she had to make a quick escape. The door creaked open. LiHoun peered into the room. Seeing her, he slipped in and shut the door behind him.

The bandy-legged old cat man drew close to her. He pressed his hands together and whispered, "Have you eaten, grandmother QuiTai?" His vertical pupils were so enlarged that the muted jungle green of his irises were mere halos.

"Yes, and you, favored uncle?"

"Well enough."

That was an unusually short answer for him.

"Is something the matter?" Her tone was sharper than she'd meant it to be. "Forgive me, LiHoun. I'm not at my best tonight."

Her hands clenched into fists as she tried to stop the sideways slip of her mind. Damn that conduit back at the Dragon Pearl for taking another pipe! Damn her venom for lingering in his system and keeping them connected now that she had no use for him. He was dragging her under, against her will, into vapor dream again.

LiHoun's unblinking gaze grounded her. "I can smell sickness on you," he said.

She showed him her ankle. "The werewolf bite isn't healing."

"My women… "

"I put your family in enough danger when – " She wouldn't finish that sentence, but he had to know she meant when she'd sent the escaped slaves to his house the night they'd run from Cay Rhi. "Anyway, we have business to discuss. The Dragon Pearl is almost out of black lotus. I doubt anyone has received a delivery since the werewolves were executed."

LiHoun nodded. "It's the talk of the runners in the quarter. Everyone is looking for a source. Some say the Devil is holding back to drive up prices. They're all worried."

"I should have foreseen this."

"I had hoped to discuss it with you as soon as I heard the rumors, but you were still in hiding. I took the liberty of making inquiries and found the werewolves' suppliers. They're anxious to move their merchandise. Some are talking about going directly to the customers."

"I have to fix this. Tonight."

"If I may be so bold, it seems that your area lieutenants would be happy to add that business to the rice and other contraband. They always grumbled about the werewolves having it to themselves."

Until recently, she'd only used LiHoun as a source of information. He'd proved himself resourceful by meeting with the black lotus dealers. Perhaps he should be trusted with more duties, for which she'd pay him generously. "You may always be so bold, favored uncle, and your thoughts mirror mine. What was the werewolves' mark-up on the black lotus?"

"Thirty percent."

"Tell my lieutenants to increase that to thirty-five percent."

"Won't that give the smugglers more reason to go directly to the customers?

"Our customers have already imagined a higher price due to the sudden scarcity of black lotus. They'll be grateful we aren't greedy enough to demand more. And five percent isn't enough to tempt the smugglers. Not for the work it would take to find customers and keep someone here to run the day-to-day business."

"Or to risk angering the Devil," he said.

"You might want to remind them of that when you negotiate an actual purchase, if you are so inclined as to take on that responsibility." If he refused, her long night would drag on until well after the sun rose. It was still early in the evening, but the hour already felt late. She hated the sense of urgency. Mistakes happened when she rushed.

LiHoun pressed his palms together and bowed low. "I am honored, grandmother."

He'd always been willing to help her. It wasn't just the coin she spent freely for his information; they'd always worked well together because, unlike most Ponongese and Thampurians, she didn't care about LiHoun's ancestry. He had her respect and she let him know it.

"Before you agree, you must know what I require of you. The Dragon Pearl needs a delivery tonight. Lizzriat was helpful to me, and a gesture is called for."

The prospect of going out in the rain to find one of the smugglers didn't seem to bother him. "I'll arrange it."

QuiTai tossed a purse of coins to him. He tucked it under his shirt so swiftly it might have never existed. She liked that he didn't count the payment in front of her.

"Lizzriat was helpful? That is interesting gossip. Perhaps her opinion of you has risen. Word has it that the Ingosolians working the Red Happiness are satisfied with your handling of Jezereet's funeral arrangements. And of her murderer."

"One wonders how they would know."

"They're discreet."

"Not discreet enough if Lizzriat knows."

QuiTai raised her hand to stop him from replying when she heard footsteps outside the door.

The door flung open. QuiTai shoved the window screen open and swung her legs over the sill. PhaJut slunk into the room and she relaxed a bit. He hadn't changed much in the years since she'd left his employ. His hair was thinner and grayer, and his stomach had turned into a tight little bowl of fat on his otherwise thin frame.

"What are you doing here?" PhaJut asked QuiTai.

"Visiting an old friend."

"In my office? You get above yourself, little sister." PhaJut turned to LiHoun. "Who do you work for, anyway?"

LiHoun barely bowed. "Your girls and boys. You don't pay me to run errands for them."

"She isn't one of my girls." PhaJut pointed at QuiTai.

"Not anymore, but I made a small fortune for you when I was. We parted on good terms. Has your opinion of me changed so much?" QuiTai asked.

"You're the Devil's concubine. I'd be a fool to trust you."

"Oh! I am hurt, uncle. Simply devastated that you would say such a thing."

"Tell the Devil I'll not sell this place to him."

QuiTai solemnly nodded, even though it made her head spin. At least he'd done her the favor of making his fears known. Prodding someone to get to the point was always more work than it should be. "I will tell him, and I will plead with him to leave you alone, for old time's sake, dear uncle PhaJut." LiHoun shot her a glance, but his expression didn't change. Maybe her sarcasm had been too noticeable. "But please, don't be angry with LiHoun. He had no idea I'd be stopping by."

"I remember how you two used to sit together on the alley stairs and whisper. Thick as rice porridge. And from what I hear, you still are."

PhaJut had never trusted her friendship with LiHoun, even though it was LiHoun's advice that had made her the highest earning worker in PhaJut's brothel.

It had been a slow night and all the customers had already gone upstairs. Lazing in the dim, sparely furnished front room held no appeal, so QuiTai had rolled a kur before going to find LiHoun. As usual, he'd been on the short flight of steps out the back door. She'd squatted next to him on the rotting wood and lit the kur.

They chatted about the weather, his family, and the new tax on fish. Once they'd exhausted all the usual topics of gossip, he watched her, unblinking, before saying what was on his mind. "Forgive me for telling a poor story, little sister, but perhaps this work isn't for you."

The stars were fading as the sky lightened before dawn. Still, she looked to them, picking out her favorites, as she thought about the wisdom of his words.

"Oh, the sex is all right, if only they would shut up! Before I started working here, I thought men came in for only one thing, but no. They want to talk. Talk, talk, talk, and they're always so boring."

She handed the kur to LiHoun.

He inhaled and then let the smoke seep out his mouth like a dragon's tongue. "They pay as much for your understanding ear as for the rest of your body."

"My ears grow deaf as they stuff them with their noise."

LiHoun laughed as he patted her hand. "As much as I enjoy our chats, as I said, perhaps you should find other work."

She made a face. "I worked on a plantation for two months. That was enough to know I'd go mad if I stayed. Then I tried working on a fishing boat. I only lasted a week."

"There's always service."

"'Oh yes, Ma'am, Thampurian lady, me so humble. Me bow many times.' Fuck that. At least here I won't lose my position for being smarter than my employer."

"But you will be put out on the street if you don't start earning more for PhaJut."

She knew he was right. Discouraged, she shook her head slowly. "My family needs the money. And it's not as if a Ponongese girl has many options. Not legal ones. I just have to find a way to be more alluring to the customers. I suppose I could giggle behind my hand more. And gaze up at them longingly." She batted her eyelashes furiously. "Oh, you big stud. My joy was complete the moment I saw you." She snorted. "I can mimic anyone, but I'm not sure I can act like that for very long before my stomach spews its contents."

LiHoun gazed at her for a long while. Then he chuckled. "Maybe, if you can't be like the other girls, you should be very different from them. On my home island, I heard of a woman who made a fine living in a brothel. When the other girls laughed, she scowled, and when they bowed their heads, she would look directly into the customer's eyes until he dropped his gaze."

"Scandalous!" But she liked the idea of this woman. "This story is meat and rice, uncle. Please tell me more."

His hands moved through the air as if painting a picture of her. LiHoun always did that when he admired a woman. "The other girls swore and got drunk, but she was always a lady. Proper language and posh manners. Aloof. She even rejected customers!"

"PhaJut wouldn't like that."

LiHoun snorted. "What the customer likes is all that matters. And from what I heard, her customers liked her so much that they begged her to take heavy purses." He handed her the small nub of the kur. "Can you treat your customers like rotted fish guts?"

"I wouldn't have to fake that." She mulled it over as she slowly exhaled the kur smoke. She could picture such a woman. In her imagination, the woman changed into her. That was a role she could play, she thought. She'd have to watch her language and refine her manners, but that was simple enough. The trick would be to make such a character seductive. But customers came into a brothel with sex in mind already, so they'd interpret almost anything she did as flirting. Men were like that. "That story was a good one, uncle LiHoun. An elegant plan."

"See? You don't even talk like the other girls, little sister. Elegant! I like the way that word sounds. What does it mean?"

He'd been right. PhaJut never liked that she went days between customers when the other workers had three or five a night, but by the time she left for the continent, she had made far more for him than anyone else under his roof. Oh, and how those customers had cried and pleaded with her when she told them that she was leaving Levapur. Some begged her to become their mistress. Chief Justice Cuulon had even offered to marry her.

She turned her attention to PhaJut, who fumed at her prolonged silence. "I only came here to visit LiHoun. I'm on my way out, as you can see." QuiTai gestured to the open window. Her feet were getting wet again. There was no hope of saving her sandals now.

PhaJut's eyes glinted with greed. "What business could you possibly have with the cat man, QuiTai? I'm sure the Devil has minions to run your errands now. Unless you're hiding something from him?"

She was too influenced by the conduit's second pipe of black lotus to finesse her way around PhaJut's clumsy attempt at cunning, so she decided to call his bluff. "Go ahead and tell the Devil I was here."

"Ah! But why are you here? Hmm? You always were up to something."

Did PhaJut really think she'd hand him information to

blackmail her with? Sometimes, people tried her patience a bit too much.

LiHoun shuffled his feet. "Little sister QuiTai needs some herbs to bring down her fever. She was asking me – "

"She has fever?" PhaJut raised his arm to cover his mouth and nose as he backed across the room. "You brought sickness into my place?"

"It's nothing contagious, you old fool," QuiTai snapped. "A cut on my ankle is infected."

"And she knows my women have medicine for it. Secret medicine from my home island. Very powerful. I sell it to all the workers here," LiHoun said.

"Then take her to your women! Get her out of here."

QuiTai's temper was almost to its breaking point. She was so miserable that if she'd been alone, she might have allowed herself a few self-pity tears. Her leg ached. Even her eyeballs were dry and gummy. And even though she felt as if her skin could ignite at any moment, she was also beginning to shiver. None of that mattered now that her mean streak had been provoked.

She swung her legs back over the sill and moved into PhaJut's office chair, a move that made him squeak with outrage. She steepled her fingers together as she leaned back. "So, tell me, dear uncle – "

PhaJut glowered at the edge in her voice.

"What sort of profit are you turning here nowadays? The Devil always likes numbers. Is it about the same as when I worked here? Let me see. If I remember correctly, you had seventeen workers, averaging four tricks a night, with the house cut being – "

PhaJut turned to LiHoun. "Both of you, out!" He glared at QuiTai. "You always were an evil bitch. The Devil should kill you while he still has a chance, because one day, you'll betray him just like you have anyone else who has ever taken you in."

"I'll share your advice with him. I'm sure he'll find it... amusing."

She wasn't sure if it was her words or the quiet voice in

which she delivered them that made PhaJut blanch and back out of the room – nor did she care.

QuiTai was furious with herself for giving in to her temper. PhaJut wasn't a bad man. He hadn't tried to cheat her more than was customary. While he shouted a lot, he'd never raised a hand to her or any of his workers. She had no reason to antagonize him.

She rested her burning brow in her hand. "Favored uncle, I'm sorry to have cost you your job."

"There will be another. I get most of my information from gossip with the runners from the other brothels and gambling dens, not from this place."

"It was still careless of me." Threats, she'd learned, was best used sparingly, and only when all other options had failed.

LiHoun helped her out of the chair. She hated showing such weakness, but she honestly couldn't have walked on her own. That damned vapor addict hadn't been useful enough to cause her this much trouble.

"I'm going to take you somewhere to rest and have that ankle tended to. Then I'll arrange a meeting between your lieutenant for this area and the smugglers. The black lotus will be delivered to the Dragon Pearl tonight," he said.

"Thank you." She shook her head though. "As I said, I won't endanger your family. Where are you taking me?" There wasn't anyone she could think of who would risk helping her.

They shuffled around the broken furniture in the hallway to the back door. It was still raining, but the drops had turned to fine mist and there was only an inch or so of water in the streets. LiHoun had to feel how hot she was, but he didn't mention it as they headed through the dark alleyways.

"You're not taking me to the Red Happiness."

LiHoun let her lean against a building as he peered around a corner. "If someone were searching for you, they'd go there first. There's somewhere they'd never think to look for you, and I'm sure they have a healer."

LiHoun talked as they took the dark alleyways through the neighborhood. QuiTai was so intent on keeping upright that she barely heard what he said. It seemed as if she'd been in pain forever, but it had been just over a week since she'd met Kyam Zul at the Red Happiness. From that day on, she'd endured more near misses with death, werewolf attacks, and miscellaneous indignities than in the rest of her life put together. This, she hoped, was the grand climax. Once she was over this, she'd settle into a predictable, orderly life. No lovers, no complications. Just business.

She tried to figure out where LiHoun was leading her, but there were gaps in time as the conduit dragged her into his oblivion. It took a moment to notice that she'd lost awareness of her surroundings and even longer to fight her way out of the vapor. The street sloped a bit too much to be the Quarter of Delights. Green jellylantern light glowed from the few windows and doorways that were open, so they weren't in a Thampurian neighborhood. That narrowed it down quite a bit. If she was right...

QuiTai pulled away from LiHoun. "Oh no." She shook her head and muttered, "No, no, no," but she saw they'd stopped at the front stoop of the apartment building she dreaded. "Kyam Zul? He probably won't be happy to see me, and he's no healer."

"Come inside, quickly. The rain is letting up, and people may venture out onto their verandas."

LiHoun was right. Besides, where else could she go? The chill was coming on again, and she didn't think she could walk to her nearest safe house. Even if she could, she'd be alone. As much as she hated to admit it, she needed help.

They slipped into the foyer. Muddy shoes sat in neat rows against the wall. She bent down to remove her sandals, but LiHoun nodded to the landlady's door as a warning and pulled her up the stairs. LiHoun keep a steadying hand on her elbow. She suppressed her resigned chuckle. Here she was, the powerful crime lord of Levapur, and she couldn't even climb a flight of stairs on her own. She didn't feel menacing or intimidating.

As they paused to rest on the third floor landing, she whispered, "I hope you know what you're doing, uncle."

"I'm not taking you to Kyam Zul."

"Then who? There's only one other apartment on the fourth floor... " She groaned as the other possibility revealed itself to her. "Let me guess. One of the escaped slaves decided to stay on Ponong, so he or she moved in with a sister or cousin from Cay Rhi who lives here in Levapur."

LiHoun's cat's eyes were full of awe when he turned to her. "The Oracle told you that?"

"No." Kyam Zul had told her about the family from Cay Rhi who lived across from him when they'd been on the *Golden Barracuda*. The rest she'd figured out on her own. QuiTai was in no mood to explain all that.

"I told them all to leave the island for their own safety," she grumbled.

"Not everyone is inclined to obey you, grandmother."

"I told you to see to it that they went."

They reached the fourth floor landing. The door to Kyam Zul's apartment was to the right, the other apartment door on the left.

"Some are even less inclined to obey me, especially this one. She's almost as headstrong as you."

LiHoun knocked on the door. A curvy woman with a worried brow opened the door a few inches. The strong smell of fish soup made QuiTai's stomach rumble. She hadn't eaten properly in days. The woman glanced over her shoulder as she blocked their view of the room.

There was a brief, hushed conversation before the door pulled open to reveal a taller woman.

"RhiHanya. Why did I know it would be you?" QuiTai meant to sound exasperated, but she knew she grinned at the woman who had helped her and the slaves escape from Cay Rhi. She'd never been able to resist the charms of women who swept through life like divas on the stage, or one who kept her head when all hell was breaking loose.

49

RhiHanya's wide smile showed the beguiling gap in her front teeth. Her hand shot out to grab QuiTai's forearm and yank her into the apartment. "Wolf Slayer! I knew we were fated to meet again. Don't hang in the hallway! Come in."

QuiTai's face mashed against RhiHanya's bosom as she was engulfed in an embrace. It was the most inviting pillow she'd rested her head on in days, but she wriggled away. The other woman watched like a nervous bird. Her face puckered with worry.

RhiHanya's voice was like a warm, soft blanket to snuggle into on a chilly night. "Well 'have you eaten' to you too, little sister."

Nothing irritated QuiTai more than being lectured about her manners, especially since hers were normally flawless.

"If you've come by to tell me to leave this island, don't bother. I wouldn't listen to that scrawny old man, and I'm not about to obey you either, little sister," RhiHanya said.

Two young boys and a girl sat at a low table near the typhoon shutters that led to the veranda. Papers filled with carefully copied letters from the Thampurian alphabet covered the tabletop. They watched silently as QuiTai limped into the room. Finding her uninteresting, they turned back to their school work.

QuiTai grimaced. Children. When she left the Dragon Pearl, she should have gone to one of the apartments she kept in Levapur and sent for LiHoun. He could have brought a healer to her. She'd made many mistakes this evening, but this one was unforgivable. She had to find a way to back out gracefully without insulting LiHoun or the Rhi women.

The apartment was no bigger than Kyam's place across the hall, and the walls and ceiling were just as damp. Steam rose from a pot on the cooking fire. A neat stack of sleeping mats sat in the corner behind a dying frame with a half-finished sarong spread on it. Only the Thampurian-style divan on the back wall seemed out of place. Perhaps it was a gift from Kyam. He'd mentioned that he was friendly with his neighbors.

"This is my cousin, RhiLan." RhiHanya pointed to the

woman who'd opened the door.

RhiLan put her hands together and bowed. Her wide eyes fixed on QuiTai.

"Auntie QuiTai is in need of assistance. A wound on her ankle is infected, and she has a fever," LiHoun said.

RhiHanya tsked as she bent down to look. "You should have drained that before it got this bad. Puncture wounds are dangerous."

"I was involved in another pursuit."

"There were more wolves than that one you ki– " RhiHanya's mouth snapped shut as QuiTai's gaze sharpened.

I shouldn't be here. Why are there never good solutions, only less terrible ones?

QuiTai turned to LiHoun. "It isn't right to ask a favor if they don't know how big the favor is." Next, she looked to RhiLan, not RhiHanya. "The colonial militia will be searching for me soon, if they aren't already. If you're caught harboring me, they will execute your family. I will not take offense if you turn me away, auntie. Your first duty is to your children, and I respect your need to protect them above all else."

Please, please send me away. Think only of your family, RhiLan. But QuiTai had seen that worshipful expression before. Normally it amused her. Now it dropped a cold stone into the pit of her stomach.

RhiLan cast a quick glance at her children. Then she pressed her hands together and bowed again. "The Rhi clans owe you an honor debt that isn't forgotten at the first sign of danger. The Wolf Slayer is welcome under our roof."

"Now you get off that ankle and let me have a look." RhiHanya lifted QuiTai and carried her across the room to the divan. "You're burning up, little sister."

RhiLan rushed to her cooking fire and put a tea pot on the flame. "Hitouh root, for fever." She pulled open small drawers in the wooden cabinet set above her chopping block and muttered as she took each item out. "Dried jikal buds to strengthen your blood. Tiuhon leaves to restore your spirit."

"And a knife," RhiHanya said as she carefully peeled the

bandage away from QuiTai's seeping wound.

LiHoun was immediately at QuiTai's side. His hair stood on end and his ears flattened.

QuiTai winced as skin pulled away with the bandage.

The children looked up from their work. Without a word, they quickly stacked their papers away and then stepped through the typhoon shutters onto the veranda.

"We're going to have to open those punctures so they can drain," RhiHanya said. She locked her gaze on QuiTai. "And flush them with water until they're clean. Otherwise, we'll have to use maggots."

While she understood and agreed, QuiTai couldn't help but shudder a little.

RhiLan put the blade of her knife into the cooking flame before reaching for her herb cabinet again. "And black lotus, for mercy."

CHAPTER 5: THE WINGED DRAGON

Hadre refused to be humiliated by his new command, even though the *Winged Dragon* should have been scuttled years ago. Once upon a time, a very, very long time ago, the *Winged Dragon* had been the pride of the Zul fleet. As he inspected the junk, Hadre found the hull sound and the ageing vessel meticulously maintained. Malk, being the son of one of Grandfather's daughters, probably never expected to be promoted from his command and thus had made the most of it. But still, the sails were in terrible shape, as if the junk had been caught on the fringes of a typhoon, and the rudder needed an overhaul.

Grandfather knew how to pick his punishments.

After dinner with his officers in his extremely small cabin, Hadre dismissed them and sat down at the scarred desk to write his weekly report. Grandfather probably expected complaints. He'd be damned if he'd humor the old tyrant.

Lately, his mouth constantly pressed into a tight line. Defying Grandfather was always wasted effort, but he couldn't have lived with himself if he hadn't tried.

It took quite a long time to compose his message. Words of frustration and anger snuck into what he'd hoped would be a polite and emotionless report. As he wrote, the paper filled with snide remarks that he crossed out. He balled it up and threw it against the unpacked trunk that held his few possessions. It bounced off the trunk and rolled under his desk. He took a fresh sheet and began again.

Sir, after inspecting the Winged Dragon, *I have found it to be seaworthy and well maintained through the excellent leadership of Cousin Malk and his diligent crew. However, I would like permission to replace the sails before we venture out of port, as it is typhoon season and I doubt they would withstand strong winds.*

The officers had not been informed about the cargo we are to take on and I was unable to ask cousin Malk before he took command of the Golden Barracuda.

His former ship's name came out in fat lines that blurred together as he pressed too hard on the pen. Grandfather wouldn't see his writing, though, so he continued.

If we are to bring a shipment of medusozoa back to Thampur, I would be obliged if you'd arrange to have the rudder refitted upon our return. However, if we are scheduled to sail to the Li Islands, it would be best to perform the necessary maintenance before we attempt to negotiate the Ponong Fangs. Please advise. HnZ

That, he decided, was the best he could do. He rose from the desk and opened a cabinet on the wall beside the door to the flying bridge. A small desk folded out. The keyboard for the ship's farwriter slid forward. He made sure the battery connections weren't corroded, consulted his journal for today's frequency, and carefully typed out his prepared message.

Hadre had already placed his journal into the desk drawer – neatness was mandatory on a ship – and was about to lock away the farwriter when the little brass bell on the side struck, indicating that he had an incoming message. The message would print out even if the farwriter was unattended, but the Zul way was to read and destroy all messages at the soonest possible moment, so while he was in no mood to read Grandfather's reply, he waited for the message to print, tore off the scroll of paper, and read it.

Have you heard if the Qui woman was apprehended? TtZ

How like Grandfather to completely ignore his message; unless the old man had sent his before he received Hadre's.

The message puzzled him. After Grandfather ordered him to take the colonial militia, Kyam, and Lady QuiTai to Cay Rhi, he'd then ordered Hadre to sail back to the harbor. Kyam hadn't said a word about what happened on the cay, although he'd hinted that he was under orders to keep quiet. His questions about Lady QuiTai had been met with averted eyes and a sudden change of subject. Why would the soldiers need to apprehend her? Did it have something to do with her escape from the fortress?

When Grandfather had arrived on the *Winged Dragon* with his odd troop of soldiers, he'd seemed to know a lot more about recent events in Ponong than Hadre did, but like Kyam and the colonial militia, he hadn't shared any information. That was typical Grandfather.

Answer me. TtZ

That's Kyam's department, not mine. HnZ

Hadre immediately regretted sending that reply, but there was no retrieving a message once it was sent. At least he hadn't added what he'd muttered under his breath: "So ask him."

Are there any signs of unease or unrest in Levapur? Is the colonial militia on alert? TtZ

"Again, you're asking the wrong grandson," Hadre muttered at the farwriter. He didn't know any of the colonial militia by name except Captain Voorus and didn't socialize with them while he was in Levapur. Why did grandfather think he'd know anything? And why did the old man expect trouble? "What are you up to, Grandfather?"

What the hell, he was already in disgrace. All Grandfather could do was exile him to Ponong as he had Kyam. The difference being that Kyam took his punishment. Hadre could sign on as crew on any non-Thampurian ship. There were plenty of smugglers around who didn't care too much about official papers, and they were always ready to take on experienced seamen.

I wouldn't know. Kyam knows Levapur and the colonial militia. Ask him. HnZ

He sent it off.

"Come on, old man. Let's see how you feel about that."

Any lesser man would have sweated out the seven minutes between sending his message and the chime sounding the reply, but Hadre simply poured himself a glass of whiskey and put his feet up on his desk.

Am unable to discuss current affairs with KtZ. TtZ

"Unable? You're too much of a coward to talk to him in case he asks you why you marooned him on this damn island," Hadre told the piece of paper in his hand.

Need insights from fresh perspective. TtZ

"Why are you always so obsessed with Ponong? You haven't been the governor for almost sixty years."

Remain in harbor. Fix sails and rudder. Re-tar the hull. Make any other repairs necessary to Winged Dragon. TtZ

"Now you're suddenly interested in the *Winged Dragon*? Or is this your subtle way of keeping me in port so I can play spy for you? I have news for you. I'm going to sit on this junk and never leave the harbor, and even if I do, I'll be damned if I'll tell you a thing about unrest in Levapur. If you want to know, you're going to have to talk to Kyam."

Hadre set down his drink and typed: *Message received. HnZ*

He was enough of a Zul to know to keep some tiles close to his chest.

A long, curved fingernail hovered over a farwriter keyboard.

She has returned.

A bead of sweat formed at his temple. It wasn't betrayal if the message could have been sent by several others, he told himself, but he knew QuiTai would see it differently.

The return message came more quickly than he would have thought. Did the old man hover over his farwriter day after day, hoping for a signal? Had he pounced on the machine when the bell rang?

What is her next move? TtZ

This conversation was a mistake, but it was already too late. How to reply? Two years ago, he would have reported every rumor. Now he was more cautious.

For now, nothing.

That seemed a safe enough answer. No one as ill as QuiTai was could make trouble for a couple of days.

Perhaps she needs further motivation. TtZ

The lump of fear in his stomach warned him that a dreadful game was underway. How could he warn her without bringing her wrath down upon him?

She probably already knew.

He nodded, willing to believe that because it comforted him. Whatever was happening, it was over his head and out of his hands. People like him were only ever the tiles in such games, never the players. All he could do was hedge his bets by staying friendly with both sides.

Chapter 6: The Marketplace

idmorning, RhiLan walked with her sons and daughter to a rundown Thampurian neighborhood on the first upslope rise. Other parents greeted her as they walked toward the same ramshackle house with their children. Near the steps leading to the small veranda, she put a coin into the hand of each of her children. As she kissed them, she reminded each not to mention their visitors to their friends or teacher.

"Learn." She wagged a finger at the eldest boy. "And behave."

His grin was so much like his father's. She tousled his hair.

The children ran up the stairs of the faded blue two-story building that had been converted into a schoolhouse. At the door, they solemnly handed their coins to Ma'am Thun, a Thampurian lady who wore an expression of constant suffering.

RhiLan had offered herbs to soothe a grumbly stomach and gently suggested that the thin woman need not lace her corset so tight, only to be sharply rebuked for the personal nature of her comments. Thampurians, she'd learned, were odd that way.

They wore clothes over another set of clothes and covered their arms all the way to their wrists. They slept inside even in the hottest weather. And while they made much of their ability to shift between forms, they never splashed in the chilly mountain streams during the dry season or waded in the gentle surf of the island's lagoons.

Still, RhiLan didn't care how foolish Ma'am Thun was as long as her children spoke fluent Thampurian and learned their numbers. If they had to live among Thampurians, who controlled most of the wealth on Ponong, then it made sense to prepare her children to be employed by them. Maybe a nice clerk position or a job in an upscale shop. Even working upslope at a plantation wouldn't be bad, as long as it wasn't in the pools. She had ambitions for her children. That's why they'd left Cay Rhi. And what a lucky decision that had been. Her cousin RhiHanya said most of the villagers were still trapped on the island. RhiHanya had faith that the wolf slayer would find a way to set them free.

RhiLan had heard rumors about the Devil's Concubine. It was hard to believe that storied being was the same woman who so politely and humbly tried to be of help in the apartment, even though she was too ill to do much. It was harder to believe the Devil would want such a sharp and angular woman in his bed. But what RhiLan couldn't accept was that people in the marketplace hated QuiTai for what *they'd* done to the Full Moon Massacre werewolves. As far as RhiLan was concerned, the werewolves had had it coming, and no one should feel guilty about that.

Besides, hadn't QuiTai shown concern over her children? She'd even put their safety before her own. From now on, if someone spoke ill of the Devil's Concubine, she'd tell them to stop spreading lies.

Chin up, she headed for the marketplace.

The streets were still muddy from the morning rain. It was hell on sandals, but then at least no one stole them from the rack on the first floor of the apartment building when they were caked with mud. In the dry season, even though they weren't supposed to, her family carried their sandals upstairs. Otherwise, they might not be there in the morning.

As RhiLan neared the marketplace, she passed a furious woman balancing a large basket of roasted jikal roots on her head. There were other tense Ponongese in the streets as she neared the town square. She couldn't decide if they were fearful or humiliated; then wondered why she imagined either emotion. Maybe something had happened in the marketplace. She wanted to ask, but the children would be home for lunch in a couple of hours, and she needed to sell at least one sarong before she returned to the apartment.

Between the government building and the dour Thampurian bank, she caught a glimpse of the marketplace. There were only a few stalls set up, as if it were still very early. Craning to see, she ignored the spice merchant who stomped past her.

Four soldiers gathered to block her way. Thampurians were a head taller than most Ponongese and solidly built, but these men were huge even by Thampurian standards. Their uniforms resembled the ones the colonial militia wore, but their shewani jackets were crisper and they had no flashy braid or jangling medals across their chests.

"No Ponongese in the marketplace," one of the soldiers said.

RhiLan was sure she hadn't heard right. "But I have a permit." She reached into her basket for the piece of paper that had cost her ten coins.

"All permits are revoked."

She bowed her head and softly said, "I'll just shop then." She tried to step around the soldier, but the others formed a wall of dark blue jackets much too close to her face.

The soldier told her, "Until further notice, no Ponongese in the marketplace, to buy or to sell."

Her chest tightened. She pointed to the Thampurian merchants setting up their stalls. "But you let them in!" She was so confused. What was going on?

The soldier spoke over head as if she wasn't there. "These snakes are deaf. No matter how many times we tell them, they think the law doesn't apply to them."

Now her face was hot and her hands trembled. The regular soldiers called her people snakes when they thought no one else could hear, but they'd never said it loudly in front of her. She was so embarrassed. She turned around and walked away with as much dignity as she could summon, but hot tears welled in her eyes.

RhiLan wondered for a moment if it was because she harbored the wolf slayer in her home. Could the soldiers sense the fear wrapped around her shoulders? She should have heeded QuiTai's warning against taking her in, but now it was too late. After the swift stab of fear passed through her, she realized that the soldiers ignored her. They didn't seem to care about QuiTai. Afraid that they'd see guilt in her face, she walked away quickly with her chin pressed to her chest. If only she could turn invisible, or maybe the ground would kindly rip apart under her feet and swallow her. She wanted to hide in her apartment until the shame went away.

At the next street corner, the Ponongese spice seller she'd passed earlier rushed over to her and stroked her arm. "It's okay, auntie. You'll be fine. We were all turned away. Come talk with us. Please, auntie. Don't cry."

Tears dropped down her face, but she nodded and followed him to the group that squatted on the veranda of a café. She'd often seen Thampurian ladies seated inside, with plates of delicate food so pretty that it had to taste like music. Of course no Ponongese would ever be allowed inside, except maybe to work in the kitchen where they couldn't be seen. She felt special and brave simply sitting on the veranda outside.

The spice seller smiled at her as he gestured for her to take a spot closer to the center of the gathered Ponongese. She set her basket at her feet and cast fleeting glances at the others. Many of them she recognized from the market, and most she knew by name. That made her feel a little better.

"We should protest to the governor!" someone said.

"How? First, we'd have to get to the government building, and that means getting into the town square."

"And who controls the soldiers? The governor."

"I've never seen those soldiers before."

RhiLan turned to the woman who'd said that and nodded. When her family had moved to Levapur, the town had seemed huge, confusing, and full of strangers, but now she recognized most people she saw even if she didn't know their names. Who would have thought she could know so many people? She could even tell the Thampurians apart; and as the other woman said, the soldiers she'd seen today were strangers. Could they possibly have been hiding down in the fortress all this time?

"If they won't let us into the marketplace, how are we going to sell our wares?" someone asked.

There were many suggestions. Some RhiLan thought were good, until someone pointed out why they weren't, and she changed her mind to agree with them. As the group traded ideas, she watched a Thampurian inside the café peer out at the Ponongese on his veranda from behind a curtain. He looked scared, or maybe he was just upset that he had no customers. It was hard to read Thampurian expressions. After a while, he edged to the back of the café and out of sight.

Next to RhiLan, a barefoot upslope woman balanced a basket of mangoes on her head. She whispered, "I'm so angry."

Why hadn't she thought to be angry instead of humiliated? RhiLan wondered. What did she have to be embarrassed about? She had a permit. The paper was still clasped in her hand.

"So, it's decided. Tomorrow, we'll meet in Old Levapur and have our own marketplace," an auntie in the center of the group said. Her face was lined from many hours in the sun, even though her hair showed no grays. A clay pot, probably full of juam nut oil, sat by her feet. "Tell everyone you see."

The others nodded.

Someone lit a kur. It passed through the group. Warm energy flowed through RhiLan's blood as the smoke filled her lungs. She looked up at the sky. It wasn't raining, but the clouds had gathered and looked grumpy enough to pour on their heads.

"What will my children eat if we have no rice?" RhiLan wondered out loud. "I planned to buy some today."

People turned to look at RhiLan. She blushed and bowed her head again.

The woman in the center of the group spoke directly to her. "Rice isn't the only food, little sister."

"But auntie, a little piece of meat gets lonely in an empty rice bowl." The man laughed, making a joke of it. Some laughed with him, but many nodded in agreement.

"Pass word around to the rice merchants that if they want our business, they must come to our marketplace tomorrow," the woman said. "There are so many more of us than Thampurians. They might not like us, but they're fond of our coins."

"But that does me no good tonight!" someone on the other side of the circle said.

"If you have no rice tonight, eat dried jellyfish," the woman said.

People gasped.

"But that's famine food," the joking man said; only he'd stopped laughing.

The woman shrugged as if resigned. "It's jellyfish or hunger. You choose."

A nearly toothless grandmother sighed as she rose. She put her hand on her back and bent this way and that to work the kinks out. "If I'm making jellyfish, I need pepper flakes and sweet seed oil. Who here has some to trade? I have fish cakes."

RhiLan bought fish cakes, fragrant anoin seeds, and a little oil. Then the café owner came back, followed by soldiers. She wouldn't give them a chance to humiliate her again. The other Ponongese seemed to feel the same way – they all hurried off into the alleyways and quickly dispersed.

QuiTai screwed her eyes tight and braced herself as RhiHanya poured water over her ankle to flush out the wound. Eyes still closed, she asked, "Is it healing?"

"Only a little new pus. We won't need to use maggots."

The tightness in QuiTai's shoulders loosened a bit. "Thank goodness. Sometimes they destroy too much muscle." She opened her eyes and craned to see her ankle.

"Only if your healer doesn't know what she's doing, or you wait too long to treat it in the first place." RhiHanya's knee popped as she rose from the hard wood floor.

"Always scolding me." But QuiTai smiled. She'd missed the comfort of daily life with a woman. Men were fine for sex, but she'd never met one who made domestic life as pleasant as a woman could.

Do not. Do. Not. Start thinking like that. This is strictly business.

"Drink the rest of that potion RhiLan made for you."

QuiTai braced herself and gulped down the rest of the drink. She'd let it cool; that was a mistake. Bitterness coated her tongue. As bad as it tasted, at least the black lotus in the potion helped her relax.

RhiHanya lifted QuiTai's legs back onto the divan then felt her forehead. "I think the fever is finally broken, but only the night will tell."

QuiTai pulled the blanket under her chin. Every time she moved, the sharp scent of her sweat wafted from her damp clothes. A wrinkle she couldn't smooth irritated her shoulder blades. If only she could bathe and put on a fresh blouse.

RhiHanya curled next to QuiTai on the divan and wrapped her arms around her. "I'll keep you warm."

"The blanket is enough."

It's bad enough that I've infected this apartment with my unhealthy stink. Why would you embrace the source?

QuiTai gritted her teeth and tried to ignore the comfort of RhiHanya's body, but it was difficult when her hair was being stroked. The chill came on strong, setting her teeth chattering and her aching legs into restless motion. She lifted her head from RhiHanya's bosom. Her breath caught as she realized how close their lips were.

"I'm warm enough now. You can let go." She hadn't meant to whisper as if they had been intimate.

Do not push your hair behind your ear or tilt your head and smile. Do not flirt with this woman. Do not entangle yourself with her.

"I don't have much patience for sickness." QuiTai tried to escape from RhiHanya's arms.

RhiHanya gripped her tighter. "So I see, but you're not going anywhere until you're healed completely."

"There's no honor debt between us. You and your cousin have paid me a great favor, but it's time for me to leave. I wasn't joking when I told RhiLan that I'm a danger to her family." QuiTai scowled. "Would you let go of me?"

"No, I won't. Not until you're well enough to free the others from Cay Rhi."

Shocked, QuiTai flinched. Every rumor she'd spread about herself had been selected to support a certain image. No one in Levapur would be foolish enough to look to her for help. Maybe those tales hadn't reached the outer islands yet. RhiHanya's faith in her had to be quashed immediately.

"I'm a dedicated disciple of the conjoined goddesses of self-interest and self-preservation. Don't expect heroics from me."

"I know your reputation. I've also seen your actions. I know which I believe more."

"I am not a nice woman. Ask anyone in Levapur, and they'll tell you that the only thing I care about is coin."

"What coin did you earn freeing me? That old cat-man gave the other Rhi money and told them it was from you. That wolf-man Petrof tried to kill you. You can't even rest in your own bed because the sea dragons hunt you. So don't try to sell your story to me. I know better."

Nothing she gave was ever enough. This crazy woman actually thought she'd try to take over a remote compound controlled by the colonial militia to free a bunch of people she didn't even know. Wasn't it enough that she'd freed the ones she had? And, as RhiHanya pointed out, given them enough money to start life over somewhere else? At what point did she end up owing her life to the people of Cay Rhi?

It was time to put a stop to this path of thoughts.

"Even I have moments of weakness."

QuiTai could see that RhiHanya wasn't going to stop defending her. There had to be another way to convince the woman.

"I have done as much as I can do for the people of Cay Rhi. They aren't my problem anymore. I have other commitments. Other responsibilities. Pressing personal matters." *Such as finding out who paid Petrof to kill me and making sure they never send another assassin after me again.* "Don't look to me for a happy ending. This is real life, and in real life, some stories end badly for innocent people."

She could read the impact of her words in RhiHanya's face. Disbelief, caution, a flash of anger, then desolate sadness.

RhiHanya said nothing for a while. When she finally spoke, she pleaded with QuiTai in hushed tones. "My pillow sister was left behind on Cay Rhi." Her gaze locked on QuiTai's eyes. "Tell me you've never loved someone. Tell me you'd let them live in captivity, and I'll call you a liar, Wolf Slayer. I know what you do to people who hurt your blood kin."

She couldn't let this woman push her into a stupid, futile, suicidal attempt to free the slaves. So what if RhiHanya was right? Once she'd killed the men who paid Petrof to slaughter her family, she was done with retribution. It paid so poorly.

RhiHanya's fingers hurt QuiTai's arms. "Tell me you don't love someone."

"I don't." She could look right into RhiHanya's eyes and say that.

"Never?"

QuiTai almost lied, but RhiHanya tilted her chin as her eyes narrowed. She knew she was going to regret this, but she spoke anyway. "I also had a pillow sister. Jezereet. She was an Ingosolian. An actress. The star of all the stages of the continent." A bittersweet smile spread over her mouth as her lips trembled. Jezereet had been so beautiful – not only her body, but like RhiHanya, she'd sparked with life that drew people to her. How could they resist? "But she's dead now. Everyone is dead."

"Some stories end that way, little sister. It's real life." From the smile on RhiHanya's lips, she'd thrown QuiTai's words back at her deliberately. "But you didn't abandon her while she lived."

"Actually, I did."

"No."

As much as it hurt to admit it, QuiTai said, "Yes."

"Prove it. Tell me this story."

Why did she let RhiHanya maneuver her into a corner like that? She could refuse, but that would be unforgivable rudeness to a woman who risked so much to heal her.

"Our daughter was killed during the Full Moon Massacre." Sadness enveloped her like a cloud on a mountaintop. Could she ever talk about the past without it overwhelming her? "People warned me that few relationships can survive the death of a child. But we weren't ordinary people. Not us. Of course we'd stay together." There was no way to explain how hard they'd tried. For years, they'd been so in love, so committed to each other. She'd tried to help Jezereet through the pain. Jezereet tried to absolve her of guilt. But in the end, in only took a few months to destroy what had once been perfect. "We were more ordinary than I thought."

"That doesn't sound as if you abandoned her."

"But I did. I felt my hurt was greater than hers and wondered why she expected me to act as if she alone knew true grief." A tear staggered down her cheek. "We still loved each other, but we couldn't be together. I moved out. Eventually, she took other lovers. You know it's not the Ponongese way to be possessive, and we both had other lovers when we were actresses. We had to. The troupe paid us next to nothing, but rich fans threw gifts at our feet. So I wasn't hurt when she found new admirers. But it was different when Petrof also flirted with her, and... I don't know." She sighed. How many nights had she tortured herself over what happened? And still, she didn't know what she could have done to change it.

"Petrof was the werewolf we met in the jungle," RhiHanya said.

QuiTai nodded. "Maybe she wanted to hurt me. Or maybe she was so distraught about our daughter's death that the black lotus Petrof offered her was her way of escaping the pain."

The last thing she wanted was pity, and that's all she saw on RhiHanya's face. "So I let her succumb to her addiction, and she died because of it." She wiped away her tears. "You understand? I'm no hero. Things got difficult, and I walked away."

"She let you walk away, little sister. I won't. That's a promise."

QuiTai knew a threat when she heard one, but she was too tired to argue about it anymore.

School mistress Ma'am Thun released her students for lunch, picked up her umbrella, and headed for the marketplace. Her heart clenched when she saw the soldiers at the edge of the town square. She hadn't done anything wrong in her entire life, but that didn't stop her from averting her eyes as she went past them. Not a word was spoken to her. Still, she exhaled relief. Then she gasped.

The marketplace was usually full of people this time of day. Stalls were normally jammed together in a haphazard maze of riotous colors, and oh! the noise and odors. But she preferred shopping there since the same goods were often less expensive than in the stores.

Today, the expanse of packed dirt was mostly bare. She saw three rice merchants, several jellylantern sellers, and a few butchers. There was only a handful of customers. It took a moment for it to sink in. There wasn't a single Ponongese. No fruit, no spices, no women with their baskets balanced on their heads singing out their wares as they walked through the crowds.

Contemplating what this might mean, she cautiously moved toward the stalls. Had the parents of her students seemed worried or upset this morning? No. There had been no difference in their shy smiles and respectful bows. What had changed since then? It had to be something dreadful if the soldiers were involved. They mostly sat down in the fortress and let Levapur be. Governor Turyat, that unctuous idler, must have ordered them to shut out the Ponongese.

She hoped he'd make an announcement explaining his reason, because her imagination already searched for explanations, and each of them made her more uneasy than the one before. The last thing a Thampurian should do was panic. It would set such a poor example for the Ponongese.

"Ma'am! Pork?" a butcher called out to Ma'am Thun.

She drew closer to his stall, which sat alone in what had been a bustling corner of the marketplace just yesterday. Beside his stall, on the bare ground of what had been her favorite place to buy tamtuks, she could see the splatter ring of oil left behind. "I don't eat pork. It causes indigestion and worms," she told the butcher. "Where are the fishmongers? I must have fish for my dinner."

He sighed. "The soldiers escorted the fishermen down to the harbor in groups, and when they came in with their catch, they wouldn't let them sell. I have no idea where they went. Maybe if you go into the Ponongese neighborhoods..."

Ma'am Thun frowned. "I'm not accustomed to climbing upslope." The thought of ascending that steep, winding road made her ribs press painfully against her corset.

The butcher placed a pale slab of meat on his forearm and offered it to her for inspection. He swatted away a fly that landed on it. "If you cook it well, you won't get worms."

She turned her head. "So, I have a choice of rice or rice for dinner."

"There's also jellylanterns."

Ma'am Thun squared a withering glare on the butcher. He shrank back. The power of a teacher's disapproval didn't diminish over the years, she noted with a bit of satisfaction. "I can't eat a jellylantern."

"The snakes do. Not the lanterns. They dry the jellies and eat them somehow."

The butcher seemed to enjoy her shudder, like a schoolboy who had placed a loathsome creature on his teacher's desk. She was far too experienced to let him see how angry she was at the idea that she'd stoop to eating something so un-Thampurian. She'd go hungry first.

Kyam's knuckles bumped against his glass when he reached for his drink. That should have been a sign that he'd had enough, but Hadre wasn't around to scold him, and he couldn't think of a single reason to stay sober. He caught hold of his glass on his second try and drained it. When he turned to signal the Red Happiness' bar keep to refill it, though, the Ingosolian suddenly seemed obsessed with a spot on the bar.

Damn that QuiTai. Had she told them to act as his caretaker? He snorted and leaned back so far in his chair that it almost tipped over. People looked away as he noisily righted himself.

If she walked in right now, Lady QuiTai would pause at the typhoon shutters that way she always did when she made one of her grand entrances, as if she were taking the stage. She'd be dressed impeccably, either in the latest Thampurian fashion or in the bright green sarong she favored. Once she was sure she had the attention of everyone in the Red Happiness, the corners of her mouth would curve up in that secretive, mischievous, satisfied smile of hers. Then she'd glide through the bar as if she owned the damned place.

She probably did.

She'd stop inches from his table and make one of those withering remarks about how drunk he was. He'd laugh, because her choice of words was always clever, but he'd also wince, because they hit their mark with unerring accuracy. And then he'd say something equally vicious, or as close as he could ever come to matching her wit.

Those conversations had been the only stone against which to hone his mind since he'd set foot on this damned island. Now she might be dead, and he'd have to figure out a way to hang onto his sanity until grandfather let him go home.

He scratched his nose. Who would know if QuiTai were alive? The Devil would. Kyam chuckled to himself and shook his head. Sure, the Devil would know, but how did one go about asking the Devil a question? The man was maishun spirit, as insubstantial as a ghost.

Someone gripped his shoulder and jostled him.

"Zul!"

Kyam lifted his gaze. Governor Turyat and his sinister shadow, Chief Justice Cuulon, loomed over him. He knew he should invite them to join him, but he wanted to be alone. Besides, he'd never liked them, and now that he had his articles of transport, there was no reason to pretend to be civil anymore.

Part of his distrust was from the tales Grandfather had hissed into his ears about how, years ago, these two men betrayed him. Grandfather had been the first colonial governor, the one who'd claimed Ponong for the king. From his stories, he'd hated every moment on the island as much as Kyam did. When he'd gone back to Thampur, he'd schemed and connived until the Zul clan had risen to the enviable position as the most profitable and powerful among the thirteen families. He'd become the king's right hand. But Grandfather was never one to let anything go.

The rest of Kyam's dislike of the men was purely their fault. They'd eagerly signed his articles of transport, but they'd also approved of keeping the islanders on Cay Rhi as slaves. If QuiTai was to be believed, they were corrupt to the core. He felt that they took every coin they could but never really governed the island. It was perhaps beyond their abilities. Or maybe, like as was the case with most Thampurians exiled to Ponong, their ambitions had long since wilted under the relentless tropical sun.

"Zul, why are you still here? Don't you want to go home?" Governor Turyat asked as he sat without an invitation. While tall with a thin build, sagging flesh at his throat showed how much weight he'd lost recently. His thin lips were too red to be natural.

Chief Justice Cuulon remained standing. Like the governor, he was tall, but his rangy build had never filled out. His temples were as bare as his prominent forehead, which glistened under the lights. Something about his strong nose made it seem as if he was always smelling something he didn't like.

Kyam didn't want to talk to anyone now, especially these two. "Governor – "

"Turyat, please." The governor chuckled in an avuncular way that grated on Kyam's nerves.

If he'd had any manners, Kyam would have insisted the governor call him Kyam instead of Zul, but he didn't.

"We need to talk in private," the Chief Justice Cuulon said. "Please come with us."

Kyam lifted his empty glass as if it needed closer inspection. "I would, gentlemen, but as you can see, my schedule today is already full of rum. Tomorrow, I will be busy nursing a smashing hangover. Perhaps sometimes next week?"

The chief justice's mouth twisted. "Typical Zul."

"Now, now, Cuulon. Don't take offense where none is meant," Governor Turyat said.

"Who said none was meant?" Kyam muttered.

Chief Justice Cuulon's cavernous nostrils flared as he drew in a deep breath. "All right. We'll talk here. You tell your grandfather that we won't stand for his interference."

Kyam expected more to the message, but they strode away. He still couldn't get the barkeep to look at him. He felt as if people were staring at him, and it felt like pity.

Kyam got to his feet. Not bad, he thought. Not slobbering drunk. Maybe the Red Happiness had done him a favor by cutting him off. Come to think of it, he'd never seen anyone dead drunk in their bar. QuiTai demanded a certain amount of decorum in her place, he decided.

He knew he held his shoulders a little too rigidly as he walked past the white wicker chairs on the veranda. Who would care if he were a little drunk? As far as anyone knew, he was still in disgrace, still living off remittance money his family sent to keep him far from home and out of sight. They didn't give a damn what he did because he was beneath their notice.

The afternoon sun stabbed the inside of his skull when he stepped out of the shade onto the street. Wasn't it monsoon? Where were the clouds? And why did the sun always shine brightest when he was drunk? The street was still muddy, though. He stepped around puddles that reflected the sky.

Four soldiers leaned against the back wall of the bank. When they saw Kyam, they stood straight and saluted. At least someone knew what he'd done for his country. He managed a wilted salute in return and continued on.

Two steps into the town square, he stopped. Confused, he looked back over his shoulder. The bank was still there. A flock of green and blue birds pecked at the dirt by its steps. He turned back. Gray monkeys played around the banyan tree's massive trunk, but there were no children. He scratched his head. The colonial government's building, with its red columns and Thampurian-style roof sat on the south end of the square, but there wasn't a single Ponongese boy on the steps calling out offers to carry packages for Ma'am or Mister Thampurian. In the center of the square, a merchant was striking his stall. Kyam didn't blame him. There were more stalls than customers, and there were no more than a dozen of those.

"What the hell?" Kyam asked, but there was no one around to answer him.

Where were the Ponongese ladies who balanced huge baskets on their heads as they strode through the market in their bright sarongs? Where was the clash of merchant's voices hawking their wares? The smells of tamtuk stands and fish and spices? It looked as if a typhoon had blown through and swept them off the cliff into the Sea of Erykoli.

Kyam walked quickly home now, his head down as he tried to make sense of it. He knew his landlady said something to him as he dumped his boots on the rack in the foyer of the apartment building, so he mumbled something back and started up the stairs.

At the top landing, he glanced at his neighbor's door. He'd been avoiding them since he'd returned from Cay Rhi. How could he take the hospitality of people when he'd let his government hold their relatives in slavery? But if they couldn't get to the marketplace, they might need his help finding rice.

Too ashamed of his state to let the children next door see him, he stumbled into his apartment, removed his jacket, and fell face-first onto his mattress.

Chapter 7: The Rhi Apartment

When a door slammed, QuiTai jumped to her feet, suddenly fully awake and ready to fight. Pain shot up her leg. She dropped onto the divan when she saw RhiLan scowling furiously at the door. The black lotus had almost worn off, but she struggled for a moment to clear the haze that hung over her thoughts. She wasn't in danger, and this was something she needed to focus on.

"Those damn Thampurians!" RhiLan banged her market basket down on her chopping block and pulled fish cakes out of it as she muttered.

"What's happening?" QuiTai asked. Her voice sounded as tired and weak as she felt.

"We can talk about this out on the veranda," RhiHanya told her cousin. "The Wolf Slayer needs to rest."

QuiTai pushed RhiHanya's hands away when she tried to make her lie down. "What's happening?"

"The soldiers wouldn't allow any Ponongese into the marketplace today," RhiLan replied. "I wonder if my man was able to get to his boat."

RhiHanya's fist rested on her hip. She couldn't seem to decide if she should scowl about the soldiers or at QuiTai.

QuiTai leaned on her side to see around RhiHanya. "Did the soldiers say why they wouldn't let you sell?"

RhiLan shook her head. "I tried to show them my permit. It has the chop of the colonial government on it. If they had only looked, they would have seen it was official. They let the Thampurian merchants set up their stalls, but they wouldn't even let me shop."

QuiTai was concerned and confused. This was bad business in more ways than one. The Thampurians couldn't be stupid enough to ruin their own merchants, could they? It was so unlike them. Normally they grubbed after every coin they could get their hands on.

"I was able to buy fishcakes for the children's lunch. I have no idea what we'll eat this evening since I couldn't buy rice." RhiLan wrung her hands together.

"Maybe your man will bring home a fish. We can go without rice for one day," RhiHanya said in a calm, reasonable tone that seemed to soothe RhiLan.

"But what about tomorrow?" QuiTai asked. "If RhiLan can't sell her sarongs, she won't have money for food."

RhiHanya spun around to wag her finger at QuiTai. "Don't go looking for more trouble when your bowl is overflowing with it already."

"You can't eat trouble, and a stomach full of it will keep you up at night," QuiTai countered. "And our squabbling is only making auntie RhiLan uncomfortable. It solves nothing."

"But we did solve the problem! We plan to set up our own market in Old Levapur tomorrow," RhiLan said with modest pride. "I've been spreading the news."

"That's a smart idea." QuiTai pulled on her bottom lip.

RhiHanya gave her a sharp look. "You don't sound happy about it."

"I have questions. Why are the Thampurians doing this? It makes no sense. I need to think. No more potions. They dull my mind. And I need—" What she needed was quiet, no distractions, and a place to pace, but how could she ask her hostess to leave her own apartment?

"But why don't you like the idea of a market in Old Levapur?" RhiHanya asked.

It was always harder to open her mind to the bigger picture when people insisted on dragging her back to one element of it. That was one thing she'd enjoyed about Kyam Zul. He could almost keep up with the speed of her thoughts, and he knew how to hold his tongue. She wondered if he'd already left Levapur or if he was in the fortress. Those seemed like the only two options. She hoped he hadn't been blamed for her escape with the slaves. If he'd been hailed as a hero for discovering the Ravidian plot, he'd probably immediately have asked for, and been granted, articles of transport. He was probably standing on the deck of the *Golden Barracuda* and facing home with a cocky grin on his face. That image brought a twinge of regret. She'd miss him.

"I guess I could go to one of the stores for rice," RhiLan said unhappily. "If I can find one that will take my money. I made the mistake of going into a Thampurian store when we first moved to Levapur. The merchant cursed me and shoved me out."

"Or... " QuiTai sat up.

Thankfully, RhiHanya and RhiLan didn't speak or even move while her brain furiously wove together the threads of an idea. Oh, it was too beautiful. Did the Thampurians really hand her such an opportunity? Pleased, she smiled to herself.

The Devil was feared for murder, blackmail, and occasional kidnappings. Those violent crimes had been the werewolves' realm, and she'd rarely been involved. She'd considered such ventures a foolish waste of time since there was little money in them, especially considering the risk. What people didn't realize was that the bulk of the Devil's business came from black market goods. That's where she'd established his power and made his fortune.

No werewolf worth his swagger would be caught dead selling something as boring as rice, Petrof had told her. They weren't lowly merchants. They were hardened criminals. Or so he'd seen himself; what he'd really been was a cowardly lowlife thug. But she didn't want to remember how she'd elevated him from that to being the Devil. It was too embarrassing.

What she chose to remember was that she'd ignored his sneers. She'd bought rice from smugglers and corrupt traders and sold it through her lieutenants. Then she'd expanded into other staple goods. They weren't exciting or flashy, but they'd made a steady profit. Of course, the Thampurian merchants had to pay that outrageous import tax to the colonial government while she didn't, so she could always afford to sell for less than they could and still earn more.

For a moment, she doubted her plan, but she'd successfully raised the price of black lotus. According to LiHoun, her customers had been so fearful of a shortage that they'd been grateful to get any, even at the higher price. Her grin spread. Only addicts bought black lotus, but everyone in Levapur ate rice, even Thampurians.

Honest people like RhiLan rarely bought black market rice or anything that QuiTai's network sold. They simply sighed and paid the higher prices from legitimate merchants because they didn't like doing business with the Devil. But the Thampurians had a different view. If there was one thing a Thampurian loved, it was a bargain. Prying money from their tight fists was going to be delicious.

RhiHanya folded her arms and scowled disapproval down at QuiTai. "I may not know you well, little sister, but I know mischief is brewing when someone smiles like that. What are you thinking?"

QuiTai put on her best stage expression of innocence. "I – "

"Uh huh."

During her stint as a magician's assistant back on the continent, QuiTai had learned the importance of misdirection. She had to make RhiHanya and her cousin focus on anything but rice by doing something unexpected and shocking. In her experience, nothing distracted her fellow Ponongese like a display of appalling manners.

She sat up prim as a schoolteacher and said, "In the meantime, we have a situation. No good guest would ever imply that her hostesses' hospitality is lacking, but she wouldn't allow her hostesses' children to go to bed hungry either. So what do I do? Do I let RhiLan spend her entire afternoon in search of rice and allow her to be insulted by Thampurian merchants? Or do I send word to LiHoun and tell him to bring us some?" With eyebrows raised, QuiTai looked from RhiHanya to RhiLan. They stared at her as if she'd lost her mind. She was quite pleased with herself.

RhiLan's face went bright red. "I couldn't – "

"Yes, you could. And you will," RhiHanya said.

Oh, how I adore practical women, RhiHanya. If you only knew.

"It's just rice, after all, cousin. It's not as if she's offering pork."

RhiLan seemed close to tears. She tugged her hair as she paced the small apartment. "If only the regular soldiers had been at the marketplace. They may be rude, but they see me every day. They know I belong there. They know I don't make trouble. They might have let me in."

Different soldiers?

RhiLan shrank back from QuiTai's intense gaze.

"Tell me about these different soldiers, auntie. Tell me everything."

During their somber dinner, QuiTai stifled her screams of boredom and smiled politely, but she wasn't sure she could hold them in much longer. The one thing they would not talk about in front of the children were the events in the marketplace, and the unspoken subject weighed heavily on the conversation though, leaving the adults in a mood to only pick at their food. RhiLan's man hadn't been allowed to pass through the town square to the harbor path, so there was no fish. Unless the other Ponongese families in Levapur could find goat or pork tomorrow, tonight might be their last meal with meat.

A meal without meat or rice is indistinguishable from an empty bowl.

The effort to join the meaningless chatter exhausted QuiTai. Every smile felt brittle as cheap jellylantern glass. Each inane bit of small talk made her teeth grind. All she could do was cast glances at LiHoun and hope he understood that she wanted to talk to him alone. She couldn't ask her hosts to leave their apartment while she chatted with LiHoun, and she couldn't talk the Devil's business in front of them, so she forced herself to sit still, listen, and make appropriate noises of concern and sympathy while frustration burned through her gut.

Finally, RhiLan rose and dragged the bathing tub from the corner. The middle son carried buckets of collected rain water from the veranda and put them on the cooking fire to boil while his sister dragged a privacy screen in front of the tub. RhiLan's man took some of their rice to see if he could barter with the neighbors for eggs and oil. RhiHanya stayed where she was, though. Perhaps she expected LiHoun and QuiTai would discuss freeing the slaves left behind on Cay Rhi, and she fully expected to be part of the conversation.

"The rain has stopped. Perhaps auntie QuiTai would like to exercise her legs with a short walk on the veranda?" LiHoun asked.

Bless you, uncle.

"She can't be seen," RhiHanya reminded him.

Stop hovering over me, woman! I don't need protection.

"I'll stay close to the wall. There's little moonlight tonight, and no jellylanterns out there. No one will see my face." QuiTai came to her feet.

RhiHanya immediately rose and supported QuiTai by the elbow.

"You've been stuck watching me all day, auntie RhiHanya. Let LiHoun give you a moment's rest."

RhiHanya gave LiHoun a long look. She didn't want to let go, but LiHoun was older than she, and thus worthy of respect, so she backed away and let him take QuiTai's arm.

As the horizon rose to meet the sun, a blessedly cool ocean breeze blew inland. Levapur seemed to have relaxed into the evening, but QuiTai wondered if behind the shutters, Ponongese were as fearful as she was of the coming days. Uncertainty was a hard pillow.

"Banning us from the marketplace was bad enough, but no fishing? How dare they? This is our island. We belong here. They don't," QuiTai whispered. If words had venom, each of hers would have struck a Thampurian dead. "And don't even get me started on how they kept the workers from repairing the funicular. Don't they understand that everything they import has to be carried up from the harbor until the funicular cable is replaced?"

It felt good to let out some of her anger, although she still had plenty left. She closed her eyes, drew in a deep breath, and then flashed a meaningless smile at LiHoun that disappeared as quickly as it had appeared. "Forgive me for slaughtering your language, uncle. It has been a long time since I've spoken in the words of the Li."

QuiTai and LiHoun squatted on RhiLan's veranda as they shared a kur. Her gaze flitted to Kyam's dark apartment.

"Another apartment shares this veranda," LiHoun said.

"Kyam Zul lived there. He's probably on a ship bound for Thampur."

"I saw him at the Red Happiness this afternoon."

The news caught her by surprise. Curiosity overrode her fury at the Thampurians. She checked her hair to make sure her braid was smooth before she slipped over to the typhoon shutters and peered in through the shutters. The apartment was dark and stillness seemed to have settled over it like dust on furniture in an abandoned house. She pressed a hand to the frame of a shutter and turned the handle. It wasn't locked.

"Allow me, grandmother." LiHoun slipped past her into the room. He returned quickly. "Paintings are tied with twine and a trunk sits in the center of the floor. The wardrobe is empty. It seems he plans to leave soon."

"Maybe he's waiting for the Golden Barracuda to sail."

"It left the harbor two days ago. There are more ships in the harbor, but only one flying the Zul family chop. It's an ugly old junk with faded sails."

QuiTai closed the shutter. The Oracle had said Kyam would be the governor of Ponong. She was never wrong, but the timing of her visions was always a mystery. Still, it was disquieting that Kyam hadn't left yet. Even more worrisome were her mixed feelings about that.

"Is your leg giving you pain?" LiHoun asked.

She realized she'd winced, but not because of her ankle. "A little, but I need to move. Lying on that divan all day is making me weak." She rested her hand on his shoulder. "I have asked far more of you in the past weeks than before. If it's a burden, be honest with me. You know that I will not take offense. But also know that you've been a great help, favored uncle, and I would be hard pressed to find a more worthy right hand."

LiHoun pressed his hands together and bowed. "You honor me with your trust, grandmother. And you've always been generous."

That put one of her many worries to rest. With LiHoun at her side, life would be much easier. There was so much she had to attend to. She simply didn't have time to train a new agent; not to mention that she'd have to reveal that she was the Devil to someone who hadn't proven themselves yet. Eventually, the news would come out, but for now it was safer to keep the myth of the Devil alive.

They reached the end of the veranda. She could barely smell food, even though they were in an overcrowded neighborhood. Many families had gone hungry tonight. That senseless cruelty sparked her anger.

Not willing to show how irritated she was, she said, "Smells like rain."

LiHoun sniffed the air. "And lightning."

"A storm is coming."

He watched her from the corner of his eye. "It may be an ill wind."

"That's the foul stench of Thampurian law burning inside your sensitive nose."

LiHoun laughed.

She could tell that he wanted to squat as they normally did and talk, but she tested her ankle with mincing steps and decided not to strain it further.

"Does your goddess tell you anything?" LiHoun asked.

His question surprised her. This was the second time he'd mentioned the Oracle, though she'd never discussed her goddess with him. Maybe he'd heard the other whores at PhaJut's shyly ask her about the Oracle on those late, lazy nights when they'd had no customers and all other talk had been exhausted. Back then, she'd only known one way to evoke the goddess, and the conduit always died. The Thampurians would have executed her for that, so she'd never seriously considered summoning her goddess. Besides, she knew the other workers and their troubles well enough to guess their futures. They didn't like to take her word for it, though. The Oracle was never wrong, but QuiTai was just another whore with an opinion.

"Lately, the Oracle seems obsessed with the dull lives of dull people."

But maybe if she stopped asking the Oracle for an answer... Hadn't her mother and grandmother always warned her that the goddess didn't work like that? Or maybe the Oracle didn't like her selfish inquires. Maybe she would bring a vision for something that affected her people.

Oh! QuiTai shut her eyes for a moment. Maybe that's what the Oracle had been trying to tell her – that she should focus on the ordinary people and not on herself.

Maybe.

"The Oracle's visions can drive people mad," her grandmother always said.

Yes, they can.

She touched the veranda railing closest to the Rhi apartment. Silhouetted by the light of the single green jellylantern in the apartment, she noticed RhiHanya hovering near the shutters. Unless she spoke Li, though, she wasn't going to overhear anything she could understand. Still, QuiTai leaned close to LiHoun's ear. "Tell me about the black lotus sales."

"Only the werewolves knew all their clients, but your lieutenants visited every den, brothel, and gaming hall in town, so the major customers now have a supply. As I told you last night, they barely noticed the price difference. We told the ones who complained that they didn't have to buy, of course. They were so afraid we'd refuse to sell them any that they quickly shut their mouths. Best of all, your lieutenants are singing your praises for enriching their purses."

"I do so love the sound of profits rolling like ocean waves. Constant and reliable."

"Rice, and meat."

A wry smile tugged at the corners of QuiTai's mouth. "Speaking of rice... "

When she'd first thought of her plan, she'd seen it as a contingency. For some foolish reason, she'd hoped and believed that the colonial government would come to its senses. Instead, matters only grew worse. Who knew what new insults would come with the next day? Now she felt she had no choice but to shove back.

"How much rice should I bring tomorrow?" LiHoun asked.

"Not too much. I don't want to insult my hostess any more than I already have. A quarter measure, I think. But that's not what I wanted to talk to you about. Uncle, this matter with the fishing fleet disturbs me. I know the governor is a bit stupid sometimes, but I can't fathom his reason for starving everyone. Or why, after years of ignoring crime in Levapur, he suddenly uses soldiers for enforcement."

"Maybe he has more to command. RhiLan said the soldiers who turned her back were strangers."

"If we can believe that her observations are correct." QuiTai raised her hand to stop LiHoun from interrupting. "I'm not saying that she's mistaken, but does she know all the soldiers on sight? I don't."

"I will have your network observe and report," LiHoun said.

"Get me an estimate of their numbers." She tugged on her bottom lip. "I suppose it's possible that the Thampurians sent extra troops to safeguard the plantation on Cay Rhi, but…"

LiHoun waited silently for her to work through her reservations.

"If that's true, then why are they disturbing the peace in the town square instead of guarding Cay Rhi? And how did they get here so fast? The *Golden Barracuda* is the fastest ship in the Zul fleet, but even it can't possibly sail round trip in three days."

Or could it? That engine she'd heard below decks had moved them at speeds she'd never imagined. In open water, it might run even faster. But between Ponong and Thampur, thousands of small islands formed a dangerous archipelago. Only a fool would try to thread through them at high speed, even if he knew the safe shipping lanes.

No. It seemed more probable that the troops had set sail before she'd led Kyam to the Ravidians, which meant the two weren't connected. The only other possibility that came to mind immediately was that Governor Turyat had asked for more troops before he knew about the Ravidians, so he'd been planning to cut off the Ponongese from the marketplace for some time now. But why? There had been no extraordinary tensions between the Ponongese and Thampurians in the past few months. Admittedly, she'd sensed something odd in the mood of the town, but Governor Turyat would be the last person to notice such things. The sudden change mystified her. Could Governor Turyat simply have brought the additional soldiers to Levapur to show his power?

If he wanted to see what one could do with power, she was more than up to the challenge.

"About the rice… I've developed quite an appetite for it. Tell my lieutenants to buy all the rice the smugglers and the legitimate importers bring to the island."

A coughing fit shook LiHoun's thin shoulders. "All?" he said faintly when he caught his breath.

"Every last grain. But spread the purchases among my lieutenants. I don't want to arouse suspicions."

"Forgive this old man for not understanding, but want do you want with so much rice?"

"Leverage, uncle. You'd be amazed how much power there is in such a simple thing."

CHAPTER 8: GRANDFATHER ZUL

*S*ince they were in no hurry to finish repairs to the *Winged Dragon*, Hadre made sure every inch of the junk was inspected. He expected the crew to complain, but they were enthusiastic about it. The officers probably felt the additional investment in the ship promised fair sailing and better payouts from the ship's profits. The crew liked the generous shore leave, since many diversions that were illegal on the continent were legal – and encouraged – in Levapur.

Grandfather continued to demand gossip from Levapur. While Hadre had visited the Quarter of Delights, he hadn't admitted it. Instead, he told his grandfather that he was too busy overseeing the repairs. He was used to life on board and could go months without yearning for land, or so he said.

His crew had plenty to say about Levapur when they returned from shore leave. Most of their talk wouldn't have interested Grandfather, but here and there he caught comments that made him hold his breath and listen intently. Those stories he kept out of his reports. He was no spy. He knew how a ship worked, but had no idea how towns functioned. Maybe it wasn't terrible that the marketplace was all but abandoned. There were still stores people could shop in, after all, but the wharf was stacked with crates that wouldn't move upslope until the Ponongese were allowed to return to work. The abandoned fishing fleet bobbed in the gentle waves across the harbor. That sent an ominous chill down his spine. What would people eat if they couldn't fish?

If only there were someone other than Grandfather he could discuss these ugly developments with. His officers were as mystified as he was by the rapid changes. Levapur had always been lawless, but cheerfully so. Now it was as dour as the trading posts on the bleak islands near the werewolves' northern fortresses.

He braced both elbows on his desk and rested his head in his hands.

He missed Kyam. Several times, he'd been tempted to find his cousin and try to work out a truce, but then Grandfather pressured him to go into town and report his findings, and he grew more determined to force their grandfather to talk directly to Kyam.

Kyam had always been far too loyal to that old man. Hadre never understood it; but then, Hadre was a ship's Captain. Once a man grew used to being his own master, it was harder to be a filial Thampurian grandson, especially to their grandfather.

As if thinking about the old man could summon him, the ship's farwriter bell chimed. If only he hadn't set the machine to the new frequency earlier, he could have ignored the muffled summons. Now or later, it would make little difference. He opened the cabinet and tore off the paper scroll.

What was your impression of the Qui woman? TtZ

Hadre was puzzled. He'd reported everything about her time on board the *Golden Barracuda* days ago, except the part about finding her and Kyam together in a cabin. Facts were all grandfather cared about. Why did the old man now want his assessment of a woman he'd met only once?

QuiTai had made a strong impression, but one he wasn't sure he could put into words. Kyam's many stories about her had prepared him for her intelligence and cutting wit, but not for her intensity. Hadre smiled. No wonder his cousin was so intrigued by her. While she'd never pass as a lady by Thampurian standards, she could have ruled a salon in Surrayya with the arch of an eyebrow and a few precise words.

Lady QuiTai is brilliant, insightful, and very quick of mind. And fearless. HnZ

Smiling wryly, Hadre said to himself, "She'd easily outsmart you given the chance, old man."

Rumor has it she has separatist sympathies. TtZ

"Is that a question?" Hadre asked his empty cabin.

If she does, she was far too canny to say so in my hearing. HnZ

I'm not interested in what she said or didn't say. I want to know if she were provoked, would she lash out at the colonial government? Is she the type? Is she an angry woman? Is she a leader? You said she was fearless. TtZ

She leapt off the walls of the fortress to escape the werewolves. She could have landed on the rocks and broken her back. The harbor is shark-infested and apparently she isn't a strong swimmer. I saw her jump without hesitating. HnZ

This is welcome news. TtZ

Not since his first ship had run aground on a moonless night and he'd woken to the sickening groan of the damaged hull scraping against rocks had his stomach dropped with such leaden fear. At least then he'd known right away why he was frightened. He'd sailed through heavy seas during winter storms that sent waves crashing over his deck and toppled his main mast. He'd survived plague that had killed half his crew in two weeks, and more than once he'd fought hand to hand with pirates for control of his ship. None of that had worried him as much as this message, and nothing angered him more than being scared by words. Words were nothing. They were maishun spirits without substance. And yet, they deeply disturbed him.

Bile rose in his throat as he carefully worded his next message.

As you said, she might have been apprehended. I haven't heard anything about her since she left the Golden Barracuda with the colonial militia. HnZ

> *She hasn't been arrested yet. Why is she holding back?* TtZ

Grandfather, musing in a farwriter message? Hadre bet the old man wished he could recall that message. Lady QuiTai hadn't been captured by the soldiers. That part was clear, but *Why is she holding back?* What the hell did that mean? Why would she hasten to be arrested?

> *Ask Kyam. He knows her far better than I do.* HnZ

Far, far better than I do, he thought. Hadre's cheeks burned as he remembered her pulling the sheet over her naked body and the smell of sex in Kyam's cabin.

CHAPTER 9: MAJOR VOORUS

*K*yam took two steps into the Red Happiness, saw his cousin Hadre drinking with his new first mate, and walked out. It seemed there was nowhere in town he could go for a quiet drink. He was an exile among exiles in a town that suddenly seemed so small he couldn't draw a free breath.

The Dragon Pearl was only a block from PhaJut's, so he went there next. It wasn't quiet, but Lizzriat, the worldly, androgynous Ingosolian owner of the Dragon Pearl, kept a quality house. Kyam was never sure if he should think of the gender-shifting Ingosolians as male or female, but since Lizzriat wore foppish suits rather than dresses, Kyam had always thought of Lizzriat as male. Besides, the other casino owners would have shut the Dragon Pearl shut down immediately if they had been able to prove their rival was a woman.

Lizzriat was in his usual place near the main entrance where he could keep an eye on the action and greet his customers. Smiling, he lightly gripped Kyam's elbow and deftly steered him to an open seat at one of the tables. Governor Turyat and his cronies sat in the other chairs. Lizzriat's smile never faltered, but a cloud of concentration settled on his brow as Kyam made his excuses and backed out the front door.

It was just as well that he hadn't taken the place at the table. He'd gambled away most of his last remittance payment on purpose so he'd have an excuse to accept QuiTai's portrait commission. She'd called his obsession with details narcissism. How she'd laugh if she knew he was living off the bag of coins she'd tossed at him as part of their act.

The least Grandfather could do, if he planned to make Kyam stay in Levapur much longer, would be to send more money. And it would be helpful if Grandfather would tell him why he had to stay on the island. But the old man hadn't acknowledged any of his farwriter messages.

As further proof that he had nothing but bad luck, as Kyam strolled down the street behind the government building, he saw Voorus at the corner – and he couldn't dodge into the nearby shop quickly enough to avoid being seen.

Voorus walked up the veranda steps with his hands shoved into his trouser pockets. He glanced around the store as if the bins of brown, black, and white rice were a quaint oddity. "Zul! I almost didn't see you. Buying rice?"

Kyam didn't see any way out of it, with Voorus ready to ask annoying questions and the merchant expectantly waiting for his order. He didn't cook often. He didn't even have a rice pot in his apartment. Then he remembered his oath to buy rice for his neighbors and thanked the Goddess of Mercy for the excuse.

"A quarter-measure, please," Kyam told the merchant. That would be enough for the Rhi family for a couple meals.

Voorus peered into a bin as if the color of the rice puzzled him. "Do you need that much? Aren't you leaving Levapur?"

Damn Voorus and his curiosity.

"It isn't for me." He regretted saying that. He paid the merchant and left.

Voorus seemingly had nothing better to do with his time than follow him. "Who is it for?"

The problem with living in a small, sleepy town was that

the only entertainment was gossip. There was no way Kyam could escape Voorus without an explanation.

"The marketplace is still closed to Ponongese, so I thought my neighbors might need rice." There. That was simple enough. And it was true.

"You're giving a gift to a Ponongese?" Voorus laughed.

Kyam stared ahead as his jaw set tight.

"You know that's just asking for trouble. Even I know they get angry if you give them a gift."

"They like gifts the same as anyone else would, but you never bring food into a Ponongese home. It implies they don't have enough to share, and that's a huge insult to them," Kyam said. "If all they had was a grain of salt, they'd find a way to cut it so everyone got a taste."

"Well, what do you know?" Voorus seemed genuinely delighted to learn that, although his easy grin and slight slouch reminded Kyam of the bored scions of the thirteen families sprawled across the dainty pink divans in his mother's salon. They could rouse from a drunken stupor and go through the motions society demanded and then pass out again and not remember a thing the following morning.

As annoying as he was, though, Voorus had a point. Such matters required a delicate touch. The best way to approach it was to cook the rice himself and invite the Rhi to join him for dinner. He'd have to borrow RhiLan's cookware, but that might smooth over any other awkwardness.

Voorus tagged along when Kyam stopped at a butcher to pick up some thin strips of pork and then at the grocer's for some vegetables. Hopefully he could make them into something edible. RhiLan was such a good cook. She knew a million ways to prepare fish so it didn't feel like the same meal every night, and her rice never crunched when you bit into it. But there was no way around the coming embarrassment unless he wanted to play the clueless Thampurian who stomped on Ponongese toes with the grace of a floundering h'vet out of water, and they'd humored him far too many times to try that ploy again.

Voorus frowned at his packages. "How many gifts are you

giving them?"

"Most of this is for my dinner."

"I wouldn't feed a pig those greens you bought."

"I didn't have much choice. The shops are nearly empty because everything is rotting on the docks and no one will carry the crates up to town."

"Don't give them to your neighbors. They'll really be insulted."

When Kyam didn't respond, Voorus nudged him with his elbow. "So you know their customs; but even you have to admit that most Ponongese are funny about strange things."

He knew he was going to regret asking, but he said, "Such as?"

"These snakes have a thousand different rules about who is in charge. Sometime it's the oldest person, which is proper thinking, but then you're in a different situation and it's someone else. At least in Thampur, if you're the eldest, everyone obeys you no matter where you go or who you're with. Direct. Easy. Sensible. Order and structure."

Kyam didn't understand how Voorus could live beside people for several years and still know nothing about them. If he had more time he could teach Voorus enough to stop looking like an ass, but who knew how soon he could leave Levapur?

A grunt of amusement shook Kyam's shoulders at the thought of being anyone's etiquette instructor.

"With the Ponongese, much depends on where you stand socially in relation to someone, which sometimes, but not always, is a matter of your actual ages. When in doubt, the old people are grandfather or grandmother, adults you don't want to anger are uncle or auntie, and anyone younger than you is little brother or sister."

If Kyam got it wrong, the Ponongese were too polite, or amused, or mortified, to correct him.

"I'll be damned if I'll treat a snake like a relation."

"It's not – " Kyam could see that it was no use trying to convince Voorus that the Ponongese wouldn't see it as a claim of kinship. "Where it gets tricky is when they defer to the person with greater knowledge or experience with a given situation. If one of them refers to an obviously younger person as 'uncle,' that's the person in charge, but only in that situation. An hour later, the same person might refer to that younger person as 'little brother.' Unless they both call each other 'uncle,' and then it gets really convoluted." The more he tried to explain it, the more complicated it seemed. In real life, anyone who paid attention could understand what was going on. Voorus didn't seem like the type to pay attention.

"See? What a mess. Some people are born to lead, and others to follow, no matter what the situation."

"Would you listen to the advice of a fishermen if you were trying to catch a fish? Sure. But you wouldn't ask him to write your will."

With a twist of his hand, Voorus waved that argument away, but his eyes lit up. "Interesting that you should use that phrase. Guess what? I've decided to study law. With these new soldiers taking over, there's no way to distinguish myself and earn my articles of transport home. But as a lawyer, I might. Never wanted to be a soldier anyway."

"Then why are you in uniform?"

"Mother's friend arranged entry to the academy, and how could I say no? It's not as if I had private tutors or the kinds of connections that get you into a university."

It took connections to get into the military academy too, so Voorus' mother's friend must have been a member of one of the thirteen families. She had good taste, and more sense than her son.

"Borrowed a set of books from one of the assistants to Chief Justice Cuulon. He hasn't even cracked them open. Said the Chief Justice tells them what's what, saves them the trouble. Once I got the hang of the language, though, I plan to figure it out for myself. From what I hear, it's fascinating stuff. For instance, did you know that it was perfectly legal to seize the agricultural terraces when we colonized Ponong? Their women owned the land, but by Thampurian law women can't hold property, so of course it all came under the control of the colonial government."

"Well, that's neat and clear, isn't it? I can't understand why the Ponongese still call it theft." Kyam swore he could hear QuiTai's words coming from his mouth. In his mind, he heard her voice, and that dry sense of humor. But if women couldn't hold property, how did QuiTai own the Red Happiness? The Devil had to be the owner. Or was it someone else? No wonder QuiTai wanted those deed documents buried where no one could find them.

"Although it's a shame they can't. My uncle seized the family home when my father died." Voorus shook his head. "Doesn't seem right. It was all my mother had."

"Why didn't it go to you?"

"Happened before I was born."

"Why didn't she claim your rights afterwards?"

Voorus glanced away. "My uncle made threats. Washed out to sea with the tide now. Anyway, a friend of Mother's bought a small place for us to live in a decent enough neighborhood, so we weren't on the streets."

The fact that they didn't fight it probably meant Voorus had been born suspiciously late after his mother's husband died. That friend who got Voorus into the military was probably Voorus' real father. Since Kyam didn't feel like being pummeled bloody, he decided to keep that deduction to himself.

Kyam juggled his packages in the hopes of reminding Voorus he had errands to run. The top one almost fell.

"You're going to drop one of those. Hire a boy." Voorus glanced up and down the street.

They were still close to the government building where the new soldiers roved in packs to scare away Ponongese. The only people in the shops were Thampurian or Ingosolian. A cat-eyed Li man squatted by an alleyway staircase behind the soldiers as he smoked a kur.

"I need a market basket," Kyam said.

Voorus drew back. "Have you gone native, man? Or has the sun cooked your brains?"

Kyam reined in his anger. He'd barely noticed all the stupid rules everyone followed in the past year and didn't want to start now. The petty taboos grated on his nerves. There was no need to act like a Thampurian. He was one. No market basket could change that.

"I need — " He almost said "rum" just to see what level of outrage Voorus' face could twist into. So he'd acquired a taste for the local brew. What of it? It was far cheaper than whiskey and much better quality than any of the imported spirits.

"I'm not going to carry anything for you, so stop asking," Voorus said. "Ha! You need a boy; I found you one." He strode across the street to the old cat-man. The cat-man tried to back away, but Voorus gripped him by the collar and dragged him over to Kyam.

Kyam wondered where he had seen this odd old fellow before. The Li Islands were a Thampurian colony several hundred miles south of Ponong in the Te'Am Ocean, but few Li lived on Ponong, just as few Ponongese moved to the Li Islands. If they wanted to escape Thampurian rule, they made the dangerous and expensive voyage to the southern continent. Chances were if Kyam had seen an elderly Li in Levapur before, it had been this man. But where? If he saw the man in context, he'd probably recognize him right away, but outside of his normal setting, Kyam couldn't place him.

Voorus grabbed Kyam's packages and shoved them into the old man's hands. "There. My good deed for the day. When you get back to Thampur, tell everyone how helpful I was. Who knows? A good word might save me." He looked at his pocket watch. "Is that the time? I'm supposed to lead drills at the fortress in an hour. I keep forgetting that I need to leave earlier now that the funicular is broken. I wonder when they'll get it fixed?"

"Never, if the governor doesn't allow the workers to pass through the town square to get to it."

With a grin, Voorus shrugged. "This island... You won't miss it, will you? Anyway, I have to go. I leave your packages in good hands."

He stepped smartly down the street.

Kyam turned to the old cat-man who stood patiently

holding his shopping. "I think I know you. Where have I seen you before? What's your name?"

"LiHoun, Mister, Sir." The old man bowed many times as he balanced the packages. "I'm honored to carry the worthy's – "

"I'll give you an extra coin if you stop treating me like a Thampurian."

LiHoun slowly grinned, showing mostly toothless gums. His demeanor changed with his tone. "As Mister Zul wishes."

Something about LiHoun still made him wary. It wasn't anything he could point to, but the muscles across his back stayed tight. Paying attention to his body's warning signs had saved his life a few times. He certainly wouldn't head down any deserted alleyways with the cat-man, and until they parted ways, he'd keep his eyes and ears open for suspicious behavior.

"Come on. I need to buy a bottle or two," Kyam said.

LiHoun easily balanced Kyam's bundles as they headed for the spirit merchant's shop.

Kyam left LiHoun on the veranda outside the spirit merchant's shop and went inside. The merchant acknowledged Kyam before turning his attention back to his other customers. Fresh wood shavings were arranged artfully around bottles stacked on wooden crates; Kyam supposed that was meant to inspire trust that the bottles were imported and not refilled with imitation local spirits, but he knew from his days at sea that the crates were too clean to have been in a ship's hold.

Kyam pretended to read labels while he watched LiHoun through the glass-paned door. LiHoun waited with the resigned patience of an errand runner. Kyam almost turned away as the other customers in the shop started talking about the marketplace. They seemed more upset about the inconvenience of having to go to the Ponongese market and their fear of the slums of Old Levapur than the injustice to the Ponongese merchants. He held his tongue as long as he could, but just as he was about to join the conversation, he saw LiHoun's back straighten.

What had caught the old man's attention? Kyam peered down the street. Five soldiers had turned the corner., and LiHoun was looking directly at them.

It was Kyam's first good look at the new soldiers. He'd passed by them before, but he'd been drunk and couldn't remember much. This time, like LiHoun, he watched them pass by.

Oddly, there were no insignias or other identifiers on the soldier's uniforms. It was as if their posting, position, and even ranks had been deliberately obscured. Who were these men, and why had they come to Levapur? From their apparent familiarity with each other, they'd served together before, possibly for years. Strangers didn't move together that way. If Voorus' quip about every Thampurian in Levapur being there in disgrace was right, there had been a scandal back in Thampur that he hadn't heard about – something big enough to put an entire troop into exile.

He should ask Hadre. No, he wasn't going to talk to Hadre until Hadre apologized for attacking Grandfather. He could figure this out without Hadre's help anyway.

LiHoun, he noticed, watched the soldiers until they reached the end of the street. Then the old man finally relaxed.

"Can I help you, Sir?" The spirit merchant asked Kyam.

Kyam turned away from the window. "Two bottles of rum, please."

He ignored the rude stares of the other customers as he paid for his bottles. There were more important matters than their approval. It felt as if he'd been yanked back suddenly into his old work as a spy, and every sense, every thought, honed in on LiHoun. The old man was watching the soldiers. Why? Who did he work for? Kyam didn't like jumping to conclusions without any proof, but the name that immediately came to mind was the Devil.

Kyam shot glances at LiHoun as they walked toward Kyam's apartment. How could he broach the subject of the Devil without alarming the old man? What if he were mistaken?

"I'm sure I've seen you before. Not many Li live in Levapur," Kyam began.

"I used to run errands for the workers at PhaJut's. Now I'm at the Dragon Pearl, but I assist their customers."

Something LiHoun said earlier came back to him. "You know my name."

"It can be helpful in my line of work."

"Fetching and carrying, or gathering information?"

It seemed as if LiHoun knew where this conversation might lead. From the twitch of his upper lip, he was enjoying Kyam's attempts to get to the point. Cat and mouse. Of course, a Li would enjoy that game.

"I saw you watching the soldiers."

They stopped at the steps to Kyam's apartment building. LiHoun passed the packages back to Kyam and put his hand out for his coins. After unsuccessfully trying to juggle his purchases and reach into his trouser pockets, Kyam set the packages on the top step.

"They are not typical colonial militia men," LiHoun said.

LiHoun wasn't even going to try to pretend he'd been stringing for the Dragon Pearl. That was unusually direct. Direct for a Thampurian, Kyam reminded himself, not a Li, or a Ponongese like QuiTai. He wondered why the Devil was interested in the soldiers. If they were cracking down on the black market, Kyam was all for it, but so far all he'd seen was their attack on legitimate businesses.

Kyam jangled the coins in his hand.

"And you're not a typical errand boy, uncle LiHoun." Kyam opened his hand.

LiHoun glanced at the coins but didn't take them.

"Two for carrying my packages. One for not bowing and

scraping. And three more if you can pass a message to the Devil."

LiHoun said nothing, but looked directly at him. There weren't many Li or Ponongese who would dare such insolence, but he had told the man not to treat him like a Thampurian. The cat-man's vertical pupils were narrow slits in the middle of murky green irises. Nothing in his expression suggested shock, anger, or wariness at the mention of the Devil.

While he had few coins left to live on, Kyam took a valuable one out of his pocket and put it on his open palm next to the others.

Kyam glanced up and down the street. No one was near. "I prefer that you tell his concubine this: someone paid Petrof the werewolf to kill her. I don't think he's succeeded – yet. He must be stopped."

"Must?"

Kyam jerked back. Had he told the wrong person? Was the Devil behind Petrof's attempts to kill her? Anger flashed through him. How many times had he seen bruises on QuiTai's neck? Was the Devil stupid enough to harm the woman who controlled his entire criminal enterprise? As far as he could tell, she was the brains behind the underground network. The Devil was just some lucky bastard who got a free ride on her accomplishments.

"Tell the Devil that if she dies, I will hold him personally responsible for failing to protect her. If she dies, I will come after him," Kyam growled, inches from LiHoun's face.

Understanding dawned on LiHoun's ancient face along with a grin. "Ah." He snatched the coins from Kyam's palm as Kyam gaped in shock. LiHoun backed down the stairs, every crooked tooth showing, eyes squinting with merriment. "Don't worry, Colonel Zul. I know how to keep a secret."

He damn well better, Kyam thought, or QuiTai was in more danger than before.

Kyam set his packages on the desk in the corner of his apartment and went to light his cooking fire. Most people left theirs burning, but he couldn't afford that. The flame wouldn't catch, and he was almost out of matches. He checked the jar of juam nut oil under the burner. There was barely any left, and he didn't have enough coins left to fill it.

He leaned against the counter and scratched his head. When he got back to Thampur, he was going to teach a class for new Intelligence recruits called Undercover Verisimilitude: how to successfully live in poverty for extended periods. Not that he'd figured it out yet. Being poor required skills he hadn't developed. Yet while it paled in comparison to his income before exile, his remittance payment was far more than an average Thampurian in Levapur lived on. Disgraced or not, he was a Zul, after all. But that money rarely lasted until his next remittance arrived, despite some attempts at budgeting. Hadre always had to lend him a bit and pay for dinner; but he could hardly go to Hadre now and grovel. Besides, the *Winged Dragon* might have sailed already.

If only he could take his packages to RhiLan across the landing and ask her to make dinner.

He realized how rude that would be. Ponongese rules of hospitality aside, it would be treating her like his servant, and he never wanted the Rhi to feel as if that was how he viewed them. It would be like twisting every kind gesture into their duty to him. He didn't want to be that kind of person.

See, Hadre? I'm not a stodgy Thampurian at heart after all. But that doesn't mean I'll excuse your behavior toward Grandfather.

Well, there was nothing to do but beg some juam nut oil from RhiLan. He had to borrow her rice pot anyway. The only thing he knew how to cook was rice-and-eggs. He hoped he didn't ruin the pork and vegetables, but it was all he could afford in the shops and if he didn't cook it today it would spoil. He briefly thought about trading the pork for eggs with the auntie who kept jungle fowl in a coop by the apartment building's outhouse, but she probably didn't have enough eggs to make the trade fair, and he'd learned never to insult a Ponongese by insinuating they needed his charity.

He detached the hose that ran from the oil tin to the burner and headed across the landing to RhiLan's door.

There was a thump and hushed but harsh whispers before RhiLan's eldest son, RhiLiet, cracked open the door. The boy usually had a smile for everyone, but today he was serious. He glanced over his shoulder and said, "It's Mister Zul." Then he turned back to Kyam as he hugged the door. "Have you eaten, Mister Zul?"

This was one of those moments when Kyam wished he understood Ponongese customs better. 'Have you eaten' was the same as 'hello' to a Thampurian, but it sounded so much like a real question that he felt he had to answer. But how did one answer?

"Um... Yes, I have, and you? Is auntie RhiLan here? Can I speak to her?" he said in a rush.

Kyam smelled an unwashed body with an undertone of sickness to the stench. If someone in RhiLan's apartment suffered from one of the three fevers, that explained the boy's wariness. Thampurian soldiers were quick to drag anyone suspected of those illnesses to the edge of the Jupoli Gorge and give them a hearty shove into the Pha River below.

The boy looked over his shoulder again. A hand gripped the edge of the door, and RhiLan peered over her son. He scooted away. She moved into the space he'd left and wrapped herself around the door as he had.

"Mister Zul. So nice to see you." Her tone was as flat as a winter lake, and he hadn't even had a chance to insult her yet.

"I was making dinner" – he waved a hand in the direction of his door – "and hoped that your family would share it with me. I may be leaving Levapur soon and didn't want to go without saying goodbye properly."

He could see the conflict in her face. She was a nice woman without a drop of unkindness in her blood. Her man and children were the same. He truly would miss them. They'd always had such a friendly relationship. And yet, she was clearly torn.

"Please, auntie. It's just a humble dinner. It may be the last chance I have to enjoy the company of your family." He gave her his best pleading look.

She held up her hand and looked behind the door. He pretended he couldn't hear the furious exchange of whispers.

"We will come, Mister Zul. Thank you for your kind invitation," RhiLan said.

He pressed his hands together and bowed. "Thank you, auntie. I'm honored." Kyam held up his oil jar. "May I borrow some cooking oil?"

She nodded as she reached for the jar.

"And your rice pot? And a skillet?"

Feminine laughter from somewhere behind RhiLan was quickly muffled. It seemed they had a guest that they didn't want him to know about. Maybe the woman was ill? Surely RhiLan wouldn't have exposed him or her family to such danger, though. Even Ponongese rules of hospitality had a limit. It was more likely that their guest suffered from one of the many other maladies that Ponong's heat and humidity seemed to make worse. He'd learned that lesson all too well his second month in exile when a simple cut on his thumb had become infected.

"Oh, and could I beg a pinch of tumejra powder?"

Merriment warmed RhiLan's snake eyes. She motioned for him to wait as she closed the door. Indistinct voices were followed by more muffled laughter. When RhiLan opened the door again, she bit her lips, but her chin quivered with suppressed giggles. "Are you sure you don't need rice and fish too, little brother?"

This was the RhiLan he was used to. Whatever worried her, it wasn't too serious. He grinned as he shrugged. "I have rice."

"I'll send RhiLiet with the pans. He'll stay to help you with your rice." RhiLan's hand pressed to her mouth. Her eyes sparkled with laughing tears. "So it's not crunchy."

CHAPTER 10: THE ORACLE'S SILENCE

*T*he hillside slums of Old Levapur clung to banded orange sand cliffs that looked as if they'd melt in heavy rain. Near the dirt road that connected the Thampurian enclave of West Levapur to the town square was an old, squat apartment building painted in mismatched pink patches. Most of the other buildings in the slum were single story shacks with tin roofs and rotting walls. Vines grew over the roofs that bowed under the weight. Jungle fowl scratched in the long weeds for grubs. Paths winding up the hillside were deeply rutted by sluggish streams that washed filth down slope, under the funicular tracks, and down the cliff into the Sea of Erykoli.

RhiLan never would have set up a market stall in such a place if she'd been alone. The other Ponongese merchants seemed to feel the same – they huddled together in a wide spot on the road between a small tavern and the apartment building. Rumor said the Devil ruled with an iron fist here and would not allow Ponongese to steal from each other, but the people of Old Levapur frightened her. Even the young had weary eyes and mean expressions.

She knew it wasn't fair to judge people she hadn't even talked to, but she worried that they'd scare away customers. If only the other merchants had picked a nice Ponongese neighborhood for their new market. The road that wound through the upslope neighborhoods in Levapur was too narrow and steep for stalls, but around her apartment, the streets were wider and almost flat.

The mango seller who had squatted beside RhiLan at the meeting jerked her chin upward. "Even the monsoon god wants us to have a good market."

RhiLan smiled at the sky. Tall clouds towered high, stark white against the blue, but they were far out to sea and held no rain in their bellies. Even the daily mist that wreathed the mountains was thin enough that she could see the outlines of their peaks. "It's a good sign."

Even though the shaky excitement shot through her, RhiLan reminded herself that this was no secret party. She drew a brown and orange sarong from her market basket and unfolded it. "I just finished this design. Do you like it?"

The mango seller averted her eyes. "Until I sell my mangos, I can't think of something so frivolous." She reached above her head and plucked a mango from her basket. Freckled red and gold patches spread over the green skin. "Nice and ripe. I found the sweetest one, just for you."

Mangos and peppers was her man's favorite dish, but RhiLan had to decline the fruit. "I only have these coins. What if I never sell another sarong?"

She rued her words as she heard them repeated back to her many times through the morning. Many people had come to Old Levapur to look at the new market, but no one dared part with their money.

Later, when the sun was high and the day turned hot, merchants with stalls retreated deep into them to rest. The basket women wandered into the fringes of the jungle where there was shade and water gathered at the base of thick leaves they could drink.

RhiLan headed to her children's school by a route that took her up slope, along the rim of the Jupoli Gorge and back down slope. It took much longer than usual, but she avoided the Thampurian neighborhoods around the government building where those soldiers waited to harass Ponongese.

The patch of open land beside the school was quiet. Normally, the children played outside after midday dismissal.

Through her life, RhiLan had never questioned why at such moments guilt came before fear. Her first thought was that she had done something wrong and should fix it. Her steps slowed as she neared the faded blue building. The silence seemed formidable. She winced as the veranda step creaked under her foot.

Maybe she'd come early.

She listened. The children's voices were low, but they were inside. Yes, she was early. She squatted on the veranda and waited. Within five minutes, more parents were squatting beside her.

The door finally opened. Ma'am Thun beckoned them inside. RhiLan's fear wrenched as she tried to think of what she might have done to anger the teacher. Or perhaps her children had misbehaved, but that didn't explain why the other parents were also in disgrace.

The converted apartment building smelled of children and old books. The foyer's bare timber grass floor was meticulously clean, although the dark varnish only lurked in corners. A gray path led to each door, and the dark, narrow stairs' bowed risers showed where years of students had trod.

The tension evident in Ma'am Thun's face and strict posture at first made RhiLan think the teacher was angry, but when Ma'am Thun spoke, her voice was thick with sorrow.

"Do not bring your children back this afternoon. The school is closed."

RhiLan had never seen a Thampurian lady cry. She was so confused that she grasped Ma'am Thun's hands between hers. Instead of pulling back, Ma'am Thun groaned as if she might faint.

The other parents squatted in the foyer.

"What has happened?" one of the other mothers asked.

"The soldiers. They said I'm not allowed to teach Ponongese children anymore. I showed them my charter. They ripped it into pieces." Her hand shielded her eyes for a moment. Then she flicked away her tears. With a deep breath, she smoothed the lace ruffle at her neck. "Well," she said in a brighter voice, as if that was all she meant to say on the matter.

Then she rang the bell that hung over the first door off the foyer. The first door opened and children filed out. The sight of their parents inside the school caused many to turn to their classmates with questioning glances.

Ma'am Thun barely inclined her head to each student as they passed her. The children, as was right, bowed much deeper with their hands pressed together. She also slightly bowed to the parents. Her smile wavered, but no more tears fell.

RhiLan wanted to stay behind and ask questions, but the door shut behind them with such finality that she didn't dare. The Thampurians were very proud. Any hint of pity would only anger Ma'am Thun.

Children, as they often did, ignored the strange ways of the adults and ran ahead, glad to finally be free for their lunch.

A father with a withered right leg slowed his steps as he waited for RhiLan to catch up to him. "I wonder what he will do."

RhiLan wondered if she'd missed the first part of the conversation. "He?"

The man looked around before lowering his voice. "The Devil."

"The Devil!" Alarmed, she stopped, her mouth open.

"You didn't know? He pays the tuition for all Pha children at this school. How else would those of us from Old Levapur afford such a luxury as education?" His boney chest filled out as he took a deep breath. "My son, he's slow with words, but no Thampurian merchant will ever cheat him with numbers!"

"But, the Devil!"

"The Thampurians better watch out, because when the

Devil is angry, people die." He bowed and hobbled after his son.

RhiLan carefully filled her tjanting pen with melted wax and then drew the tip over the new sarong she was making. The wax was too hot, and the line flowed into the others to ruin the intricate design. The wobbly lines she'd drawn looked like her daughter's efforts.

"The Devil! My children went to a school financed by the Devil!" She couldn't hold back her despair any longer.

It felt as if her apartment were too crowded for RhiLan. She wasn't used to having so many people underfoot in the afternoon. QuiTai sat at the low table with RhiLan's daughter RhiTeek in her lap as she helped the children practice their letters. RhiHanya swept the floor.

"It was just a school, cousin. It isn't as if he was teaching them to pick pockets," RhiHanya said.

"How do we know what went on? Ma'am Thun seemed so respectable."

RhiHanya glanced at QuiTai. "Maybe the man was misinformed."

"He seemed to know. He approved!"

"Everyone knows," QuiTai said. She pointed to a place on RhiLiet's page and told him, "That letter is a dragon scale. There's a little point at the tip. Yes, like that."

RhiLan felt as if she'd been dismissed. "I didn't know! Why do you corrupt such a good thing?"

QuiTai made a face as if she were reluctant to speak. "I grew up in Old Levapur. My mother had the foresight to send me to Ma'am Thun's school even though it meant going to bed hungry many nights. Other parents in the slums wanted to send their children but couldn't afford to. I taught what I could to the ones who were interested, but teaching requires a mindset I don't possess. Once I was in a position to pay tuition for others, I did, much to the relief of those I tried to teach."

"See?" RhiHanya said.

"But she gets her money from the Devil." RhiLan gasped. "I'm sorry, Wolf Slayer. No offense."

QuiTai inclined her head. "None taken, auntie," she said even though RhiLan was certain her frighteningly serene guest was irked.

If you are what becomes of a child with a Thampurian education, perhaps my children are better off out of school, RhiLan thought. She immediately regretted feeling that way. The Wolf Slayer had done nothing to her to deserve such a waspish sting.

"So what do you plan to do about this?" RhiHanya asked QuiTai.

"About what?" QuiTai asked.

RhiHanya paced the apartment with that roll to her hips that warned RhiLan that her cousin was spoiling for a fight. She'd been foolish enough to insult the Wolf Slayer, but she had an excuse. Her cousin was a fool to continue prodding her to argue when she was already angry. While RhiHanya was much curvier, QuiTai looked like the type who would strike fast, and fatally.

"Your school being closed," RhiHanya said to QuiTai.

"It isn't my school."

"Uh huh." RhiHanya's head bobbed with attitude.

RhiLan felt pressed from all directions. The Thampurians, her overbearing cousin, the Wolf Slayer, and now even the Devil seemed to have staked out territory in her mind so that she could barely think without bumping against one of them. If only there was a polite way to get the Wolf Slayer to move out. And then her cousin.

"Maybe I should go to the market," RhiLan murmured.

RhiHanya turned on her. "At least you can leave this apartment. We're stuck here. Right, auntie QuiTai?"

Rather than answer, QuiTai gently combed through RhiTeek's waist length black hair. "One day, when you are fertile, you will wear your hair in a braid like your mother and cousin," she told the girl.

"Can I have a clip like yours?" RhiTeek asked.

QuiTai smiled down at the girl but said nothing. RhiLan didn't want any more of QuiTai's charity.

"Only I want an orange one. Green is ugly," RhiTeek said.

"RhiTeek!" RhiLan was mortified. It was bad enough to say such a thing to an ordinary guest, but to this one, who sat coiled around her daughter, it was alarming.

QuiTai chuckled. "Orange is a good color. It says that you're happy and strong, like the sun."

"What does green mean?" RhiTeek asked.

RhiLan sucked in a breath between clenched teeth.

Brow furrowed, QuiTai finally said, "It means I like green."

"Oh." RhiTeek shrugged and bent over her letters again.

RhiLan exhaled in relief.

"It means she's dangerous," her middle boy said. He looked at QuiTai for only a moment with his solemn eyes. It was the first words he'd spoken in her presence.

"Are you dangerous?" her eldest boy RhiLiet asked, suddenly much more interested in QuiTai than he had been.

"Yes," QuiTai answered RhiLiet in her unnervingly flat tone that made one wonder what she might be thinking.

"Stop it this instant! Have you no manners? Wolf Slayer, forgive them," RhiLan said. Her heart raced. She didn't think QuiTai would harm her children, but she swept over to the table and yanked RhiTeek out of QuiTai's lap. She grabbed RhiLiet by his hair, since he had been the rudest, and dragged him to his feet. He twisted and turned under her grasp, his chubby cheeks flushing bright pink as he yowled. "We're going to the market, children."

QuiTai rose. "If I may impose, RhiLan, could you do me a favor?" She grabbed a few coins from the purse that hung always from her waist. "Buy a few things."

RhiLan wanted to say no, to ask this woman to go away, but she was beginning to fear QuiTai, so she took the coins. "What do you need?"

"Anything. Not food, though. From what you said, no one is willing to spend money. Someone has to be the first. If they see you willing to spend money on something you don't need to survive, it will have a greater impact."

"Can I have a hair clip?" RhiTeek asked.

"Not for several years, little sister," QuiTai told her.

RhiLan bristled at QuiTai's nerve. "Many, many years," she said. "And definitely not until you show better manners to our guests." She glared at her boys. "And that goes for you two. No sweets."

RhiLiet was still pleading his case when they left, but his younger brother said nothing.

RhiHanya chatted as she bent over the sarong on RhiLan's frame to pick off the ruined wax designs. "My cousin doesn't have the temperament for an adventure."

If only she could have gone with them. I need quiet time to think.

QuiTai couldn't figure out what to do with herself. She could recline on the divan and pretend to sleep, but her mind would still be wide awake and frantic for activity. Every letter and newspaper LiHoun brought her had been read so many times she could almost recite them from memory. She crossed the room and opened a typhoon shutter.

"You are not going out on that veranda in daylight," RhiHanya said. Her fist was on her hip.

"I'm bored."

"You and me. So liven my afternoon by taking a step outside. Go on."

They'd both feel so much better if they could get out of the apartment, or distract themselves from the heat and relentless boredom somehow. Unfortunately, sex was out of the question. Or was it? She saw RhiHanya's scowl. Angry sex could be fun.

But you couldn't get away afterward, could you? Better not entertain that thought much longer.

"I wish LiHoun would stop by."

"That's fine for you, talking in those cat-words so I can't join the conversation. That's rude, you know."

RhiHanya definitely wanted a fight. QuiTai was in no mood to help her, so she bowed her head. "I'm sorry. It is."

QuiTai looked around the apartment. There was nothing new to see. By now, she knew every inch of the room, every item in it, and far too much about the people who lived there. If she'd had any skill with a needle, she would have searched their mosquito nets for holes and repaired them. Her gaze alit on the double boiler RhiLan used to melt the wax for her batik work. Steam still curled over the pot.

She went to the cooking fire and put the kettle over the fire. Then she opened each of the drawers in RhiLan's spice cabinet.

"You're making yourself tiuhon tea, right?" RhiHanya asked. The edge was still in her voice.

Irritation prickled QuiTai's temper like a heat rash. It took every ounce of control to keep it out of her voice. "My fever already broke."

"So?"

QuiTai growled. "Oh, all right. I'll make tiuhon tea. But if I have to drink it, so do you."

"I'm not sick."

"Neither am I." She took a deep breath. She would not be dragged into a fight, especially not one as stupid as this.

RhiHanya seemed to have reached the same conclusion. "If that's what it takes to get you to drink it, then go ahead and make a cup for me too."

The plot that formed in QuiTai's brain wasn't one of those that hit with the full force of clarity. This one was far stealthier. It crept up on her as she waited for the water to boil. Instead of seeing a whole plan, she only saw the first step. Tiuhon tea was bitter and strong enough to hide other flavors. She glanced at RhiHanya, who was still picking at the wax on the sarong. Then she slid open the drawer with the black lotus and palmed the vial.

Minutes later, she handed RhiHanya a scalding cup of tiuhon tea and settled on the divan with her own cup. They chatted idly about inconsequential matters, each trying hard to be polite when they wanted nothing more than to snap and make snide remarks.

RhiHanya's thoughts tailed off, unfinished. She yawned loudly. "Sorry."

QuiTai reclined on her elbow and closed her eyes to slits as if she, too, were drowsy. Thunder rattled the typhoon shutters. Rain sprayed down moments later.

RhiHanya yawned so hard that tears fell from the corners of her tightly closed eyes. "I can't think why I'm suddenly so tired." She pulled a sleeping mat off the pile in the corner and stretched out on the floor. Before long, her breaths turned to a deep, even rhythm.

"And that's why I rarely accept a drink from anyone," QuiTai told RhiHanya as she sat upright, her eyes fully open.

The final stages of her plan had come to her as she watched RhiHanya drink the bitter tea. She set aside her cup and limped across the apartment to the spice drawers. No one would notice the daub of black lotus missing from the vial that she placed back exactly where she'd found it.

She went to RhiHanya and knelt beside her head.

"I'm not a nice woman." That didn't explain why she'd laced the drink with black lotus. RhiHanya wouldn't hear her, but she still felt as if she owed, if not an apology, at least a reason. "I can't sit here and do nothing for days on end. I need information. I need a conduit to the Oracle. And you were foolish enough to trust me."

She pressed her lips to RhiHanya's and milked a drop of her venom into her mouth.

QuiTai saw RhiHanya's pillow sister and fleeting glimpses of the Ravidians taking the villagers captive. But the majority of the Oracle's vision was about the escape from Cay Rhi.

Show me the future, Goddess.

The scene shifted, but not to the future. She saw LiHoun

talking with her on the apartment veranda, although this time they spoke in Ponongese, and they discussed a plan to free the slaves.

QuiTai sat back on her heels. That was wrong. They'd spoken Li. Besides, the plan was deeply flawed. Only an idiot would attempt something like that.

Why are your visions wrong, Goddess? You're never wrong. And why don't you speak?

She was seeing RhiHanya's dreams, not memories. That explained the difference between what she knew to be true and what she was seeing. She pushed those aside and dug deeper into RhiHanya's mind. A flood of memory came to her, but it was only about RhiHanya's life on Cay Rhi. There was nothing about the men who had paid Petrof to kill her. Once again, the Goddess failed. It was an unprecedented string of failures.

This would take a great deal of thought.

The visions she saw were usually of past events. These came through the conduit and were always from the conduit's perspective. From their memories. She'd seen plenty of her conduit's memories, first from the vapor addicts and now RhiHanya.

Of course. That's what the Oracle is really for – searching their minds for guilt or innocence. They can't hide their memories from her. The way I use her is wrong, which is why she's punishing me.

Her thoughts turned to years ago, when her mother and grandmother had trained her in the Oracle's ways. It had been years since she'd taken part in a true Qui ceremony. The Thampurians had been quick to ban the Qui's practices when they took over the island. They called it human sacrifice. To be fair to the Thampurians, it was.

How could she ever forget that innocent woman who died at the hands of the Qui? Guilty people she didn't care about, but killing an innocent was just murder, no matter how convinced you were that you had the right to do it.

That woman, the one accused of murdering her neighbor. She'd denied it even as they forced the red tar's smoke into her nose and mouth. My mother lifted me so I could add my venom to hers and Grandmother's. The Oracle showed us the woman's innocence and grandmother proclaimed it as the woman's heart slowed. But then a strange thing happened. All her memories linked together like parts of a story, and I knew who had killed the neighbor. The Oracle spoke, but no one heard what she told me.

For years I wondered about that, until a few days ago in the Dragon Pearl when Lizzriat said she heard nothing from that Thampurian when I did. It's obvious now. The Oracle doesn't actually speak from the mouth of the conduit. I hear her in my head. That's why Mother and Grandmother didn't hear the Oracle proclaim the name of the real killer.

But why didn't that woman tell her accusers everything she knew? It would have saved her. She knew who killed her neighbor. She had it all locked in her memories.

Unless the woman didn't know what those memories meant. She couldn't see the big picture.

Hand over her mouth, QuiTai's eyes widened. She'd never had such a terrible thought before.

No. This is sacrilege.

Rising, she shook off RhiHanya's black lotus lethargy and paced the room, quickly striding from one end to the other. She pushed open the typhoon shutters and gulped in air as the rain splattered on the veranda.

Grandmother and Mother were linked to the conduit the same way I was through our venom. It opens a connection from our minds to the conduit's and to the Oracle. Grandmother and Mother saw everything I saw, but they didn't put the woman's memories together. They didn't see it any more than the woman did. They've never had the ability to gather information and read the meaning that connects it together. But I do.

"No. No. No."

She stared up slope at the tiers of apartment buildings, her hands balled into fists. Was there nothing of her past that she could keep? Her daughter, Jezereet, her parents and aunts all gone. Even the terrible things like Petrof and the werewolves had been wiped away. Now this?

This is why you couldn't get the visions you wanted from those vapor addicts in the Dragon Pearl. They didn't know anything you wanted to see. Their memories don't contain the information you seek.

Everything she tried to hold rotted in her hands. A world stripped of magic and wonder was as bleak as the rocks of the Ponong Fangs.

She collapsed on the divan and drew her knees to her chest. RhiHanya's memories clamored for her attention. She shut her eyes, as if that could make them go away. QuiTai groaned, "Leave me alone."

A voice, familiar but unwanted, echoed in her mind. *"You are an Oracle, and the Oracle is you."*

The Oracle had spoken. And she was never wrong.

CHAPTER II: OLD LEVAPUR

Kyam walked through town with his head bowed against the pouring rain. If he was going to be stuck on this island for the foreseeable future, he would at least make good use of his time. Tracking down the Ravidians and stopping their scheme had whetted his appetite for espionage. He was sober – mostly because he couldn't afford to waste his dwindling supply of coins on drink – bored, and ready to put his mind to work.

There were few mysteries in Levapur that interested him. He wondered who his neighbors were hiding in their apartment, but he couldn't bring himself to spy on such good people. The newly arrived soldiers were only a puzzle because he didn't like Governor Turyat or Chief Justice Cuulon enough to ask them what was happening. They'd make him grovel and then probably wouldn't tell anything. Or he could pump Voorus for information. Something so easily solved wasn't nearly challenging enough, though. He could search the deed documents in the government building to find out who really owned the Red Happiness, but digging through musty files sounded dull. He wanted action.

He grinned as he remembered one of his last assignments before he'd been exiled. Stealing hull plans for the new Ravidian fleet had been his kind of espionage – lots of action, some narrow escapes, and of course the satisfaction of helping his country. Thwarting the Ravidian scheme on Cay Rhi had been almost as good, but he'd never be lucky enough to find that sort of adventure in Levapur again. The town was too drowsy, its intrigues too domestic.

But Voorus had handed him a clue to something interesting. Someone had paid Petrof to kill QuiTai. Was that assassination attempt successful? Voorus didn't think so. If Kyam found out who hired Petrof, then he'd probably also know if QuiTai were still alive. That, he knew, was the real mystery he wanted to solve.

It occurred to Kyam that if QuiTai were alive, they were probably now enemies. He knew how she felt about the colonial government, and she was smart enough to realize she held a secret that could bring the governor and chief justice ultimate disgrace in the eyes of Thampurian society and anger the Ponongese. Like Voorus, he wondered what she was waiting for. Was she building a rebellion inland? He couldn't let her do that. He regretted that the colonial government had no real control over Ponong outside Levapur. The Ravidian scheme on Cay Rhi proved that the isolated plantations could fall under enemy control and no one would know for weeks or months. If QuiTai used the escaped slaves to stir up anti-Thampurian sentiments, the colonial militia wouldn't know until her army marched across the Jupoli Gorge Bridge, and then it would be too late.

He hoped she'd been sincere when she told him that she'd sacrificed the werewolves to stop further bloodshed. She claimed she could see that future and had done her best to stop it, even though it made some of her own people hate her. As far as he could tell, she'd never outright lied to him. Omitted truths, certainly. Twisted words as if they were hushoin art paper, constantly. And selectively revealed information like a practiced seductress removing her clothes. But she hadn't lied about wanting to contain the escalation of violence, had she? He hoped; but he couldn't quite bring himself to believe.

Captain Voorus rubbed his eyes. Reading by jellylantern light strained his sight. His chair scraped against the floor of his apartment as he dragged it closer to the window. He wished Thampurian buildings were more like the Ponongese ones, with wide verandas wrapping around each floor. He would have liked to sit outside while he read. Monsoon clouds covered the sky, but they glowed in the midday sun. Unless the wind picked up, the cover overhead would shelter him from the fine rain.

He flipped through the pages of the volume of colonial law he'd borrowed. There was nothing in it about inheritance law that he could find except mystic sentences that said things such as *Refer to Thampurian law, section...* followed by a string of numbers and letters. When he'd asked the law clerk about those notations, he'd been told that meant he'd have to read it from a book of Thampur's laws. But there was only one set of books like that on the island, and the clerk swore Chief Justice Cuulon would have them gutted if they dared touch them, so he'd done the next best thing. He'd asked his mother to buy the books and send them to him. She didn't have much money, but sometimes she could go to her rich friend and beg for gifts.

Once he had the Thampurian law books, he'd see if there was any hope of reclaiming his inheritance from his father; not that it would do him a damn bit of good as long as he was in exile. Unlike the privileged Kyam Zul, he didn't even know why he'd been sent to Ponong or what it would take to earn his way back, but he suspected that an inheritance would help. If there was one thing he'd learned on Ponong, it was that government officials could be bought.

While he waited for the law books to arrive, he decided to use the one he had to learn how to decode the confusing texts.

The words looked like Thampurian, but they seemed to have different meanings. He'd already been over to the government building five times to ask the law clerks what a sentence meant. They'd made it clear they didn't want to talk to him anymore.

He thought if he looked up a law he knew, it could be a valuable key to deciphering what the laws meant in everyday terms. Voorus searched for a simple entry, such as the law against Ponongese baring their fangs to a Thampurian, but he'd flipped through the books several times and he still hadn't found it. It had to be written down somewhere. Since he'd come to Ponong, they'd hung at least five Ponongese a year for that crime. Everyone knew that was the law. Even the chief justice said so; he signed the death warrants, after all. But Voorus couldn't find the damned law in any of the books.

QuiTai and LiHoun squatted on RhiLan's veranda as they shared a kur. Her gaze flitted to Kyam's dark apartment and then away, but not quickly enough.

"Thank you for delivering my newspapers and letters. They were a welcome diversion," QuiTai said.

"Any news of note from the continent?"

"Troubling developments, uncle. Foreigners denounced as the source of all troubles, rising patriotism, plays censored or closed for offending official thought, new restrictions, paranoia. It doesn't look good. Each country is withdrawing into its borders. But those are their problems, and we have plenty to concern us here."

"Our rice bowls are full," he agreed.

While she organized her thoughts, she watched a stand of palm trees on Levapur's first hill bend under the onshore breeze. LiHoun waited. Inside the apartment, RhiHanya hovered near the typhoon shutters, probably hoping that they'd lapse into Ponongese or Thampurian. Thankfully, the rest of the family was at the market in Old Levapur.

While she'd never been a deeply religious person, the loss of the Oracle made QuiTai uneasy. It had been such a nice dream that someone with great power watched over her, loved and protected her. Now she'd woken and felt like a child in the middle of the night who heard strange sounds. Maybe she could force herself to believe again. There was comfort in faith, like a jellylantern glowing in the darkness. But now that she knew the truth, she didn't think she could ever accept the falsehood again. She wondered if her mother and grandmother had known they were Oracles. Had they deliberately led her to believe in something they knew to be false?

I've always had to rely on myself. If I'm honest, I never trusted the Goddess to do anything for me. I always did it myself. So what did I lose when I lost faith? Nothing real. In a way, maybe this is better. I know I can trust myself. False deities? They've never done a damn thing for me. And I guess I always knew that.

But what about my vision of glass covered in blood? That didn't come out of any conduit's memory. It helped me when I fought Petrof.

For a moment, she had hope, but her logical mind turned it back.

My visions were usually vague, and only after something happened that sort of aligned with the vision did I pronounce it as fulfilled. Maybe the dirt Thampurian saw one of the Ravidians slice his hand on glass when the container of sea wasps broke, and I tapped into that memory but didn't remember that I had. After all, I was under the influence of the vapor too. Then when I saw the shattered jellylantern, I believed it would save me because that fit the vision I believed in. Interpretation is art, not science. Faith is not logic. I know which one I trust more.

She pushed her braid over her shoulder and lifted her chin. LiHoun seemed to notice her focus return to him.

"Colonel Zul asked me to pass on a message," he said.

QuiTai was instantly alert. "He knows you work for me?"

"He guessed that I work for the Devil."

Of course he would. "He's far too clever, that one."

LiHoun grinned as he inhaled kur smoke. The bright orange embers nearly touched his pointed finger nails before he took it from his lips. "Not clever enough sometimes."

"What do you mean?"

"He said someone hired Petrof to kill you."

"He knew Petrof was trying to kill me, but the last time we spoke, he didn't know it was on another's orders. I wonder how he learned about that." She waved away the offered kur. Her blood burned, and she had too much vitality for the cage that confined her already. "Was that message for me or the Devil?"

"For you, but for the Devil if I couldn't warn you."

So Kyam hadn't figured out that she was now the Devil. Not yet. She had no doubt that he'd eventually figure it out. He couldn't make the mental leaps she did, but he had enough determination to methodically take every step until he reached the same conclusions.

She idly scratched her arm. Contact with black lotus wouldn't addict her, thanks to the Ponongese's natural immunity, but it certainly made a pipe more alluring. "I'm trying to decide if it's an advantage that Colonel Zul figured out that you work for the Devil."

"I think he's more interested in knowing if I work for you."

"His interests aren't my concern. But maybe he's heard other information we could use. After all, he can get into places we can't."

"You don't care about his interests?"

She didn't like LiHoun's sly smile. "Should I?"

He shrugged.

"Uncle LiHoun?"

"He saw that I was observing the new soldiers. Unless there are more down in the fortress that I haven't seen, there are thirty of them."

"Thampur has doubled their troop strength in Levapur." That bothered her. Someone expected trouble.

"Colonel Zul was also watching them."

She gritted her teeth. "That man is constantly crossing my path."

"You find him irritating?"

"Very."

LiHoun seemed to find that amusing. "That's something, at least."

Exasperated, she glared at him. "What are you hinting at?"

"We're storing the rice in the werewolf's old lair."

"This is the second time you've changed the subject, uncle."

"I thought you wanted to talk business. We can discuss the Thampurian if you prefer."

It seemed LiHoun was in a mood to tease her. She wasn't used to that. Why did he think she had any interest in Kyam Zul? She'd told him about being taken to the fortress and her escape, their timely rescue by Captain Hadre, and most of what happened on the *Golden Barracuda* and Cay Rhi, but she hadn't so much as hinted that she'd seduced Kyam. It wasn't an important part of the story. Besides, it was none of the old man's business. But if she avoided talking about Kyam, LiHoun might think she wanted to avoid the subject.

She looked directly into LiHoun's eyes. "Okay. Let's talk about him. I'm curious. How did he figure out that you work for the Devil?"

LiHoun almost seemed abashed. "I was counting soldiers for you. Captain Voorus hauled me across the street to carry Colonel Zul's shopping, seeing as the soldiers had cleared the streets around the town square of all Ponongese."

QuiTai tapped her bottom lip with her forefinger. "These soldiers, they knew you weren't Ponongese? They let you stay when they chased away the Ponongese? You dress almost like us. From a distance someone could easily mistake you as a native, and as you well know, once a Thampurian soldier makes a mistake, they'd rather kill the witness than admit they were wrong."

"They accosted me, but the leader inspected my ears and hands and peered at my eyes. As soon as he declared me Li, they walked away."

"So they're specifically targeting Ponongese for these humiliations." It was further proof that her forming theory was right. Now was the time to be careful about jumping to conclusions, though. While she normally enjoyed the speed of her thoughts and ability to act quickly on them, this time she hesitated. She needed more information. It was time for her to come out of seclusion and gather facts.

"Their uniforms are high quality, grandmother, and lighter weight than the material the colonial militia wears. Someone wanted them to be comfortable in this heat. And that same someone made sure there wasn't a single identifying mark on their clothes. I misspoke when I said that the man who inspected me was their leader. I have no idea what rank he held, or any of the others. They called him Mister. Not major, not colonel, not captain. Mister. And he referred to them the same way. No family name."

QuiTai's forehead furrowed. "But they were Thampurians? Could you have mistaken another race? The Li, the Ponongese, and Thampurians look quite a bit alike from a distance, despite our obvious differences."

LiHoun didn't seem convinced. "I think we know of all the Thampurian colonies and continental races. They sounded like Captain Voorus, not posh accents like Kyam Zul. Not that they spoke much, but I heard enough to convince me they're Thampurian."

"I don't like this. It's as if... " She shook her head. This was no time to jump to a conclusion, but the facts seemed to support the scenario that unfolded before her. She had to get it right though, so she would force herself to approach it methodically.

Why would someone from Thampur meddle with Levapur's insignificant economy? It wasn't as if Ponong were a valuable colony. Jellylanterns were a good, solid business, like rice, but most of the profit came from the jellylantern factories in Thampur. Ponong just supplied the bioluminescent jellies.

Could the soldiers be in Levapur because of the harbor? It was the biggest and most protected harbor in the archipelago, a good place to stop for fresh water and food before sailing through the Ponong Fangs, but a large junk could conceivably carry enough provisions to sail the long way around the island chain. A smaller junk with a reckless captain could bypass the harbor, sail through the Fangs, and pray he reached the Li

Islands before his water barrels emptied. But why would they have to? The Thampurians already controlled the harbor. The only thing they had to worry about was some other country wresting it from their grasp. That struck her as a remote possibility, unless the unsettling rumors in her friend's letters and the continental newspapers were true.

Frustrated, she growled. That couldn't be it.

So why would someone from Thampur waste money stirring up trouble on Ponong?

If this were an invasion by a foreign power, she could understand them taking over the other Thampurian colony, the Li Islands. It was far more profitable. Much as Ponong was the only place green light medusozoa could live, the Li Islands were the only known source of juam nut oil, which powered everything from the lamps vapor addicts used to cook black lotus to the engines that powered the funiculars that climbed Ponong's steep slopes to the plantations.

And those secret engines aboard the Golden Barracuda.

She shook her head again. The soldiers were in Ponong, not the Li Islands. It couldn't be someone from Thampur behind the trouble, because it made no logical business sense to stir up trouble in your own colony. Besides, why would anyone pay soldiers to ruin such a small economy? She might not like the Thampurians, but she appreciated their business acumen. So it couldn't be someone from Thampur. The person who brought the new soldiers to Thampur had to be here on the island, and it had to be part of some personal vendetta. It still wasn't logical, and it was certainly an expensive way to wreak havoc, but if there was one thing she'd learned about Thampurians in Levapur, it was that they'd go to any length, or expense, over petty, stupid little power struggles. But who was fighting whom?

And there she was again, acting as if her ideas were facts. Kyam Zul had scolded her about that often enough. Of course, she'd been right every time. This time, though, she was going to wait for evidence.

She clasped her head in her hands. "Illogical behavior makes my brain weep." She drew a deep breath through her nose. There was no profit in that train of thought. Time to focus on current problems. "So. Voorus unfortunately put you under Colonel Zul's employ, and Colonel Zul caught you observing the soldiers... " She gestured for LiHoun to continue his story.

"Then he asked me to pass his message to the Devil."

"What does he profit by warning me?"

LiHoun stared at her as if incredulous. Several times, he seemed on the verge of saying something, but he held himself back. Finally, he spoke. "The Zul clan is devious."

"So I've heard." There was nothing she could do except keep a few steps ahead of him. "I guess I should count myself lucky that I only have to worry about Kyam. I'm not sure I'd fare as well against Grandfather Zul."

LiHoun gasped.

Her eyes narrowed as she regarded him. "Are you ill, uncle?"

"Gas." LiHoun beat his fist against his chest until he belched. "His exact words: 'I'd prefer you tell his concubine what I have to say. Someone paid Petrof the werewolf to kill her. I don't think he's succeeded – yet. He must be stopped.'"

Had he just changed the subject? She hated that flicker of doubt, but she would remember it. "Anything else?"

"He said, 'Tell the Devil that if she dies, I will hold him personally responsible for failing to protect her. If she dies, I will come after him.' Then he left. He has not sought me out since."

QuiTai groaned. The Oracle should have warned her that Kyam Zul was a romantic; but then, she was her own Oracle. She should have put the pieces together because the clues had always been there.

"Just like old times at PhaJut's." LiHoun laughed so hard that he fell into a prolonged, phlegmy coughing spell. That explained why LiHoun teased her about Kyam. He wanted to know if she had feelings for the Thampurian. Such nerve!

"Every time I decide he's a thoroughly jaded debauch, he manages to lose my esteem." She tsk-tasked. "He's a foolish little brother." That, she thought, should be enough to stop LiHoun's ill-advised inquires about her affections.

LiHoun laughed and coughed until his face was flushed with the effort to draw a breath.

"Do you need tea, uncle?"

He waved his hand. "No. I'm fine."

"Okay. Then may we talk business now? Thank you. Please bring me the purple and black box from my safe house near PhaJut's place." She rose. "I've worn out my welcome with the Rhi, and I can't conduct business from here. I need to talk to my lieutenants directly. I need information. I need to look at something other than the inside of this damned apartment or I will go insane." She flicked her braid over her shoulder. "But most of all, I need to walk through the streets of Levapur and observe for myself."

"The soldiers will probably arrest you the moment you're seen."

"That's why I need my purple and black box. And darkness. The moment the sun sets, my convalescence ends."

After the first day of the Ponongese market, RhiLan thought perhaps QuiTai had wasted her money. Few merchants turned around and spent the money she gave them. Although she'd protested, QuiTai gave her more to spend this morning. Still, merchants had been cautious. But after the sky cleared, more people came to shop, and many were buying. It was almost like a festival. Basket women called out their wares as they moved through the crowd. Even the people of Old Levapur came out of their shacks to enjoy the afternoon.

Without Thampurians around, everyone could speak Ponongese without fear of being beaten. Her children sat enraptured by a story teller who related the traditional tale of the fisherman and the moon goddess. She realized they'd never heard it before. All they learned in school were the colorless Thampurian stories about their gods and heroes.

She needed to tell those stories to her children. Like most Ponongese adults, she had memorized them the first time she heard them, but her children were so used to reading from a book that they didn't bother to keep the stories in their hearts. Ma'am Thun didn't encourage them to memorize anything. Before long, there wouldn't be a Ponongese left who could remember news and relate it faithfully word for word. Why the Thampurians didn't teach that skill she'd never understand. They were a mysterious, and often foolish, people.

The storyteller came to the end of one story and began another.

"I haven't heard that one in ages," RhiLan said wistfully.

Her man laughed. "Your favorite." He took her basket of sarongs and gestured for her to join to audience. "Have fun."

She flashed a wide smile at him before picking her way through the crowd to squat next to her children.

Ma'am Thun glanced over her shoulder as she traveled through back alleyways near the town square. She suspected many Thampurians would shop at the new Ponongese marketplace, but like them, she didn't want to be seen. As a precaution, she'd worn her mourning veil.

She'd eaten eggs and rice for dinner the night before, and for breakfast. She didn't mind it in the morning, but it disturbed her sense of correctness to eat such an informal dish after sundown. It simply wasn't done.

Unhappily, she sensed that the longer she stayed in Levapur, the more she lost of her Thampurianness. In the heat and humidity, it bubbled and flaked away like paint on the buildings. In its place, strange allowances took hold, and you could only try to hold onto who you used to be before you started letting things slip.

By now, I probably can't go back to Thampur, ever. I've been corrupted in so many little ways that I won't even realize how wrong

I've become until I see that horrified expression on the faces of old friends. And of course they'll be sympathetic, and pretend not to see, but the whispers will start, and I'll never be accepted even if I never make another error.

Ma'am Thun was actually quite pleased by that thought. It relieved her of the duty of wanting to return to Thampur. Every other Thampurian in Levapur spoke wistfully of their return from disgrace. It drove them to excess drink, suicide, or black lotus as they obsessed on senseless schemes to win forgiveness. How freeing it was to say, "I can't go back, so I might as well stop making myself miserable."

Why would she ever want to go back? Her husband, a man of vicious temper, had had the nerve to die under questionable circumstances. It had looked like an accident. It had been an accident, if falling into a canal while drunk and drowning rather than shifting into his sea dragon form could be called an accident rather than abysmal stupidity. But upon his death, his family had cut a funeral shroud for him of such fine character that the word murder was whispered, and gazes had shifted in her direction. What could her family do then but put her on a ship headed for Levapur? They'd salvaged their name at her expense. She suspected that many other Thampurians in Levapur could tell similar tales of abandonment for the sake of honor if they ever broke the taboo of discussing their exile.

That prohibition against mentioning their pasts worked in her favor. In Levapur, she was the gracious lady who tried to help the unfortunate Ponongese by educating their children, not a suspected murderess. Certainly she would never be invited to dine with the governor or have lunch with the wives of the rigid upper cast of society, but that discrimination was exactly the same as she would have faced in Thampur. There was comfort in the pretense of normality. What wasn't normal, for Thampurians, was the awe and respect afforded to her by the Ponongese. She quite liked that. It was much easier to accept her position in society as long as it was clear that there were people below her, people who could never rise.

It wasn't that she hated the Ponongese. She never called

them snakes, not out loud. She had a fondness for their simplicity, their innocence, their desire to please her. They asked for her advice, although she knew they rarely took it. They made sure their children behaved properly and apologized profusely if they didn't. That was more respect than her husband or family had ever shown her.

She peered around the wall of the bank that sat on the edge of the town square. The white sliding doors to the balcony on the third floor of the government building looked like scowling eyes under the heavy brows of the roofline. If she'd been the fanciful sort, she would have stretched the likeness of an angry father to the entrance portico's columns and thought of them as bared red teeth. She wasn't that fanciful, although she couldn't shake the feeling that the government watched the virtually empty town square and all who might pass through it. If only the marketplace had been its usual chaotic mash of noise and smells and people, one could cross it to the road to Old Levapur without being seen; but then if the marketplace had been there, no one would have reason to go to Old Levapur to shop.

That, she decided, summed up life in Levapur perfectly.

Ma'am Thun squared her shoulders before marching forth on the town square. There were more monkeys than people to be seen. It seemed as if Thampurians had decided to buy their rice, pork, and jellylanterns in the shops rather than marketplace stalls.

How very Thampurian of us to shun what others are shunning simply because others seem to be shunning it and never, ever pause to wonder what started it.

Still, she held onto the bottom hem of her mourning veil so it wouldn't fly up as she quickly passed by the few stalls that were left. The merchants didn't even bother to call out to her. Everyone had given up.

She felt much less exposed when she reached the road to Old Levapur. On one side, a steeply ascending orange, black, and white streaked sandstone cliff. Odd formations in the sandstone that looked like wax spires that had melted and dripped were occasionally traversed by a thick vine, and tenacious air-rooted flowers clung where they could. The other side of the road dropped off so sharply that she could have leaned over and touched the tops of trees. The funicular tracks to the harbor were somewhere below.

Almost around the turn of the dirt road, she saw men in uniform. They strolled rather than marched, so she slowed her steps, even though they were probably headed to the same place she was. It had been a bit of a shock to realize how much people in Levapur relied on the Ponongese for their food; worrisome, maybe, if one believed that the Thampurians were somehow self-sufficient on this island. She knew many Thampurians who spouted such nonsense. Ponongese cooked their meals and cleaned their houses. Ponongese carried and fetched and bowed and served here because no Thampurian would be caught dead doing such things in Levapur, even though almost all servants in Thampur were Thampurian. Besides, where was the loss of face in having Ponongese servants? It just proved that everyone was in their proper social order.

She hoped they had fish at their market. She'd heard that the Ponongese fishermen weren't allowed down to the harbor, but she believed that somehow they would find a way to take out their rickety little fleet. Ponongese always had some way around Thampurian rules. She also needed fruit and vegetables.

Ma'am Thun wasn't a woman given to cursing – out loud – so her nose pinched as she realized she'd have to carry her purchases back to town. Carry packages! She'd heard rumors there was a Ponongese trail along the rim of the Jupoli Gorge, but wasn't it bad enough that she had to venture into Old Levapur? Did she really have to follow some native game trail back home if she hired a boy to tote her shopping?

Her growing scowl was for Governor Turyat. He was to blame for this mess. While they'd never spoken, she would certainly make sure to have a word with him now. She'd march up the steps to the government building, sweep past his secretary, and politely yet firmly tell him to kindly desist in his actions. There were only so many indignities she was willing to suffer.

She froze as she heard a scream. In the jungle, it was hard to tell which direction sounds came from, but she was certain it had come from ahead. There were more screams, as if a great many people had suddenly been surprised by pain. She spun on her heel and quickly walked toward the town square, never once glancing behind her, because whatever was going on was really none of her business.

With a little huff of disgust, she decided she'd just have to eat pork for dinner.

In the years he'd lived on Ponong, Voorus could count the number of times he'd been in Old Levapur on one hand. He didn't even have to use his thumb. The slum made him uneasy. All those snake eyes watching him, as people leaned silently in the doorways of their shacks or squatted in groups put a knot in his gut. He didn't want to go there now that there was so much tension between the Ponongese and Thampurians, but the goods in the Thampurian shops were so ridiculously expensive compared to what the Ponongese charged, and many of the shops had bare shelves. Thankfully, several other members of the colonial militia also had shopping to do. Hopefully, the sight of their uniforms would be enough to keep the Ponongese in line. He wasn't sure how long that would last.

He and his men strolled toward Old Levapur. It was one of those bright, hot afternoons where the humid air seemed to push against every step like a strong wind. The jungle lurked on the edge of the road. He felt sometimes that if he looked away for a second, it crept closer. They passed a tree covered with iridescent blue butterflies.

"There'd better be a market when we get there," a lieutenant said as he swatted away a vortex of gnats that swirled past his face. "I'd hate to think we walked all this way for no reason."

"The Ponongese all said there would be one," another soldier said.

"Have you ever noticed how they say the exact same thing when they tell you news? It's like they memorize it."

Voorus nodded. For a brief moment, his suspicions flared. The Ponongese could be luring his men into a trap. Just as quickly, he dismissed the thought. As long as he'd been in Levapur, he'd heard the Ponongese parrot each other's news word for word, without deviation. At first he'd thought it funny, but by now he was used to it. It was just their way. Besides, it wasn't as if anyone had invited the Thampurians to shop at the new Ponongese market.

"Has anyone asked the governor why he closed the regular marketplace to the Ponongese?" the lieutenant asked.

"I've tried," Voorus said. "He hasn't been in his office all day, and he's refusing callers at home."

"Go to the Dragon Pearl. He's there at least three nights a week."

One of the soldiers snickered. "If you were married to his wife – "

A sharp scream jolted them. Voorus looked to his men and nodded sharply. They came together in formation and drew their batons. By the time they heard the following screams, they were already running toward Old Levapur.

The story teller was at RhiLan's favorite part of the tale when a man shouted in Thampurian, "You are ordered to disperse! This assembly is illegal. Anyone who doesn't leave immediately will be arrested!"

Confused, RhiLan rose. Thampurian soldiers surrounded the little marketplace. Without another word, they stepped forward and started swinging long, black batons. A fishmonger fell as blood spurted from his temple. People screamed and ran, but the soldiers blocked the road.

RhiLan picked up RhiTeek. Her frightened daughter wrapped her skinny legs around RhiLan's waist and buried her face into her shoulder. RhiLan gripped RhiLiet's hand. Her middle son fell as people shoved past them. She called out for her man but couldn't see him in the crowd. The soldiers beat people who curled up on the ground, their hands over their heads.

She screamed his name. Her voice mingled with the other screams of terror.

RhiLiet tripped as he helped his brother up.

"Run! Upslope!" RhiLan yelled.

The panicked mob shoved and pushed her as she fought her way upslope. She yanked RhiLiet along and hoped he had a good grip on his brother. At times she was crushed so tightly between people that her feet didn't touch the ground, although the mob carried her forward. The breath was crushed from her lungs. She fought her rising panic. Her sweaty hand gripped her son's hand tightly. If she let go, he would be lost, and they'd be trampled.

The stampede carried her to the ridge above the Jupoli Gorge. They followed the running crowd along the narrow footpath. She heard the Pha River rushing below. If one of them fell through the thick plants growing along the ridge, they'd never survive.

Why? she wondered. Why would anyone do such a horrible thing?

Behind her, she still heard the screams and wails of the people being beaten. Tears ran down her cheeks.

I've abandoned my man. I got away with my children and left the others behind. She felt a sudden burst of sympathy for QuiTai and her cousin. *This is how it must have felt to run from Cay Rhi. How do they live with their guilt?*

She wondered how she would live with hers.

Where the road widened, Voorus first saw the bright yellow of a stall's awning. Then he saw one of the new soldiers, his arm rising high and coming down again and again while something brown and orange writhed at his feet. The screams were horrible, like the anguished cries of prisoners taken to the private cells in the fortress.

"Stop! Halt this moment!" Voorus yelled.

The soldier straightened and looked directly at him. Though blood splattered his face, he showed no emotion.

As the soldiers stopped beating the people, Ponongese fled. The sharp screams had turned to moans and pleading. The orange soil was dark with blood and the air was already ripe with the stink of it. Voorus could barely focus long enough to count the wounded or dead. There were at least four Ponongese who had seen their last sunset.

Voorus pointed to the nearest soldier. "By what right do you attack these people? What have they done?"

The other soldiers drew together. There were thirty of them and only six colonial militia men. Voorus was too angry to care about the overwhelming odds. He wanted to spew his breakfast across the road, but he had to take charge of the situation. "Tell me!" he shouted. "Who ordered you to do this?"

The new soldiers formed a block and sauntered down the road toward the town square.

Voorus knew tears of rage flowed freely from his eyes. He'd never wanted to kill another man before.

"Should we follow them?" The lieutenant's voice cracked.

Voorus saw a young Ponongese girl standing twenty feet away. She didn't seem harmed, but she didn't move. She simply stared at the bleeding people on the ground. When he took a step toward her, she screamed.

"Oh, no, honey, it wasn't me," Voorus crooned to her. "It wasn't me." He knew he was pleading with a child, but he couldn't bear the way she looked at him.

Her screams rent the air as he reached for her.

A Ponongese woman with a bloody face ran from the door of an ugly pink apartment building to the girl. She hugged the child until the ear-piercing screams muffled against her belly. The child's shoulders shook as she sobbed in great, gulping breaths. The woman gestured for Voorus to step back while she spoke gibberish.

The lieutenant grabbed his arm. "Sir, we should go."

"What is she saying?" Voorus spun around. "Do any of you speak Ponongese?" Why didn't she speak Thampurian?

"She says we should leave, now," the lieutenant said.

"But we – "

The woman was still talking. She gestured toward the road more emphatically. Voorus stepped back as she moved toward him.

"She says others may come soon, and they might think we're the soldiers who did this. She said to go before they come. Or, at least, I think that's what she means. She's talking too fast," the lieutenant said.

Voorus didn't know how to explain their innocence. He could barely tell one Ponongese from another. How could she possibly believe that he wasn't the same as the other Thampurians in uniform? He'd feared that the Devil's whore would inflame rebellion; he'd never imagined that Thampurians would be the ones to spark it.

"I'm so sorry. So, so sorry." Voorus gestured to the people on the ground then to the girl she held. "Tell the child I said that," he told the lieutenant.

The lieutenant drew back in outrage. "Sir!"

Voorus realized what he'd said. Right or wrong, the Thampurians had to present a unified face to the Ponongese. Siding with the snakes was unthinkable. "Don't tell her that."

"Damn right I won't."

Before Cay Rhi, everything had been so simple and straightforward. The right thing used to always be the Thampurian way. Now it was a murky mess.

"Captain, what should we do?" a plaintive voice whispered near his shoulder.

Voorus angrily shoved away his tears and straightened his shoulders. By the Goddess of Mercy, he hated being a soldier. He fought for control over his emotions. His men looked terrified. Many of them openly cried.

If only the Ponongese understood that these men had

decided to let the Devil's Concubine and the Rhi slaves escape into the jungle. These men were good people. They believed the same things he did, in law and order and moral right and wrong. They were as sickened by this attack as he was, yet in the eyes of the Ponongese, they were probably just as guilty as the ones who had carried it out. It wasn't fair.

How many Thampurians in Levapur would have felt the same way he and his men did if they'd been here or on Cay Rhi? Probably many of them. No one could say such things out loud, of course. It would be social suicide. But did Thampurians deserve to die in the rebellion that would surely begin now, just because they didn't have the guts to speak out? Who would have guessed insisting on justice for the Ponongese would ever be a matter of life and death for a Thampurian?

He wanted to toss down his uniform jacket and go home, but he couldn't abandon his men; and the gods knew Levapur needed real leadership now more than ever, because after this, there would be no stopping the violence.

A man on the ground rolled on his side and coughed up blood. Curious Ponongese were coming out of their homes on the hillside. They didn't seem angry, yet, but they vastly outnumbered his men.

"Let's go; but a dignified retreat, gentlemen. We don't want them to think we're running away," Voorus said. He stepped backward while never taking his eyes off the gathering crowd. Fear could be the death of them.

CHAPTER 12: THE RETURN OF QUITAI

*Y*ou're going to leave us?" RhiHanya blocked the apartment door so QuiTai couldn't leave. "Didn't you hear what RhiLan said?"

QuiTai knelt before RhiLan and took the woman's hands into hers. "I will put my informants to work looking for your man," she said gently. RhiLan nodded, although QuiTai wasn't sure if her hostess was really listening. She glanced at the terrified children. "I will do my best," she promised them.

Only the middle boy responded, with the barest nod of his head.

"RhiHanya, I will send LiHoun to you at least once a day. He will bring food." QuiTai was deeply worried when RhiLan didn't react.

LiHoun was as grim as she'd ever seen him. "Uncle LiHoun will not let you starve, little brothers."

She went to the children, who leaned against the wall as if they wished they could hide behind it. Their eyes were wide. Even the oldest boy, who rarely stopped grinning, was solemn.

"I know you want to search for your father, but you must trust me, just as I must trust you to obey your mother and auntie RhiHanya. None of you are to go out on the streets for any reason." She met each of their gazes in turn and waited for a nod of agreement.

"But you're going out," RhiHanya said.

QuiTai fought to keep her expression calm. "I didn't think you'd be the one to give me trouble."

"You can be hurt just the same as us."

QuiTai drew on her deep brown velvet Thampurian jacket. "I don't have children to protect."

"Let her go," RhiLan said. "Get her out of my home."

RhiHanya stomped over to her cousin and shook a finger at her. "How dare – "

"Your cousin's right and you know it. I thank you for healing me, but it's dangerous to let me stay." QuiTai let enough edge into her voice to let RhiHanya know she was in no mood to argue.

RhiLan seemed to agree.

RhiHanya grabbed QuiTai by the elbow and dragged her out on the veranda. Seething, QuiTai jerked her arm away.

"What are you going to do?" RhiHanya asked.

"What I promised to do. Send out my informants to find RhiLan's man. Or his body," she added in a whisper.

"You're not going to let them get away with this."

"You don't want me to risk going out on the streets, but you expect me to take on the entire colonial militia?" QuiTai buttoned her cuffs.

"Let me go with you. We'll go to the inland villages and tell the people about the attack today. We'll tell them about the slaves on Cay Rhi!"

"You want to start a rebellion?"

"Yes!"

Somehow, QuiTai had expected this conversation. Still, she groaned and put her hands over her eyes for a moment. She was angry too, but emotion wasn't the answer. "Give me time to figure out a peaceful – "

"Peaceful?"

QuiTai shushed her.

RhiHanya lowered her voice, but she was no less passionate. "Peaceful? You want me to be a good slave and not raise my voice? People were beaten, little sister, perhaps to death."

"Yes. People may have died. May have. But many of our people will most certainly die if we rebel against the Thampurians."

"They brought it on themselves. Just like the werewolves."

QuiTai didn't want to admit that she'd given over innocent werewolves to the mob in the marketplace. She'd lost her taste for blind vengeance. "Someone is behind this, and trust me, I will make those responsible pay for their crimes. But I need time to figure out who it is. Things are chaotic enough right now. That doesn't make my task any easier. If a rebellion starts, it will be the innocent who bleed on the streets, not the guilty. They've planned for this. They know they need to hide. Give me time to hunt them down and put an end to this before it gets worse."

"Everyone knows the governor is to blame."

"Everyone doesn't see how intricate this plot is. I'm not convinced that he's the only one behind it, but I don't have any proof yet. I need time."

RhiHanya crossed her arms over her chest. "You have three days, Wolf Slayer. Then I take matters into my own hands."

There was no changing her mind. "A week," QuiTai begged.

"Three days."

QuiTai and LiHoun skirted the edges of shadows as they neared the Quarter of Delights. She clutched his arm for guidance, as she could barely see through her inner eyelids and the small glass lenses that made her eyes look Thampurian.

The streets were as empty as the night of the full moon. Not even soldiers walked in the darkened streets. During the full moon, while people avoided the street, they normally sat on their upstairs verandas. It could be pouring rain and they'd still come out of their apartments to chat with neighbors. But tonight, Levapur cowered behind tightly closed typhoon shutters. Even the light from jellylanterns was trapped inside.

The scent of rotting plants and garbage filled QuiTai's nose. After four days in RhiLan's apartment, the stink of the town was almost overwhelming. It could have been her imagination, but she felt as if it was worse now, as if the schemes of the colonial government had intensified the decay.

"Do you want me to gather your lieutenants?" LiHoun asked.

QuiTai shook her head. "I don't want to risk their safety. I shouldn't even have you out here."

"Yet you are out here."

"You sound like RhiHanya."

"The Rhi woman has shown her wisdom many times."

When Petrof or the werewolves questioned her decisions, she could easily dismiss them as idiots. It was harder to ignore LiHoun, even though his sudden protectiveness annoyed her. Perhaps she wasn't the only one grappling with a loss of faith.

"I have many things to do and a short time to accomplish them." A logical plan of attack was forming in her mind, but she needed more time to figure it out. "It will be best if we go separate ways at this point."

"I won't leave you, daughter."

Humbled, she blushed. It wasn't lack of faith in her, but concern. That, she hadn't expected. "Favored uncle." For a moment, QuiTai couldn't go on. She gently squeezed LiHoun's arm. "Dearest friend. I'm touched beyond words. And I do need you, but not beside me. Go to my lieutenants and tell them that I want to know the fate of RhiLan's man. Our sources in Old Levapur might know, but I don't know if the soldiers are still there, so please, be very careful. I'd rather break my promise to RhiLan than lose you."

"You can barely see," LiHoun reminded her as he guided her around a puddle.

"Distance is a problem, but up close I can see enough."

"I wish you'd let me stay with you."

Although there were few people on the street, she leaned close to LiHoun and kept her voice low. "Did we buy all the rice imported into Levapur this past week?"

"Yes. The old werewolf den on the other side of the Jupoli Gorge is packed to the rafters. It's humid up there. I worry that it will start to go bad."

"Don't worry. We're about to get rid of it. Tell my lieutenants that from now on, they will charge our Thampurian customers the market price for rice rather than the black market price. Tell them we'll meet tomorrow at the seventh door to discuss the effects and fine-tune my plan, but for now, simply match the Thampurian price for rice."

LiHoun squinted. "The Thampurians might buy it from the legitimate venders instead."

"They might, but once the legitimate merchants realize they can't replace their inventory, they'll raise their prices."

"Then you'll undersell them? I see. You increase you profit."

"Indeed I will make more, but we will match the market price coin for coin. No discounts. Except for our non-Thampurian customers. They will still pay our old price."

LiHoun's ears flattened against his skull. "Is that the right move, grandmother? With everything that has happened this week, you must be very certain of your actions. I'm sure this is one of your elegant schemes, but it seems designed mostly to anger the Thampurians."

"It is."

"Then what happens?"

"When they're angry enough, they'll demand that Governor Turyat do something about it. Then I will tell him to let the Ponongese back into the marketplace and to call off his soldiers so that I can safely be seen in public again, and to give me the names of the men who paid Petrof to kill my family, because that's the only thing that will bring the price of rice down."

LiHoun quietly grumbled.

"I respect your words of caution, wise uncle. A person who won't hear dissent is deaf to rational thought. But this is the only way I can think of to strike back at the Thampurians without actually hurting anyone. They won't starve. They'll just be poorer."

"You're lucky indeed that your Oracle warned you to prepare for this."

QuiTai bristled. She didn't want to think about the Oracle.

"But I see a complication. Of course, your Oracle probably foresaw this, but... "

What had she missed? "The Oracle didn't tell me anything. This is my plan, so please feel free to share your council," she said.

"Most Ponongese don't buy rice from you. So won't they end up paying the higher price too?"

He said it gently, but she sharply rebuked herself for overlooking such an obvious truth.

"You're right. Spread the word that the Ponongese can buy cheaper rice from us."

"They won't like this any more than the Thampurians."

"It's only a temporary measure. They can go back to buying rice from legal merchants when the price drops. Besides, it's not as if they've been able to buy any rice since the marketplace segregation began. At least we'll see to it that their children don't go to bed hungry."

He sighed. "You've always been able to predict how people will act. Every time I doubt you, I am proven wrong. But this plan can't work forever. Eventually, more shipments of rice will be delivered to this island, and the soldiers will make sure the legal merchants get all of it."

"I expect that. But trust a Thampurian to make a coin off suffering. They'll keep the prices high."

"So will the smugglers. They'll hear about this. Then it will cost you a fortune to buy more."

"That's why I bought all that rice. I will continue to sell it to the Ponongese at the lower price until there's such a glut that the legal market price drops back to normal, even if it means paying the higher price for a couple weeks to keep them supplied with cheap rice."

LiHoun didn't seem convinced. "You're going to lose so much money."

"The Devil won't cry if he loses a few coins." The corners of her lips curved. "But the Thampurians? They will howl."

RhiHanya turned on her cousin the moment QuiTai and LiHoun left. "How could you push her out like that?"

"She's bad luck."

"Do not! Do not even say such a thing to me. If it weren't for her, I'd still be on Cay Rhi with the other slaves."

"And ever since you showed up at my door, look what's happened! The marketplace, the school, the beating today!"

"You are not going to blame me for that." RhiHanya stared down her cousin.

RhiLan wrung her hands. "If we don't upset the Thampurians, maybe they'll forgive us – "

"Forgive! What have you done?"

"Nothing! I've done nothing! We've done nothing. But they obviously think we have. So we'll stay calm and behave ourselves and show them they can trust us, and eventually, they'll let us back into the marketplace," RhiLan wailed.

RhiHanya put her hands on her hips. "Always the peacemaker, cousin. Right? Always the one to make excuses for your mother when she beat you and you'd run to our house, crying. And my mother would fix you up and heal your wounds and beg you to stay with us forever. But you'd go back to that woman and pretend if you were good it would never happen again. Only it did, didn't it?"

"Shut up!" RhiLan curled onto the divan, her face to the wall, and put her fingers in her ears.

"Keep on pretending. It isn't going away, and it won't

get better. Mark my words." RhiHanya glared at her cousin's children, who stared at her with wide eyes. "But we won't let it get worse."

The middle boy ran his fingers over his chin much as his father did, even though he had no beard to stroke. "You told the Wolf Slayer she had three days to do something."

RhiLan sobbed louder; RhiHanya nodded.

He rubbed his chin again. "She wears green because she likes it." Then he nodded once, as if that settled the matter in his mind.

LiHoun slipped through the alleyways with speed and grace that would have amazed anyone used to his usual bandy-legged gait. QuiTai had eight lieutenants, but only the five in Levapur needed to know about the rice scheme. He hoped he wouldn't have to convince them the plan would work. They rarely questioned orders from QuiTai, but he was nervous, and it might be contagious.

QuiTai hadn't told him to, but he would warn them that there might be trouble. He would say she wanted them to take their enforcers everywhere. He would say she said for them to be careful of the soldiers. He was frightened for everyone.

CHAPTER 13: THE DRAGON PEARL

QuiTai had lied to LiHoun: her vision through her inner eyelids was dangerously bad on the darkest streets. From now on, even though it was ridiculous at night, she'd wear a mourning veil. Her eyes would be barely visible through the dense lace, and she'd be able to see.

She bumped into people and things and apologized to both in cultured Thampurian tones. Considering her destination, that was probably the most convincing detail of her disguise.

In the well-lit Thampurian neighborhoods, more people were out on the streets than in the Ponongese areas. Still, QuiTai read anxiety in their fretful body language when they drew close enough for her to see them. Levapur was on the brink of something, and it wasn't going to end happily for anyone.

Some stories were like that.

The stupid part was that she didn't have to do this. She could retreat to one of her hidden homes, be the Devil, and reap her profits. There was no reason to risk her life. It wasn't as if anything she did would ever be enough. Free some of the slaves from Cay Rhi? She should rush back in with a foolhardy plan to free the rest. Pay the tuition for some children to go to school? She was grooming them for the Devil's work. Try to provide her people with cheap rice? She was turning them into the Devil's accomplices.

The corset under her Thampurian clothes fought against her deep sigh. How she hated that strangulating squeeze!

Where were the conjoined twin goddesses of self-interest and self-preservation when she needed them? Maybe, like the Oracle, they weren't real. Not for her. Forces beyond her control were at work, trying to make her react. But what was it that they wanted from her? RhiHanya wanted blood. Strangely enough, QuiTai felt that was what the other side wanted too. There was no question in her mind now that all this trouble was meant to get her attention. Most of the moves had affected everyone in Levapur, but closing the school had been a uniquely personal message. A cold lump of fury settled in her throat. All she could do now was take control as best she could and fight both sides every inch of the way to the edge of chaos.

You are a spectacular idiot. They snap their fingers, and you jump even when you don't want to.

When the gold and sapphire façade of the Dragon Pearl came into focus, QuiTai bit her lips mercilessly in the hope that they would turn deep red like a true vapor addict's. It was too bad her clothes were so finely tailored to her slim frame, but one couldn't have everything. To complete her disguise, she set her face into an expression of furtive hunger and desperation.

If anyone at the gaming tables watched QuiTai climb the curving staircase to the vapor den, she didn't see them. It was just as well, she thought. If she'd known she'd caught a curious eye, stiffness in her bearing or self-consciousness in her movements might have signaled that she was aware of being watched. A real vapor addict would only have had eyes for the second story.

She passed the door of the shared den. Tonight, she wouldn't waste time with ordinary citizens.

QuiTai flinched as the shape of a person appeared before her. She scolded herself for not remembering the plush carpet that deadened footsteps. Thankfully, she recognized the bluish face and paprika curls before her fangs sprang forward.

"If you're looking for – " Lizzriat broke off with a gasp of recognition.

She gripped QuiTai's arm and yanked her down the hallway into a room QuiTai guessed was an office. Lizzriat's personal scent and the faint fragrance of her masculine perfume scented the air. The door slammed behind her.

"What are you doing here?" Lizzriat asked.

"Are Governor Turyat and Chief Justice Cuulon here tonight?"

"You can't be here." Lizzriat leaned against the wall, arms crossed.

"You know I wouldn't endanger you on a whim. Much is at stake. You heard about the raid on the Ponongese market today? I tell you that blood will run in the gutters if I don't figure out how to fix this before it spirals out of control."

"Taking on the entire colonial government single-handed? Even if the Devil backs you – "

"I'm in no mood for small talk, Lizzriat. I need access to the governor and chief justice, and I need it now. So tell me if they're here."

Lizzriat shook her head.

QuiTai's heart sank. This business of trying to discuss delicate matters with dimmed sight wasn't going to work. She needed to see the nuances of Lizzriat's expression. She removed the glass lenses from her inner eyelids and put them into the vials she kept in her purse.

The details of the room came into focus as her inner eyelids rose: Lush Ingosolian furnishings cluttered the ornate little room; fringe and rich fabrics swathed every piece of furniture except the desk; picture frames and little porcelain statues crowded onto every surface.

Lizzriat's lacy cuffs almost covered her hands. As usual, she wore a man's suit. Tonight, the hat atop her curly hair tilted at a rakish angle.

"And here I thought you were part of what's wrong with

this island," Lizzriat said.

QuiTai's grin was part relief, part self-mockery. "This week, I'm playing the part of the reluctant hero. When this is over, I'll return to my usual role as scourge of Levapur."

"Couldn't talk anyone else into sacrificing himself?"

"If you have anyone else in mind... "

"Kyam Zul was here just minutes ago, also asking to see Governor Turyat and Chief Justice Cuulon."

QuiTai wasn't sure if she wanted to curse or thank her stars that Kyam was on the same trail she was. She had no idea why he wanted to talk to them, but it was possible that he too was trying to get to the bottom of the market fiasco. She'd have to talk to him soon, even though it might be an awkward discussion.

"I showed him into their private room, but he found them in no condition to help."

"Then they are here."

Lizzriat didn't seemed happy that she'd let that slip. Her mouth twisted in varying expressions of anger and unhappiness until she finally sighed. "I don't know why I risk my neck to help you."

"It's my charming personality."

"Or the fact that you could cut off my black lotus supply."

QuiTai clutched her hands to her chest. "Finally, someone who understands me."

Lizzriat chuckled quietly. "You could say I'm well aware of whom I'm dealing with. Don't take this the wrong way, but you're poisonous."

"I have a stomach full of worship and it's giving me indigestion. So I'll take it as an insult – with a grain of tikkut. I'd hoped to keep our relationship cordial."

After examining her flawless, buffed nails, Lizzriat finally met QuiTai's gaze. "Cordial is such a cold, formal word. A Thampurian word. I prefer something a bit warmer, and from what I've heard, most of your relationships are torrid."

QuiTai smiled weakly, acknowledging but dismissing Lizzriat's suggestive tone. "I take it the governor and chief justice are in vapor dream?"

Her graceful shrug proved that Lizzriat wasn't offended. Some flirtations weren't meant to lead to anything; they were simply undertaken for the pleasure of it. Then she nodded.

"Excellent. If you please, show me the way."

"I don't know what you did to that customer the last time you were here. All you did was hover over him. I watched him carefully, but he showed no signs that you'd harmed him. Do I have your word that you won't hurt the governor or the chief justice?"

"They will not be harmed, and they will have no memory that I was here."

"They'd better not." This time, there was a hard edge to Lizzriat's voice.

Lizzriat gestured to the insensate figures of Governor Turyat and Chief Justice Cuulon sprawled across dreamer's beds as if to say, "Here they are, for what it's worth."

Unlike the sparse den that common people shared down the hallway, the private room reminded QuiTai of an Ingosolian room of ardor. Copper and purple striped paper covered the walls. She assumed the thick velvet drapes hid typhoon shutters that led to a private veranda. The carpet was so dense that QuiTai's heels sank into it with each step. In the light of the oil lamp burning on a low brass table, gold and jewels glinted from the dreamer's beds.

"I won't ask what you plan to do, but I insist that you do it quickly," Lizzriat said.

QuiTai nodded. "Ten minutes, maybe a few more."

"I'll come back for you." Lizzriat put her hand on the door but didn't slide it open. "Don't kill them. I have enough troubles without two dead Thampurians on my hands. Disposing of bodies is so difficult, don't you think?"

QuiTai batted her eyelashes. "I wouldn't know."

"Of course you wouldn't. What was I thinking?" She smirked, nodded to QuiTai, and left.

QuiTai didn't have time to waste. Governor Turyat supposedly knew everything that went on in Levapur, but she knew him to be a bit of an idiot. Chief Justice Cuulon was the real power behind the colonial government. Besides, she'd used him as a conduit before.

She gathered her heavy skirts as she knelt beside the chief justice. After a quick glance to make sure Lizzriat wasn't peering through the door, she leaned so close to his face that his rumbling snores blew in hot gusts across her lips. It was possible that there were spy holes drilled into the walls, so she let her braid fall across her face to block the view, opened her mouth, and brought her fangs forward.

The drop of her venom hung heavily at the tip of her fang before oozing into Chief Justice Cuulon's open mouth. For a moment, she wondered if her new crisis of faith in the Oracle would affect her ability to link with his memories, but suddenly she was at a gambling table and she knew she'd connected with him.

He set a tile down on the felt. The image on it writhed into another form. He picked it up and made a joke, but his pulse raced. He stared at the tiles in his hand. Some images on the tiles melted, others turned into nonsense symbols. That was the first layer of vapor, the dreamer's dream. It rarely made sense. She delved deeper, as she'd been taught.

QuiTai realized her breaths were too fast and shallow. She was growing dizzy. Wearing the corset had been a mistake. She forced herself to slow the rate of her breathing, even though it felt like suffocation. She didn't have time for this nonsense. If she'd always been the Oracle – an Oracle – then there was nothing different about this time. She knew how to follow threads of memory to the event she wanted to see. She'd always been able to do that.

What first?

She was back at the gambling table with him, only it was a different night than in his vapor dream. Several soldiers entered the Dragon Pearl. Chief Justice Cuulon panicked. The jolt sent her pulse racing too. His thoughts became like a feral animal wanting to run but too afraid to let him move. She hated that feeling, like those dreams she'd had as a child where a boar crashed out of the jungle undergrowth as she helped her mother collect herbs, and her legs wouldn't work or she could only move in slow motion. His heart pounded along with hers as if in a race that neither of them could win.

What was it about the soldiers that frightened him?

He had tried to appear unruffled, but he glanced at the soldiers constantly. Not being able to control his flitting gaze frustrated her. But between those looks she was able to piece together information. The soldiers weren't the usual colonial militia. Their uniforms were better quality and bore no insignias. If she hadn't known from the chief justice's thoughts that they were soldiers, she would have thought she was looking at a private army.

If he or the governor had brought these soldiers from Thampur, why did he want to hide from them?

"Memories are a web, not a time line. They connect to similar memories. The more connections, the stronger the memory. Picture the scene as the center and trace outward from it. Soon you will have enough fragments to tell a story," grandmother had lectured.

But there were so many fragments! And every time the chief justice spied a soldier, she felt like burrowing under the dreamer's couch and covering her eyes.

This is getting me nowhere I want to go. What's this link? Chatting with the governor in this room, but when? If only people would glance at a newspaper and focus on the date with each memory, or say something like 'I'm glad Typhoon DurMat didn't hit Ponong two days ago.'

She searched the connected memories. In one, he stood in the upstairs hallway of the Dragon Pearl with the governor.

"She's still out there! She can ruin us!"

Governor Turyat had scratched his arms, reminding her of Jezereet. "If only Zul hadn't tricked us into taking slaves – "

Anger and fear welled up in Chief Justice Cuulon's chest at

the mention of Zul. "Shut up!"

Governor Turyat had ignored the chief justice as he looked around. "Where is Lizzriat?"

She'd felt Chief Justice Cuulon's surge of longing for the vapor, but he said, "This is no time to get lost in the vapor, Turyat. She's escaped, she has the slaves, and she could bring us down at any second. We have to find her!"

QuiTai clasped her hands over her mouth. She had heard this discussion. She knew the date it took place.

Chief Justice Cuulon heard bumping against the sliding door that led to the commoner's den. A slight smile tugged at her lips as she remembered her brief struggle with Lizzriat.

The memory muddled at that point, as if often did when the conduit attached no importance to the events, but it had a strong connection to another memory. She followed the strongest thread.

The governor and chief justice had been in this same room. Lizzriat had lit the oil lamp on the brass table between the dreamer's beds and then scooped the black lotus tar from a vial into two pipes. She'd knelt by the table and started to cook one over the lamp flame. The governor had leaned forward with glittering eyes and inhaled the scent, but the chief justice had gripped her wrist.

"We will cook our own," Chief Justice Cuulon said.

Anger flashed over Lizzriat's face but was quickly replaced by a placid countenance. She rose. "As you wish. Gentlemen." She bowed and left the room.

With a rush of impatience and disgust, Chief Justice Cuulon grabbed both pipes before the governor could. "This is serious. Zul is making his move. Mark my words, those soldiers are under his control. He brought them here on that miserable junk the *Winged Dragon*, and rumor has it that he was on board."

Which Zul? Hadre? She couldn't believe it. Besides, why would it be worth mentioning that Hadre had been on board a Zul ship?

The governor's gaze never strayed from the pipes.

"He's going to use the slaves on Cay Rhi to discredit us

back in Surrayya. He swore he'd get his revenge on us when we forced him out years ago. I warned you not to let the soldiers keep the Rhi as slaves. Our secret died with the Ravidians on that island, and we would have been safe if only you'd listened to me."

QuiTai sat back, her hand over her mouth. She looked at the ceiling as she gathered her thoughts.

I don't have time to mull over this. Sort through the facts later. Collect them now, while you can.

She lifted her heavy skirts and moved over to Governor Turyat. It was going to make her nauseous, but she had little time left and she wanted to see his memories too.

QuiTai glared at Governor Turyat's prone body. His head lolled against a red pillow, exposing the loose, wrinkled excess skin on his neck to her. As before, she shielded her mouth as she milked a drop of venom into his mouth.

How have you manipulated your memories to make it possible to live with what you've allowed to happen, Governor?

His mind was a mess. His connections were weak, and there were far fewer of them than in the chief justice's memories. How did he retrieve anything? How did he rule? If strong memories were the ones people attached the most importance to, then he thought only black lotus and sex workers were important. However, it was clear that he feared the new soldiers as much as the chief justice did, and he had no control over them.

"Please let the Ponongese back into the marketplace," he whined to the soldiers' leader when they visited his office in the government building. "You're going to anger the Devil's Concubine. You have no idea how dangerous she is, or her power over the snakes."

The soldier smiled.

Sweat trickled down QuiTai's face. While she'd expected the disorienting whirl from being connected to two conduits at the same time, she'd forgotten how bad it could get as memories overlapped. Her brain simply couldn't handle more than one vision at a time.

Her heavy Thampurian clothes clung to her back, and she

felt as if she had another fever. Any moment now, she was going to throw up. But at the same time, she was sinking down into vapor dream. Unnerving blank moments disrupted her train of thought.

"Will you two shut up," she said as she shoved her fingers into her ears. It made no difference. Their connection was inside her head, not buzzing around it like a mosquito. She kicked the train of her heavy skirt behind her and paced the room to escape the tendrils of vapor chasing her.

"If they find out we took money from the Ravidians, they'll hang us."

QuiTai spun around. Which one of them had that memory come from? She'd long suspected that they'd been as corrupt as the Harbor Master, but these two had helped the Ravidians? She'd kill them both.

"You have no idea what you've brought down on your heads," she told the insensate men. Despite her promise to Lizzriat, she advanced on the governor. Unlike Petrof, he was going to die quickly.

Their memories still flowed to her. She no longer tried to sort out which man's mind they came from as she bent over the governor.

There were footsteps in the hallway. The door began to slide open. QuiTai pressed her fangs against her roof of her mouth with her tongue and forced her temper to cool. It was just as well she'd been interrupted. Until she learned what they knew about Petrof, she had to let the governor and chief justice live. That was fine. She could wait. Patience was a Ponongese virtue.

Lizzriat rushed into the den and shut the door behind her. "Your time is up."

QuiTai needed to get out of the claustrophobic den. The smothering heat and dense fabrics threatened to suck all the air out of the room. If she never touched velvet again, she'd die happy. Besides, she didn't need to be near the conduits to tap into their memories.

"A moment. I must put my lenses back on."

Lizzriat shuddered when QuiTai lowered her inner eyelids. If she blanched when the glass disks were put in place, QuiTai couldn't see it.

QuiTai groped for Lizzriat's arm. With an apologetic smile, she said, "Lead on." But if Lizzriat thought she was helpless, she was wrong. All QuiTai had to do was raise her inner eyelids. Her lenses would pop off and be lost forever, but she'd have her full sight.

They returned to the office. "I have a secret exit. I'll take you down it," Lizzriat said. "But first..." She pulled a black scarf from her desk drawer. "I'm sure you understand."

QuiTai let Lizzriat drape the scarf across her eyes. It was better that she not admit how blind she was.

Warm fingertips traced down her neck behind her ear.

"Under different circumstances, this could have been fun, *krith amaci*," Lizzriat whispered.

Before QuiTai could reply, she felt Lizzriat leave her side. She strained to hear Lizzriat's movements. Although she didn't sense danger, her pulse raced. Her neck still tingled from Lizzriat's touch.

"Out of habit, I've been using a female pronoun for you. What do you prefer?" QuiTai's voice sounded unnaturally loud to herself, and her attempt at normal conversation strained.

"I thought you were beyond such matters."

"In bed, yes, but Thampurian only allows two genders and I prefer to use the one you like."

"I prefer Ingosolian; it's so much more civilized. But here, in Thampurian territory, use *he*." There was a quiet click before muffled footsteps crossed the thick carpet back to QuiTai's side. "I'd hate for the Thampurians to decide I was female and take my Dragon Pearl from me."

"I will not make the mistake of thinking of you as female again."

Rather than take QuiTai's elbow, Lizzriat wrapped an arm around her waist and led her across the room.

We're going around the desk.

She extended her arm and brushed the space before her with her fingertips. Lizzriat forced her hand down. They shuffled forward.

"First step," Lizzriat said.

QuiTai carefully moved one foot forward. After a brief, disorienting moment, her foot landed on a solid step.

"When my people perfect them, I'll send you some instant jellylanterns. I think you'll find them useful," QuiTai said. She wasn't sure why she needed the comfort of small talk when she was helpless. Normally, such conversation bored her.

"Instant jellylanterns?"

"Glass tubes about the size of a kuriwei fish. They don't give off light until you break the seal between the liquid half and the powder. Shake them up, and suddenly you have a jellylantern." QuiTai bumped against a wall. She placed her palm against it as she climbed down the steps.

"Clever," Lizzriat said.

"A Ravidian invention."

Lizzriat sucked in a breath. "Ravidian? I'd rather be in eternal darkness."

"I'm not buying the jellylanterns from them; I stole the idea."

"Isn't it illegal for – Hah! I forgot for a moment who I was speaking too. I'll take a dozen."

"As soon as I figure out how to manufacture the glass tubes, I'll send them to you."

Lizzriat stopped QuiTai and removed the blindfold. "We're here. Let me check the alleyway."

QuiTai tried to see but the darkness was too complete. "I appreciate your help."

"Did you get your information?"

Something in Lizzriat's voice warned QuiTai that she – no, he – had spied on the room. QuiTai tried to remember anything she'd said out loud. What did she owe this Ingosolian? Nothing, maybe. But she didn't feel right telling a lie to someone who could have called for the soldiers.

"Not as much as I would have liked."

"Too bad." Lizzriat's arm drew from her waist. "The alleyway is clear now. You're on your own from now on."

QuiTai nodded. She felt the quick press of lips to her cheek before a firm hand pushed her through the hidden doorway and into the rainy alley. From the smell, she assumed she was near an outhouse.

CHAPTER 14: AN UNEXPECTED MEETING

After nearly a week in RhiLan's tiny apartment, Qui-Tai craved quiet. Nowhere in Levapur was as tranquil and hushed as the neighborhood where apartment buildings gave way to walled family compounds.

Her grandmother had often mentioned that the rare swath of flat land had been fields for crops before the Thampurians seized it. Once upon a time, the terraces her people had carved into the sides of the mountains had been rice paddies. Once upon a time, the Ponongese had been able to feed themselves. Now they were forbidden to grow anything. They could harvest food that grew in the wild, such as fruit, jikal roots, fish, and wild boars, but everything else had to be imported.

The Thampurians were about to learn their laws could cut both ways.

No one was on the wide lane that meandered through the Thampurian Quarter. It was rumored that their Ponongese servants had fled the compounds when the soldiers attacked the market in Old Levapur, but QuiTai hadn't heard yet if that was true. She hoped the Thampurian ladies were stooping over their own cooking fires. Thampurian men had it much easier since they viewed their women as servants anyway. The men probably didn't care who made their dinner as long as it appeared on the table before them.

Since no one was likely to see her in this still, quiet place, she paused to remove the lenses from her eyes. With her inner eyelids raised, the details came back into focus: limbs of the trees on the side of the road stretched overhead and tangled together; rain dripped from the pointed tips of leaves. She hopped the puddles between islands of gravel on the road to avoid the slimy mud.

As she traveled deeper into the neighborhood, the compound gates were further apart and the walls were higher. Inside the smaller compounds, the houses were close enough to the lane that she could see the second story windows, but by the time she heard the ocean waves crashing against the nearby cliffs, she could only see the roofs of the buildings behind the walls.

Near the end of the lane, she stopped at a high carved wooden gate. A brass bell hung from a gracefully arching bracket beside the gate. She didn't ring it. No one had invited her, and she knew no one would be inside. The gate swung open for her. She was surprised, but grateful, that it wasn't locked.

The gate opened into a formal first courtyard almost as big as RhiLan's apartment. A blue tiled privacy wall bearing the Zul family chop sat in the middle of the courtyard. A stone basin brimming with rain water sat in the corner. If a servant had let her in, he would have offered her a dipper of the water with which to ritually wash her hands in the Thampurian manner. QuiTai, however, felt no need to cleanse herself of anything that might offend lurking ancestral ghosts.

She didn't give the ornate festoon gate a second glance as she passed through it; she'd seen similar carvings on the red and gold columns of the government building. Her heart broke a little more each time she saw Ponongese boys playing on the steps of the government building as they waited for a Thampurian to hire them to carry shopping or run errands. She always wanted to force them to look at the snakes writhing under the cruel claws of the sea dragons and remind them that they should be angry about the crude depictions of the Ponongese people, but she knew that outrage was a difficult state to maintain. It sapped your heart and soul but did nothing to hurt your enemies or change the future. In the end, all it did was leave you exhausted and frustrated. But she wished they wouldn't act as if it didn't matter that they had to see themselves depicted that way everywhere they looked.

And how could she scold them for not caring, when so many times on the stage she'd played the part of the comical servant – rolling her eyes, dressing like a savage, speaking in broken language? She'd refused to go along with it after a while and demanded dignity, but it had always been a battle. It would be the worst hypocrisy to pretend she hadn't taken such roles.

"It didn't use to be this way," she wanted to tell the children. "Once upon a time, this island was ours alone. We were a free, sovereign people." But how could you convince children that such tales were true when you had never seen it either? All she had were her grandmother's stories; and the next generation would never hear such tales directly from the witnesses.

The main courtyard was beyond the festoon gates. Built by Grandfather Zul when he'd been the first colonial governor of Ponong, the compound had once been a raw, uncouth statement of Thampurian power. Now it was a ghost mansion where jungle vines pushed aside courtyard tiles and deep green ferns sprouted from walls.

A large, stately two-story residential building with a Thampurian roof and architectural details sat on one side of the inner courtyard. Typhoon shutters on the second floor opened onto a veranda, the one nod to Ponongese design. The kitchen was in a separate building at the back of the compound. That's where she and Kyam had slept when he'd brought her to the compound to hide from Petrof. Perhaps she should have been insulted that he'd kept her in the servants' quarters rather than allowing her into the family home, but she doubted he'd done it because she was Ponongese. He'd said that there was no furniture to speak of left in the main house, so the servant's quarters would be more comfortable, and she'd believed him.

Kyam had told her that he rarely went to his family's compound. She also believed that, although she wasn't sure why he shunned such a prestigious address with spacious living quarters. He preferred to live in his tiny apartment in a run-down building amongst the Ponongese. It was one of his maddeningly attractive traits.

Because she tried to be honest with herself, even when it made her wince, she admitted that she'd enjoyed most of her adventure with Kyam. It wasn't often that she had to work so hard to stay ahead of someone in a mental game. He'd forced her to remain sharp, honed, focused. And he'd been rather fun to talk to. Not to mention how easy he had been to look at.

She scowled. Enough of that. On Cay Rhi, they'd agreed to pursue the interests of their own people and parted ways. She assumed he was keeping his end of the bargain, as she intended to keep hers. Unfortunately, that meant that they probably would never work together again. Life being what it was on Levapur, they would probably find themselves at odds. She looked forward to matching wits against him.

A warm smile played across her mouth. She quickly quashed it. This was no time for those kinds of thoughts. She had some serious thinking to do, and now that she'd come to the perfect quiet hideaway in which to mull over the events of the past week without interruption, she wasn't about to start daydreaming about his hands tugging impatiently at her sarong or his devouring kisses.

QuiTai was curious about the interior of the mansion. Did chandeliers of long-faded jellylanterns wait in the darkness like ambush spiders? Did jungle vines slip through the slats of typhoon shutters like moonlight and creep along the walls? Would ghost footprints show on the dusty floors? Or did servants come every week to scrape mushroom ears from the walls and polish the banister in anticipation of a master who might never come?

She lightly pulled on the grand entrance door. It didn't budge. The doors to the second floor veranda probably weren't locked, but her Thampurian clothes made climbing impossible. As she'd cautioned Kyam, just because one was curious didn't mean one had a right to know, so her questions about the mansion would have to remain unanswered.

She turned to the low second building in the compound. The door was slightly open. She couldn't remember whether she or Kyam had closed it, but despite neglecting the property, he had enough sense to make sure it didn't become home to a troop of monkeys. Cautiously stepping forward, she tried to keep a cloak of shadow around her.

The scent of hot juam nut oil was faint but grew stronger as she drew closer. Whoever was inside had recently used the cooking fire, although she didn't smell food. She concentrated on sounds. Under the splatter of rain dropping from the eaves to the courtyard tiles, someone gulped a drink and sighed. From the depth of tone, she was sure it was a man.

Had Kyam somehow guessed that she'd come here? He was smart, but he wasn't psychic. Maybe he'd followed her. He knew she could pass as Thampurian when she wanted to. But when had he guessed her destination, and how did he know a quicker route?

She should steal away before he knew she was there. It was a long walk through Levapur to her nearest safe house in the jungle, but what was inconvenience compared to safety? She didn't know that it was Kyam inside. If the man were someone else, matters could get dangerous. But what if it were he?

Her heartbeat throbbed painfully in her throat, and she moved in slow motion to the window and peered through the shutter. The man inside was undoubtedly Thampurian. His shoulders were broad, and even though he sat on one of the low stools beside the cooking fire, from the length of his outstretched legs, he was tall. Unlike Kyam, he wore some sort of uniform jacket, although if it had borne a soldier's epaulets, the silver threads would have glinted in the low light.

She watched him drink from a nearly empty bottle as he stared into the cooking fire. Like her, he seemed to have something to mull over. She almost hated to interrupt him, but she now had a strong suspicion who he was, and a warm smile had already spread across her face.

She slunk several steps away from the building and then walked toward it again, this time making sure the sole of her boot scrapped across a tile. By her third audible step, she heard him rise with a bit of a groan. He wasn't the type of man who expected trouble, so he didn't try to move silently. She lifted her hand to knock on the door, but it slid open.

His eyes widened seconds before his pleased grin. "Lady QuiTai!"

"Captain Hadre Zul." Relieved, she beamed as she extended both hands to him.

After placing dry kisses on her hands, he backed away from the door and gestured for her to come in. "Have you eaten?" he asked.

"Yes, and you?"

He nodded.

Hadre busied himself with host duties, apologizing profusely for the stool he offered her instead of a proper chair, and placing the kettle over the fire. Once they were settled, he stared at her. "This really is the most unbelievable luck. I was just thinking about you, dear lady. But why are you here?"

She accepted a cup of tea from him after it had brewed. He didn't seem to notice her hesitation before pretending to take a sip. It smelled like regular tea, but she wouldn't taste it until she was sure of his intentions.

"I understood from your cousin that this property was infrequently in use, and I had a great desire for a private, quiet place to think," she said.

"I'm almost sorry that you found me here, then. I came

here for the same reason. I can shut the door of my cabin and tell my first mate that I'm not to be bothered, but the watch calls out and the conversations of the crew drift from the main deck through my windows, and that damned bell on my farwriter interrupts me with no regard to my train of thought. And I knew that Kyam wouldn't come here. I have no such guarantee from any public venue in Levapur."

That comment struck her as odd, but she didn't think it wise to pry. While she hadn't sought Hadre, she was glad to have this chance to talk to him. "I'm surprised to see you too, and not just in this unlikely retreat. I was informed that the *Golden Barracuda* sailed days ago."

Hadre's scowl reminded her of Kyam. While Hadre was better at hiding it, it was clear he had a temper to match his cousin's. "It did."

She wondered if he'd been removed from command as punishment for his part in the Cay Rhi adventure.

"I'm now captain of the *Winged Dragon*."

She had no idea which junk was the *Winged Dragon*, but the *Golden Barracuda* was the Zul family flagship, equipped with experimental technology. The *Winged Dragon* had to be a lesser post. "But still, you have not sailed."

He glanced away. "The ship is in need of repair."

She didn't doubt that was true, but it seemed he didn't want her to know something about the circumstances. The more he talked, the better chance she had of figuring it out on her own. People never realized how much information they let slip. Unfortunately, they didn't have a long acquaintance. There wasn't much idle gossip she could use to lull him into lowering his defenses. But as she took a deep breath in preparation of launching into the only subject they had in common, he suddenly turned to her.

"What are your feelings for my cousin?"

Shocked, she found her mind suddenly blank. Finally, she managed a coy smile. "That's rather direct for a Thampurian."

While her tone was light, he looked as if she'd slammed something sharp across his knuckles. "Forgive me. When you're on board a ship for months on end with only a male crew, you forget how to treat a lady."

"Don't – "

"Ky-ky and I have had a falling out. I'd hoped to find you and ask you to talk to him, but you're devilishly hard to find. The only people who showed any interest when I mentioned your name were colonial militia, so I stopped asking. But that wasn't getting me anywhere, until, well, here you are. So could you have a word with my cousin? Maybe he'd listen to you."

"Surely – "

"He saw me in the Red Happiness and cut me. Spun on his heel and marched out."

If anyone else had interrupted her like that, she would have made it clear not to dare try it a third time. Hadre was talking to himself more than her, though, and he was clearly worried. Besides, a man who had turned his ship around on her orders deserved every modicum of respect and generosity she could extend to him.

"But you're going to have to be careful. Much more circumspect than I was," Hadre said.

What could have come between Kyam and Hadre? She'd only spent a day with them, but they were obviously close. Now, only a week later, they wouldn't sit in the same room together. They'd exchanged angry words at the Red Happiness, but that fight over their grandfather wasn't enough to destroy their friendship, was it?

"A delicate subject?" she asked.

He laughed as he shook his head. "Do you know much about Thampurian religion?"

This was an odd turn in their conversation, but she trusted he steered the course for a reason. "Ma'am Thun made us memorize the Thampurian gods' tales, but she never implied that they were more than stories."

"In a way, this is one subject where Ponongese and Thampurian beliefs are similar. From what I understand, you have priestesses who preside over death rituals, and ones for births, justice," – he nodded knowingly at her as if he understood about the Qui – "and you have gods and goddesses, but like your priestesses, they don't interfere with daily life."

QuiTai nodded.

"We also have gods and goddesses, but they're more concepts than actual beings with supernatural powers. But where there's a void of power in Thampur, someone will always step in." Hadre drained his cup of tea and set it on the ground. "Convince someone that you have a celestially ordained right to control every aspect of their life... Take a fatherless boy who loves you, respects you, worships you, and convince him that the only way to earn your love in return is unwavering obedience..."

Impatient, QuiTai tapped her foot.

"I'm sorry to be such a poor host, but – " He gestured to an empty rum bottle. "My tongue has been loosened. Anyway, there's nothing angrier than a true believer when his faith is challenged."

QuiTai startled. Did this man somehow know she'd lost faith in the Oracle?

"Or when warned that the person they worship means to harm them," Hadre said.

"Are you still speaking of your cousin?"

Hadre rested his elbows on his knees and sunk his head into his hands. "We were brought up to worship our grandfather. That's the Thampurian way. Not as a god, but as the ultimate authority over our lives."

"Grandfather Zul." QuiTai breathed his name. So their fight over him had been enough to estrange the cousins. For a man who lived so far away, his name came up far too frequently in conversations in Levapur. She'd admire his reach if it didn't seem to have an iron fist at the end of it.

"I'm an apostate. Too much time as my own master and out of the cloistered family compound back in Thampur. You'd think that after spending so much time traveling around the continent, living undercover for months on end, and answering to different masters, Kyam would have come to the same conclusions I have; but instead, when faced with facts, he clings more tightly to his belief in our grandfather. I don't understand it."

QuiTai began to see the origin of Hadre and Kyam's estrangement, but she still wasn't sure what Hadre expected her to do. What message did he want her to deliver to Kyam, and why did he think that she would have better luck making Kyam listen?

"Such irrational behavior doesn't sound like the Kyam Zul I've come to know." She recalled the respect with which he'd spoken of his grandfather, though, and couldn't deny that it had bordered on worship.

"We're speaking of religion, Lady QuiTai. Rational thought is the antithesis of faith."

That was too raw a subject for her to touch on lightly. "I have no quarrel with faith."

"Neither do I. But I do with men who claim to speak with the voice of a god."

He really was drunk to talk like that. "Is your grandfather mad, then?"

Hadre snorted. "Worse. His mind is sharp as yours, and his schemes are brilliant, if you're not caught up in them. He manipulates Kyam heartlessly for his own aims." He shook his head. "And Kyam knows it, but the family let that old bastard sink his clutches into Kyam after his father died, and there's no prying grandfather's grasp loose now. Not that I'm much better off. I stand against grandfather, in my own way." He smiled apologetically and shrugged. "And yet, he gets what he wants from me anyway. Maybe it's better to delude yourself with faith rather than struggle against tyranny. Either way, you suffer, but if you believe in the cause, at least you feel as if your pain had a purpose."

As they sat in the darkened kitchen, each traveling down their own path of thoughts, she decided that she didn't care how Hadre and Kyam worked out their problems. It was none of her business. She was hardly the influential voice in Kyam's ear. However, as long as she and Hadre had this chance to talk, she might as well get a few answers to her own questions.

"Are the new soldiers in Levapur real Thampurian soldiers,

or are they Grandfather Zul's private army?"

She expected denial. She expected Thampurian bluster and an artless change of subject. Instead, Hadre slapped his thigh and laughed.

"You truly are an amazing woman, Lady QuiTai. One of these days, you'll have to tell me how you do it."

"So you know."

"Grandfather brought them here on the *Winged Dragon*."

She sucked in a breath. "He's here? In Levapur?" The bigger picture unfolded before her. It was as if she were back in Ma'am Thun's schoolhouse looking at the wall map that showed Thampur as the center of the world. The Ponong Archipelago were mere dots, almost an afterthought compared to the mass of the continent. Thampur sat in the middle of everything, with dashed lines showing trade routes radiating out from it as if it were the center of a web. While she had no proof, she was certain now that the events of the week were no part of a little domestic power struggle. Pluck Ponong's line of that web, and the vibrations were surely felt in Surrayya.

"Grandfather sailed back to Thampur immediately. He probably didn't want anyone to know about his plan."

"He sailed back on the *Golden Barracuda*? At top speed, how long would that take?"

Hadre gave her a sharp look. Then he frowned. "You can't sail at top speed through the rock island archipelago that lies between Ponong and Thampur, and there are spy ships patrolling the Sea of Erykoli. We don't want anyone from the continent to know about that technology, and you shouldn't ever mention it again. Grandfather would have your neck in a noose."

"How long did it take the *Winged Dragon* to bring him here?"

From Hadre's expression, he wasn't about to tell her that either. As she recalled, it had taken about two weeks to sail from Ingosol to Ponong when she'd made the trip, but Thampur was much closer. She guessed that the *Winged Dragon* could have crossed the distance in five or six days. That meant it had left port the day she agreed to help Kyam track the Ravidians.

"If you can't risk the junk at top speed in the Sea of Erykoli, what use is such power? Unless... " A broad smile spread across her face as she pictured the rest of Ma'am Thun's map. Once a ship passed through the Ponong Fangs, it entered the vast expanses of the Te'Am Ocean. "Oh, of course. The Li Islands. How short-sighted of me."

Hadre's face had gone pale. He'd covered his mouth as if afraid of what he might give away, but then he seemed to realize that there was nothing left to let slip. His hand dropped. "You are a very dangerous woman."

"I believe that your cousin already warned you about that. However, I gave you my word that I wouldn't discuss anything I saw on board the *Golden Barracuda*, and it's bad business to break promises."

"There are governments that would pay handsomely for that information."

"Certainly. But I wouldn't live long enough to enjoy it, and even if I did, there are some things money can't buy." She leaned forward, hands between her knees. "Before Grandfather Zul took it away, did you ever get to take the *Golden Barracuda* out at top speed? What was it like?"

Hadre seemed reluctant to say anything, but she could tell he found her earnest interest irresistible. He shook his head and chuckled, a mannerism so like Kyam's that her breath caught.

"Once, on the Te'Am. You should have seen the *Golden Barracuda* fly." Hadre gazed over the cooking fire as if it were the open ocean. "My navigator almost threw himself overboard when he thought I was going to try to run the Fangs at top speed. It was harrowing enough at one quarter speed. That contraption you saw in my cabin came in handy. We were able to plot our course – " Hadre kicked his empty bottle of rum again. "I'd make a poor spy."

Now that he'd given away what he thought was his biggest secret, maybe she could pry the information she really wanted from him. "A promise is a promise, Hadre. I won't breathe a word about it. Now, about those soldiers... "

"I'll make a bargain with you, Lady QuiTai. You tell my

cousin that he has to escape from this island before he's stuck here forever, and I'll tell you anything you want to know about those soldiers."

"Kyam might have been angry, but he heard your warning and advice. What difference would it make to hear it from me?"

"Do you love him?"

Why did they always go back to the unanswered questions?

"I just lost my spouse. We might have been unable to live together, but I very much loved Jezereet right until the end, and still do. I have no desire to be in love with anyone and don't expect to be for quite a while."

"Do you care for him as a friend, then?" Hadre asked, exasperated.

"We aren't friends. We had a business arrangement and were working together only until the terms of our agreement were met."

Hadre's face contorted with fury. "Stop playing word games with me. Just tell me if you give a damn about his future."

"I have been trying to drive him away from this island since the first hour he set foot on it."

That hadn't been out of concern for Kyam, but Hadre seemed to take it that way. His anger disappeared, and he apologized nicely for his outburst.

"You should have seen his face the first time he told me about you, Lady QuiTai. I'd never seen him so enraged. Over time, it was evident that his opinion of you... well, it didn't soften, but he'd come to respect you. I think he very much looked forward to your *queltumonz* after a while."

Her eyebrow rose. "Did he use that term?"

"Never! But the Ingosolians have such a flair for summing up complex matters of the heart, and er... " Hadre coughed into his fist and glanced away. "In a single word. Don't you think?"

"Our arguments weren't foreplay."

Hadre blanched at her rather direct language. "When I don't like someone, I stay away from them. You two sought each other out, repeatedly. 'Passionate' is how witnesses described your verbal battles. And you were in his cabin, in his bed, undressed." Hadre's face was noticeably pink by now. "I'd hoped you'd developed some feelings for him."

"Most certainly. Loathing. Animosity. Repulsion." She ticked off each word on her fingertips.

"Lady QuiTai! Please be serious."

"We had a business arrangement. There's nothing more between us."

"Then there's nothing to keep you apart either. You're a formidable woman on your own, but together, you two are a force of nature."

He was right, but she and Kyam simply weren't meant to be together. One of them would have to abandon their goals, and she would never stop being the Devil for Kyam any more than he'd give up his life for her.

"Despite what you saw in his cabin, we are not lovers."

"You finish each other's sentences. He made rice-and-eggs for you and you ate it, even though he's a terrible cook. Call your relationship by any word you want to choose – the Ingosolians probably have a term that would fit – but don't tell me that you don't care for him, because that would be a bold lie. So I beg of you, use whatever influence you have to convince him to escape Ponong."

Why did everyone believe she had near-supernatural powers? She couldn't lie to this man and make him think she could talk Kyam into leaving the island. Hadn't she spent over a year trying to do just that?

QuiTai flicked beads of water off her velvet skirts. Despite the rain, the night wrapped around her with seductive comfort. Her eyelids drooped. Too many days cooped up in RhiLan's apartment had sapped her strength. Against her better judgment, she sipped her now tepid tea. Hadre wanted something from her; he wasn't likely to poison her tonight.

"I see no profit in this venture."

Hadre rose. He ran his fingers through his hair. "If you speak with him, if you persuade him, I will tell you everything I know about Grandfather's soldiers." He shrugged apologetically. "I'm a Zul. I know how to bargain."

"Can he leave?"

From the look on Hadre's face, that was another delicate matter. "He has signed articles of transport, but for now, they're useless. Don't ask me for details."

"Then how would he leave if I were able to convince him?"

Hadre wrestled with that question for a while. He ducked his head, abashed. "I hoped you had connections that wouldn't be particular about paperwork."

She also rose. "I see. What if he won't listen to me? How can I prove that I kept my end of the bargain?"

"I trust your sense of honor. However, I don't expect a miracle. I know who you're up against."

"Kyam has faith in his Grandfather; you have faith in me. Not the best judges of character, are you?"

"On the contrary." Hadre escorted her to the door even though it was only a few feet away. "We can meet here, in three days. Same time."

"Here, tomorrow night. I only have two days left. I need that information."

He gently gripped her forearm. "What happens in two days?"

"A massacre." She stepped out of the room and crossed the dark courtyard, sure that Hadre would watch her every step until she passed the festoon gate.

Report to me. TtZ

He bristled at the demand on the farwriter roll. Even though written words had no tone, he imaged a haughty voice.

Anyone who bought and sold information learned over time when to withhold rumors. It was essential to always have a backup for those times when talk ceased and scent trails faded. Such was the natural ebb and flow of life. Like the monsoon rains, gossip always returned. Patience was as much a part of selling information as cunning. The trick was to never panic.

Those words made his heart feel as if it were submerged and struggling for a breath though.

She has gone back into hiding.

She has agents who can do her bidding even if she's hidden herself. Has she spoken of retaliation against the colonial government? Did she go to the inland villages? TtZ

She's too canny to speak such dangerous words out loud.

She is thinking.

QuiTai was always thinking. It showed on her face, even if her thoughts didn't. It was like reporting that a bird was flying.

The reply was a long time coming.

I, too, am thinking. TtZ

They were like players reviewing what they held, calculating odds and sizing up their opponent. He wondered which one would make the next move.

CHAPTER 15: DÉJÀ VU

Kyam had walked almost all the way down slope to the harbor before he changed his mind about re-uniting with Hadre. He knew the *Winged Dragon* was still in port as Hadre replaced the sails and tried to make the old junk more seaworthy, but he couldn't bring himself to apologize, and he doubted Hadre would be able to either. So he turned around and climbed back up the steep, winding road to the town square.

During monsoon, the rain seemed endless, but today the sky was cloudless. As if making up for lost time, insects buzzed loudly. The large ring-tailed lizard basking on a rock barely opened its eyes as Kyam passed. Brilliant pink flowers blooming overhead perfumed the air.

The winding road crossed the already rusting funicular tracks. Rumor had it that it could take weeks to fix the werewolves' sabotage. All that damage, just to kill QuiTai. How did the Devil let it happen? If he didn't care for her – and there was no evidence that he did – didn't he at least care what happened to the people of Levapur? Everything shipped to the island had to be hauled up the road from the harbor, but no Ponongese were allowed into the town square. Who would carry the heavy crates? Not any Thampurian he knew. They wouldn't even carry their own shopping.

It was hard to care about the funicular any more. Since he'd found Governor Turyat and the chief justice in dream at the Dragon Pearl, he hadn't done anything to find out who'd paid Petrof to kill QuiTai. It was this damned island. The longer he stayed, the worse his apathy grew. QuiTai could take care of herself. She'd find out who wanted her dead and handle it herself. How she summoned that much energy was a mystery. Maybe that was why she kept her rage stoked like a furnace. He was angry too, but he couldn't force himself to do anything about it.

He ran his finger under his collar. His clothes stuck to his skin. Not for the first time he wished he could have worn a light sarong like a Ponongese man. It would cause a scandal, though, and he didn't want to give his grandfather any excuse to keep him away from Thampur much longer.

If only Grandfather would answer his farwriter messages.

By the time he reached the crest of the road, he was too sapped to question why quarrelsome voices carried across the marketplace. He remembered that he was out of rice, but he saw the lines at the few stalls and decided to make do with what he could find in his apartment. That wouldn't be much. With the humidity so high, food spoiled quickly. Like most people in Levapur, he bought only what he needed for a day or two. But if the choice was between going hungry and standing in a long line in the blistering sun, he'd go hungry.

He decided to go home.

The landlady's apartment door flew open the moment he pulled off his boots in the foyer of his building.

"Mister Zul!"

She must have spent all day with her ear to her door, waiting for her tenants to walk into the foyer. He bounded up the stairs as if he hadn't heard her.

"Mister Zul! Rent!" she shrieked.

He tried to get his key into the lock before she reached him, but she moved quickly for such a round old woman.

"Rent!" Panting, she put her hand out for the coins.

There was no avoiding her. Reluctantly, he counted out the payment. She counted it again, gave him a sharp look, and toddled down the stairs.

He unlocked his door and walked in.

Someone was in his apartment.

It felt as if he'd suddenly been yanked back to his first day in Levapur. For a moment he didn't even dare breathe. He was afraid if he moved or spoke, QuiTai would disappear like a shy maishun spirit fleeing through the jungle.

Sunlight filtering through his typhoon shutters cast stripes of light and shadow across the bare wood floor. The bright band of gold around her vertical pupils glowed out of the darkness that fell over her eyes. On the day they'd first met in this apartment, she'd been dressed much the same, like a Thampurian lady rather than a Ponongese. His trunk was even in the middle of the room as it had been when he'd discovered her waiting for him. She'd sat on it just like that, her hands folded in her lap, ankles crossed, back so straight it made his spine ache, her chin lifted just a bit as if inviting him to speak first.

She had to be real. He smelled that elusive mixture of spice and wood that clung in the hollow of her throat. She had to be real. He blinked to make sure his eyes weren't playing tricks on him. She had to be real. No one else could make him want to punch the wall without saying a word.

"You!" If he remembered correctly, that's what he'd said to her that first day too. He'd been no less furious with her then than he was now.

She didn't so much as flinch when Kyam stomped over to her, bent down, and punched the trunk on either side of her slim hips. He leaned forward on his knuckles and glared into her impassive eyes. He felt her slow exhale on his cheek. Not a spirit, then. He could grab her by the arms and she wouldn't evaporate like mist through his fingers.

The corners of her mouth curved up and she blinked languidly, the way she had after he'd pleased her in that narrow cabin bed on board the *Golden Barracuda*. Now he knew exactly why the Devil's fingerprints were so often on her throat. He wanted to shout, to shake her, to kiss her so hard she'd back away from him in alarm. Just once, he wanted her to be frightened of him. He wanted her to regret how much he'd worried about her. Instead, he gathered every pittance of control he had left and slowly growled, "Did it ever occur to you to let me know you were still alive?"

Even though a long moment passed before she spoke, he didn't believe for a second that she'd given her answer any serious thought. At best, she seemed mildly surprised by his question. "No," she said.

Kyam strode back to the door. If it hadn't been his home, he would have walked out and slammed the door so hard the building would have collapsed. Did she really say *no*? His thoughts were so intense he couldn't put them into words. All he could do was make sounds of disbelief and contempt as he tried to get himself under control. He ran his fingers through his hair while he stared at the wall. Why did this woman make him so insane?

"Are you unwell, Colonel Zul? You seem less articulate than usual."

The anger he'd tried to rein in exploded. He spun to face her. "Why?"

"I'll thank you not to bellow at me. I can hear perfectly well, as can your neighbors. And if you want an answer, please include at least one verb – and a pronoun if you're feeling generous – with your interrogatory. 'Why' is a rather vague question."

A year ago, she'd robbed him of his possessions. Now she stole his ability to talk. A million words came to mind but none could pass through his tightly clenched teeth. His hands rose in a gesture of angry pleading and shook.

She waited for him to speak with the patience of a cat on a

sunny perch.

He wasn't angry that she was alive. He had to remind himself of that. She was so cold, calculating, and unfeeling. He thought he'd earned better from her. His lips pressed together as he shook his head. He'd made a fool of himself over her.

"Scoot over." He lightly swatted her thigh and plopped down beside her on his trunk.

She stared straight ahead. He refused to be caught stealing glances at her, so he did too. Neither of them spoke. She could make silence do terrible things to his mind.

"Thank you so very, very much for almost getting me killed on Cay Rhi, Lady QuiTai. Half the soldiers we needed to fight the Ravidians chased you instead," he said.

She coughed delicately into her gloved hand.

In his experience, the only time women made that little throat clearing sound and sat up that straight was as they prepared to verbally flay a gentleman. Somehow, he knew she'd speak in a low voice, at least to start. That was the way it was done.

"I made it quite clear that our business arrangement had come to a natural end, and that I would seek my own path from that point forward. My actions shouldn't have come as a surprise to you, Colonel Zul."

He shook a finger at her face. "I − " She had a point. He hadn't been surprised, but he wasn't about to let facts douse his righteous indignation. "A few of the soldiers accused me of helping you. If Captain Voorus hadn't shut them up, I could have been thrown into a fortress cell."

"Could have been, but you weren't."

He hated the mocking tone dancing through her voice, as if she were on the verge of laughing at him. She tilted her head and smiled at him, charming and heartless as a viper, while she waited for him to speak.

"I'm beginning to hate you."

She shrugged. "Who doesn't?"

Kyam rubbed his forehead. He was getting a headache. "The slaves you freed."

"Ah, yes. We must not forget about them."

Voorus' warnings about a Ponongese rebellion came back to him. Was she hinting that he and the colonial government shouldn't forget that she could incite her people to riot?

"Or the Rhi who remain in slavery," she said. Her smile was gone. She didn't bother to soften her tone with flowery words or flirtatious looks, but there were layers of meaning behind that statement. He wasn't scared of her, and had never been, but the chill she cast reminded him how very dangerous she was.

"Is Petrof dead, or are you still chasing each other?"

He might have imagined it, but he thought he saw the dimple by her lips deepen, as if she were suppressing a wry smile. She knew he'd deliberately changed the subject. He couldn't ever hope to fool her. Yet she went along with it. Suddenly, she was charming and gracious.

QuiTai straightened the tassels of her skirt's waist scarf. "How kind of you to ask, Colonel Zul. Yes, it seems that my unfortunate little tiff with Petrof has come to a satisfactory resolution."

He was in no mood to play her word games. "You'll never use the word 'killed,' will you?"

"I have enough rope, thank you. I'm not about to ask you to give me more with which to hang myself."

Normal conversations weren't competitions, but each one with her was a battle. Had he ever won?

Resigned to losing this battle, he asked, "How is your sea wasp sting?"

She pulled off her glove and lifted her hand for his inspection as she fixed her gaze on the door. He gently wrapped his fingers around hers and watched her profile as he pressed his lips to the dark pink scar. Nothing, as usual. Not even a hint that she felt a thing. He turned over her hand and kissed it. At least that time she blinked. Did he imagine a slight movement of her mouth or a narrowing of her eyes? Kyam wondered why he craved a response from her.

"Someone in the government paid Petrof to kill you," he said.

"Hmm."

Did that mean she already knew?

She finally turned back to him, but her expression was still unreadable. He could feel the warmth of her thigh against his, but she was distant. She was dressed as a Thampurian, which meant she was here on business. Was she once again completely the Devil's woman? Had she ever been anything but that?

Kyam couldn't stand to be near her another second. He jumped to his feet. "What do you want, Lady QuiTai?"

Was that a flicker of relief on her face? Maybe it was a trick of the light and shadow she used like a veil.

"Why are you still here, Colonel Zul?"

"It's my apartment." How did she like word games used against her?

"Why are you still in Levapur? You have signed articles of transport."

"For all the good they do me."

Her eyebrows rose.

His wagged his finger at her. "Oh no. No, no, no. We are not going to discuss that. We aren't going to discuss anything. As you said, our business is concluded. You got what you wanted from me."

"And vice versa." She rose.

This wasn't the reunion he'd pictured. It wasn't what he'd wanted. They'd drawn close during their adventure, and it was hard to accept that moment was gone forever. Yet he sensed this was exactly the way she planned it to be. As usual, she was in complete control of the conversation, steps ahead of him.

He was surprised when she stood on her toes to place a chaste kiss on his cheek. "I'm relieved that you weren't blamed for the events on Cay Rhi. It would have pained me if you'd been arrested. I couldn't have done anything to free you, of course. That would have distressed me even more. Helplessness leaves a vile flavor in my mouth."

She seemed sincere.

He had to stall her until he could say the right things. "Is that why you finally decided to reappear? To tell me that?"

"No, Colonel Zul. I came to say goodbye."

He was surprised how final that sounded. If only he could start over from the moment he walked into his apartment... but she'd slipped away from him again, elusive as ever. "I never finished your portrait."

"We don't need that ruse anymore."

Again, she was telling him that she didn't expect them to meet again. He didn't know what to say to change that. Regrets already haunted him, and she hadn't even stepped out of his apartment yet.

"We made a good team, QuiTai."

Unlike before, this time she seemed to give a great deal of thought to her reply. "Smugglers can take you to any free port on the continent. From there, you can travel overland to Thampur. You know LiHoun. Tell him if – when – you're ready."

She opened the door.

The one emotion she'd never hidden from him was sadness. He didn't know if the glimpse of it on her face was her final gift. It struck him that she was being kind in her peculiar fashion. She pitied him, and he didn't know why.

Before the door even closed, he'd sunk his head between his hands.

Chapter 16: The Rice Riots

M a'am Thun shut the front door of her schoolhouse. She checked the sky. Puffy white clouds drifted in the blue expanse, roiling from within – that meant the weather would change soon. She patted the handle of her umbrella on the crook of her arm and walked down the steps to the street.

She had enough money to last a few more weeks, unless QuiTai demanded she return the tuition already paid for classes that might never meet again. Those damn soldiers. Who told them they could march into her school and ruin her life?

She nodded smartly to her neighbors as she passed them. Everyone seemed tense. Some people didn't return her greetings. She felt as if she were being snubbed, which burned her pride. What had she done to deserve such curtness?

If QuiTai wanted the money back, what could she do? She might have to sell some of her possessions. The humiliation felt unbearable, even though it hadn't happened yet. Perhaps if QuiTai stopped by she could ask her former student for a loan.

Her step faltered. Taking tuition money was one thing, but

borrowing from a girl who had once been so poor that she'd worn the same sarong every day was quite another. And where did QuiTai get her money? From such unsavory business! From that criminal, the Devil. That was the puzzling part; not that she'd ever understand the way the Ponongese thought. QuiTai didn't need the Devil to make her way in the world.

Years ago, she'd had such hopes for QuiTai. Such a mind! Going to university in Thampur had been completely out of the question, of course, even though QuiTai had asked to take the entrance exam and passed it. Thampurian universities didn't admit women, and they certainly didn't admit barefoot natives. She'd offered letters of reference for QuiTai to enter service in Thampur, although she couldn't think of anyone who would hire a Ponongese servant. To this day, she shivered when she remembered the look on QuiTai's face – and yet, QuiTai sent students to her and often paid their tuition. The quiet, serious child had blossomed into something rather mystifying.

But she had money to spare. As filthy as it was, it spent the same.

Perhaps there was something to be said for abandoning polite society. Ma'am Thun sniffed through her fleshy nose. There was no such thing as polite society for the Ponongese, and no matter how civilized they behaved, they'd never be allowed into the tight circle of privileged Thampurians in Levapur. She'd led an exemplary life and hadn't received so much as an invitation to a salon or lunch from the compound dwellers.

Would QuiTai let people know if she asked for a loan? No. The girl had always kept her own counsel. You never knew what was going on behind those strange eyes. And oh, the endless questions! QuiTai would never take anything at face value. You had to prove everything to her. It was almost a relief that she only came to the school to deliver the tuition payments because even now she asked uncomfortable questions.

Ma'am Thun gripped the handle of her umbrella tighter. What if QuiTai never visited now that the school was closed? It wasn't as if they talked about old times over tea. Their monthly chats were always brief to the point of being brusque – a few questions about the students' progress, who excelled at which subjects, and sometimes a discussion about books and equipment, and then the purse would come out and the coins stacked in that exacting manner on the edge of her desk, signaling that the conversation was over.

If QuiTai would not come to her, she would have to seek her out.

She realized that she'd already accepted that she'd have to beg QuiTai for money. After her exile from Thampur, she'd learned to take a realistic view of such matters, no matter how offensive they were. All you could do was pick the shame you'd have to live with. Borrowing money seemed far better than selling her possessions.

Ma'am Thun wondered how one went about finding QuiTai. She'd never had to do that before. QuiTai always came to her. Levapur was small and rife with gossip; surely someone knew where one could find the most notorious woman in town. But what if she were seen asking? Oh, no. That simply wouldn't do. Perhaps it was possible to simply pick a café near – but not too near – the Quarter of Delights, drink tea, and wait for QuiTai to pass by.

At the corner, a group of Thampurians stood outside a rice merchant's shop. They looked angry. Ma'am Thun needed rice, but the shops always charged more than the merchants in the marketplace. Whatever had caused the crowd was none of her business, so she crossed to the far side of the street and went past.

One street before the town square, she saw another crowd of angry Thampurians outside a rice merchant's shop. Fear and uncertainty prickled her mind. A Thampurian lady with twin boys tried to enter the shop, but a man grabbed her arm and yanked her back. The lady yelped as Ma'am Thun also squeaked in surprise. She'd never seen a Thampurian gentleman in Levapur act like a common ruffian, although his clothes proved he was no member of the top tier. Words were exchanged, but it wasn't her problem, so she hurried away before she found out the reason for their argument.

It was with no small amount of caution then that she hurried on to the marketplace. Unlike the past days when the few, forlorn stalls had been all but neglected, now there were long lines of Thampurians waiting at some of them. Her disgruntled frown deepened as she realized all the lines were for the rice sellers.

With a tiny huff of exasperation, she picked what seemed to be the shortest line and stood behind a fashionable woman in russet velvet. When the line didn't move for a while, she leaned over to see around the woman's large beribboned hat to watch the prolonged, animated discussion between the man at the front of the line and the rice merchant.

The woman's head turned suddenly. She leveled narrowed eyes on Ma'am Thun. "Do not even think of jumping the queue."

Her jaw dropped. "I would never think of doing such a thing. I simply wanted to know why the line does not move."

"The line does not move because people like you try to insinuate themselves ahead of others." The women turned away. Her straight back and tense shoulders spoke volumes of outrage.

"Even if one were exchanging social pleasantries, I do not see why it would take so long to buy a measure of rice," Ma'am Thun grumbled.

Someone bumped her from behind, sending her against the woman. After a frosty glare, the woman sniffed and turned around again, ignoring her protestations of innocence. Receiving no satisfaction in that direction, Ma'am Thun in turn scowled at the men behind her. He shrugged, slightly apologetic, and pointed to the five people behind him as the culprits.

"This is insufferable. I should go to another line," Ma'am Thun told him.

The man spread his hands. "If I had no manners, I'd let you, but one of the merchants is out of rice already, so the lines have doubled at the other stalls. Best to take it in good humor or your morning will be wasted for nothing."

Finding the gentleman – although from the state of his shewani jacket, he was a mere clerk – much more agreeable than the woman in front of her, Ma'am Thun decided just this once to talk to someone beneath her station. "There were no lines yesterday. What happened overnight that every Thampurian in Levapur suddenly must buy their measure?"

"I wish I'd bought some yesterday. The price was thirty percent lower then."

"What?" She turned around to glare at the rice merchant.

"You haven't heard?"

"Heard what?" Panic again fluttered in her heart. "What has happened?"

"The black market price for rice went up this morning. The merchants heard the rumor and started raising their prices. So people are buying more than they need, and the price keeps going up. By noon, it will have doubled."

Her fingertips touched her cheek. "Oh my! I hadn't heard.

As the man had mentioned, the line behind them grew longer. She wondered if QuiTai might talk the Devil into selling her rice at a little discount.

"Hey! What's taking so long?" someone shouted.

People bumped into her as the back of the line grew restless. She gave up trying to apologize to the woman in front of her. Staying on her feet was enough of a challenge. Someone tried to cut into the queue near the stall, and she heard the shouts and a melee broke out. Pushed forward by the people behind her, she moved closer to the front of the line. The shouting and fighting grew worse. The lady in front of her held a hand to her hat as it nearly fell off. Then suddenly everyone surged forward.

The merchant tried to protect his merchandise, but people jumped over the table to reach the sacks of rice at the back of the stall. The table was knocked over and the scale hit the ground with a thump. Men grabbed sacks of rice and tried to run off, but others jumped them. Bags split open. Rice spilled onto the wet dirt.

Ma'am Thun shoved her fist into the gash in a burlap sack and grabbed a handful of rice as a man pushed her aside. She backed away, clutching her fist to her chest.

A once beautiful and expensive hat sat in a puddle on the ground. She stomped on it quite decisively before rushing away.

She heard shouts and the thud of blows landing. Soldiers ran past her into the marketplace. She walked at a fast clip, never looking behind, as she cradled her handful of rice.

Levapur had always been a sleepy town. Tonight, it was dead. Few people were out on the streets. Voorus was glad of that. After the small riot – no, Thampurians didn't riot. After the unfortunate events in the marketplace, he hoped people were reflecting on their actions and hiding their faces in shame.

He should have smelled dinners cooking and heard the clatter of plates. Someone should have been laughing or scolding their children. If it hadn't been for the glow of jellylanterns in the windows, he would have thought the town had been deserted. The quiet made his nerves jumpy.

Although policing the streets technically wasn't part of his duties as a soldier, Voorus hadn't minded it until recently. He and his men could keep order when the only troubles were a few drunks in the Quarter of Delights and the occasional domestic squabble. The past few weeks, though, were a reminder that the colony needed a regular police force. Not more soldiers. The soldiers who had recently arrived were causing more problems than they were solving. It was as if they wanted to provoke the Devil's whore into starting an uprising.

He'd tried every day to talk to Governor Turyat. No one in the government office would admit they'd seen him. The servant who answered the bell at the governor's compound wouldn't allow Voorus through the gate. Chief Justice Cuulon was unreachable too. Something had to be done before matters got out of hand. His only hope was to corner the governor in the Dragon Pearl's vapor den before the man took his pipe.

Voorus heard breaking glass. He closed his eyes for a moment as he sighed. Lately it seemed that all he did was run toward bad sounds to find a terrible scene waiting for him. This time his men weren't with him. It was a Thampurian neighborhood, though, so he hoped to find something simple, like a fire. A fire would be good. People banded together to fight them.

He rounded the corner. About twelve Thampurians were gathered before a rice merchant's store. It was hard to count in the dim moonlight. Some people were stepping through the broken windows to grasp bags of rice. The rest menaced a figure on the ground. The fallen man could have been a looter, but Voorus would sort that out after he saved the man's life.

He grabbed his baton while his other hand tried to capture the whistle bouncing wildly against his chest as he ran.

"Disperse! This is the militia! I order you to disperse!"

Several people ran away with burlap sacks of rice over their shoulders, but the rest stood defiantly as he drew closer.

He finally got a grip on his whistle. It sounded desperate and panicked, as if giving away his thumping pulse. He hoped some of his men were close enough to hear the shrill summons.

Steps away from the men, he realized the other seven weren't going to run like the looters had. From their cruel smiles, they knew he was alone, and they wanted a fight.

The nearest man looked as if he'd spent a lifetime lifting heavy crates. Voorus wasn't as muscular, but he'd trained for fights at the military academy. He ran at the man with his baton ready. While the man raised his hands to protect his face, Voorus slammed the baton low against the side of his thigh. As the man collapsed, Voorus gripped the end of the baton and pushed against the man's knee, then stomped on his ankle. The man screamed as he rolled on the ground.

Voorus was already on the next man, but he couldn't work fast enough to take down all seven. He heard running footsteps leading away from the fight, and then someone else tackled him to the ground. He kept swinging as he was forced onto his back. Bile burned his throat as he fought to keep his dinner down when a man landed on his stomach. He bucked until the man tipped forward. Their faces were inches apart. Before one of the other men could pin his arm, he hugged the man on top of him, gripped both ends of his baton, and rolled it hard against the man's ribs.

"He's breaking my back!" the man screamed. "Get him!"

Voorus almost got enough leverage with his scrambling feet to roll the man off him, but the other men grabbed his legs and arms. He desperately kicked and twisted to get away from them. They grunted as his boots hit soft flesh, but there were just too many of them. A harsh blow on the side of his face stunned him. Pain flamed through his shoulder. The baton wrenched out of his hand. He gripped lips and gouged everything he could with his thumbs.

"Uh!" One of the attackers slapped his hand to his throat and toppled over.

"My legs!" a man screamed. "I can't move my legs!" Then, oddly, he stared at his hand and giggled as he slowly collapsed.

Voorus threw punches, but his assailants seemed to fall to the ground of their own accord. He sat up. Sharp pains in his back, legs, and arms warned him that his injuries went deeper than bruises.

He jumped as a hand clutched his arm.

"Thank you! Thank you for saving me!"

Voorus finally got a close look at the man who had been at the center of the mob when he rushed in. The man's huge nose twisted oddly to the side. Two streams of blood dribbled out of it. Mud coated his jacket and pants.

Voorus drew up his knees and lowered his head to them to stop the spinning in his brain. He knew from his trembling that he was close to going into shock. "What's going on?"

"They demanded I sell my rice at yesterday's price," the merchant whined. "Then they wouldn't let anyone come into my store. And they broke my windows!"

Voorus nodded. This was the first shop he'd heard of being attacked, but one of the merchants in the marketplace had been attacked by a mob too. "Maybe you shouldn't have been so greedy."

"A man's got a right to make as much profit as he can in times like this." The merchant rose on his knees then got to his feet. He took two stumbling steps before he yelped and collapsed on the ground.

Voorus knew he should get up and do something. He knew he should care that the rice merchant had fallen face-first into a puddle and might drown in the murky water, but he couldn't work up the empathy. He was too dizzy and confused and by now was shaking all over.

The rice merchant rolled over, but from his limp arms, Voorus knew he hadn't done it himself. He turned weary eyes to the merchant's feet.

A Ponongese man with a neck thicker than his head gripped the rice merchant's ankles. Several people stood behind him. They looked like the crew of a Ponongese pirate ship, even though two were women. He saw long timbergrass tubes in their hands and remembered hearing once that the Ponongese hunted with darts dipped in their venom. Their victims should have been paralyzed, but from the happy, vacant smiles of the men on the ground, he suspected black lotus.

The Ponongese group parted. One of the men solicitously helped a petite Thampurian woman swathed in dark velvet draw nearer. He thought he knew most of the society women in Levapur, but he couldn't begin to guess who she might be. Clothes that elegant probably cost more than he made in a year. But why would any Thampurian woman surround herself with such dodgy Ponongese escorts; and with Levapur teetering on the edge of chaos, why did the men in her family allow her out of their compound at night?

Voorus shook his head and instantly regretted it. His head felt as if it might float away from his shoulders. Black and white pinpricks flashed at the side of his vision. He lifted his gaze up the nearing velvet skirt, past the tasseled waist scarf, to the darkness under the fashionable hat.

Voorus swatted at the sharp prick on his neck and felt the barb lodged in his skin as gloved hands lifted the thick mourning veil to reveal the face under the hat. "I'm dead," he groaned. But suddenly, it seemed so absurd, so funny that she would be the one to rescue him, that he giggled.

Voorus was dragging himself out of a bad vapor dream when an incongruous thunderclap jolted him back to reality. He was in a room. The ceiling was simple lathe and plaster with whitewashed beams, common enough in Levapur and Thampur, but he knew that he'd never seen this particular ceiling before. Rain drummed against the roof and splattered on the ground outside.

He smelled something warm and homey cooking, though he couldn't name it. A rough blanket draped over his bare legs and feet, but there was no pillow or sheet on the cot. The leather strips creaked as he rolled on his side. Except for a table beside the bed and a low, three-legged stool such as one would find by a cooking fire, there were no furnishings. The room felt abandoned. There wasn't even water and a basin to wash the smeared mud from his face. At least there was a white light jellylantern in the wall sconce so he could see.

He heard voices outside the room, but the rain drowned out any distinct words. One voice was clearly from a man, the other from a woman. QuiTai! He struggled to sit up. That bitch had taken him prisoner. Voorus untangled his legs from the blanket and rose carefully, so the creaking cot wouldn't give him away. He got to his feet. He wished he had something to hold on to. He tried to control his labored breath so he could listen to the voices. The low murmur continued. He took a step toward the window. Every muscle ached.

Four more steps took him within reach of the carved window screen. There was no lock on it. She'd obviously expected him to sleep much longer, or she was a poor judge of how to keep a prisoner.

He gulped. He'd tried to hang her. Had she kept him alive just to execute him? He imagined hundreds of blood-thirsty Ponongese being whipped into a frenzy as a noose tightened around his neck. He'd seen the aftermath in the marketplace when QuiTai had left those werewolves on the steps of the government building like offerings on a heathen altar. What a goddamn mess. He hadn't been able to sleep for weeks afterwards. The werewolves had been torn to pieces. The worst part, he'd been told, was that the werewolves had been alive when it started.

Chief Justice Cuulon had told him that QuiTai, and all the Qui clan, were priestesses of a cult that committed human sacrifice. The cult had been all but destroyed when the werewolves killed the clan, but QuiTai escaped, and she'd gotten her revenge against the werewolves. The colonial government could never prove she'd done it, but everyone knew. Immediately after the mob tore apart the werewolves, he and his men had found her at the Red Happiness, deep in vapor dream, and from the smell of the room, it wasn't her first pipe. The whores all swore she'd been there since the day before, but he'd known they were lying. Why they hadn't been allowed to arrest her baffled him, but the orders came from Thampur to let her get away with it. The mob might have killed those werewolves, but she'd made it happen, which made her more guilty in his eyes. Mobs didn't think. She'd planned it out in her cold, monstrous way. Then he'd almost had her, but she'd escaped from the fortress before he could hang her for her crimes. Now, she had him.

He wondered how long a man could live while a mob ripped his arms and legs from his body. He hoped the heart or brain knew to shut down when the pain got unbearable, but he'd tortured enough prisoners to suspect he couldn't count on that mercy.

Voorus opened the window screen. He was on the ground floor – that was a relief. The rain fell so hard beyond the eaves that he couldn't see far, but he was almost sure he saw a compound wall beyond the silvery veil. He glanced around the room again and realized he was in the servants' quarters of a kitchen building. That baffled him, but escape was more important than trying to figure out his strange prison.

He leaned against the wall to rest. He didn't think he could climb up on the window ledge, even though it was only waist high. Experimentally, he lifted a leg. Beads of sweat dappled his brow as pain shot up his back. As he fought for breath, he realized the voices were closer. Before he could summon the strength to escape, the door opened.

Captain Hadre Zul ducked as he entered the room.

"Thank the Goddess of Mercy! Zul!" Voorus cried out. Maybe his men had come right after the black lotus swept him into dream.

"He's awake," Hadre said to someone behind him.

QuiTai appeared at the doorway. "I don't suggest trying to leave that way, Captain Voorus. Your boots and trousers are drying in the other room, and running through town half naked is bound to cause talk."

Voorus stared at her. "No. You're working with her?" he asked Hadre. He was going to be sick.

"Have some manners, Voorus. She saved your life. And for the love of the sea, man, cover yourself." Hadre's cheeks were pink.

Voorus knew he couldn't climb out the window. Even if he did, he couldn't outrun Hadre, and who knew where QuiTai's thugs lurked?

She stayed in the hallway outside the room, but her gaze never left Voorus. He felt as if his soul were being judged. Then he saw her gaze move down his body. He grabbed the blanket and fashioned it into a sarong. That seemed to amuse her.

QuiTai finally turned her attention away from Voorus. "Tiuhon tea for the Captain, I think, Hadre. He's been through an ordeal, and a restorative is called for."

To Voorus' surprise, Hadre nodded and left the room. Outraged, he sneered at QuiTai. "You dare use his first name? You dare order him around? Captain Zul is descended from one of the thirteen families."

Her eyes narrowed slightly. "I dare a lot of things, Captain Voorus, and by the end of the night, you might be glad I do. Now sit down before you fall. One of your pupils is slightly smaller than the other, which I believe means you suffered a hard knock to the head. We can't send for the ship's doctor just yet to tend to your injuries, and you do not want to experience my nursing skills."

"You're not going to kill me?"

QuiTai's mouth curved up in that smile he'd always wanted to punch off her face. It was as if she knew something no one else did. "If I wanted you dead, I would have ignored your distress call and let those men finish what they'd started. After all, you can't hang someone for failing to prevent a murder."

She had a point. He hated how her answers always sounded like insults, though. Back on Cay Rhi, he'd been certain several times that she was mocking him.

The situation thoroughly confused him. A Zul and the Devil's whore were working together? Maybe he was still in vapor dream. Bright white light flashed through the window screen. Thunder shook the room immediately after. He decided this was real.

If this was no vapor dream, he had to do something. Next to the Devil, she was the most wanted criminal in Levapur. "In the name of the colonial government, you're under arrest, QuiTai."

She scratched her ear. "I refuse. Ah, I see that confuses you. Let me put it this way: Play nice. I did. I didn't have to."

Her superior tone did nothing to improve his mood, nor did her reminder that he owed his life to her. Despite the power of her lover, she was nothing more than a whore. He was a Thampurian, and he had to act like one.

"If you lead a revolt in Levapur, the government will just send more soldiers, and your people will suffer," he warned her.

He expected her to be shocked that he'd guessed her plans. He expected her smug face to slowly register defeat. Instead, she nodded gravely, her smile now gone.

"Exactly, Captain Voorus. That's why we must talk about the events of the past few weeks, figure out who is behind them, and stop this nonsense before someone gets killed."

He jerked back in surprise. Voorus glared at her as he tried to work up suspicion. She couldn't mean that. Yet he couldn't convince himself that she was deceiving him. He'd been trained to detect lies during interrogations, and every signal her body and face sent was utterly frank.

If she was serious, that explained why she hadn't incited a rebellion. Maybe he'd been wrong about her. He knew she wasn't liked by many Ponongese in Levapur, but they respected her. They feared her. If one overlooked the fact that she was a common criminal, she was a lot like the men who ran Thampur.

He had no idea how QuiTai planned to keep the peace, but if anyone could, he believed it would be her. He hoped she had a good plan. He never would have believed he'd look to a Ponongese whore for guidance, but it made as much sense as anything that happened in Levapur.

He shuffled over to the cot. His thighs flared with pain as he sank onto it. "Start talking."

"We will wait for Hadre. This concerns each of us, and we all have important pieces of information to contribute. Together, we will see the bigger picture."

"Is that why you saved me tonight? For my information?"

She perched on the small table. Her hands folded in her lap. "All my life, I've been told that Thampurians are more civilized than the Ponongese. I thought I'd rejected those teachings, but apparently some of the poison wormed its way into my brain and affected my thinking. I will not make the mistake of underestimating Thampurians' capacity for violence again."

He had no idea what she was talking about. All he knew was that she hadn't answered his question. "Why did you come to my rescue?"

"Because you were horrified by the other soldiers' attack on my people in Old Levapur."

"Who told you that?" Of course she knew what had happened. The Devil had spies everywhere. For the first time, he was glad the criminals' network was so well organized. It shamed him that the Thampurians couldn't make the same boast.

QuiTai leveled her spooky eyes on him. "I don't like you, Voorus. I don't want to trust you. But your true nature has been revealed, and people of honor are too rare to sacrifice to a mob."

Voorus took the cup of tea Hadre handed to him.

Hadre settled on the low stool with some difficulty. Such seats were meant for servants. Tall Thampurians looked ridiculous on them.

"I hope you're behaving yourself."

"Never," QuiTai said. He could have sworn she was amused.

"I meant Voorus, but I assume you knew that," Hadre said.

"He tried to arrest me."

Voorus didn't know why Hadre scowled at him.

"I'm sure he felt compelled to act dreadfully Thampurian in the face of a confusing situation. Thankfully, I believe he's worked that out of his system," QuiTai said.

She had no respect for authority. How was he supposed to keep order if people simply ignored him?

"You'll end up in the fortress eventually, and then we'll see how smug you are," Voorus said.

QuiTai leaned forward, her strange eyes full of mirth. "I absolutely shiver in fear, Captain."

There she went, mocking him again. He took a sip of the drink Hadre had handed him. He winced. "This tea is horrible."

"It is, isn't it? But it will help you stay alert for a little while. How does your head feel?" QuiTai asked.

He wasn't sure how to react to this woman. Even if his head hadn't been hit, he was certain that his mind would still be reeling. She wasn't behaving the way he expected her to. One moment she was bitingly sarcastic; the next, almost solicitous. After a moment of thought, he realized that she answered civility with civility and aggression with sarcasm. He'd never met a woman who could dismiss a man so completely. "The throbbing is a bit better," he admitted cautiously. This was a test. If she said something rude, he'd be proven wrong about her.

"A good night's sleep will help. Unfortunately, we can't wait. I don't think anyone saw my lieutenants carry you here, but these are dangerous times, and as you're well aware, there are spies everywhere in Levapur."

So that was how to handle her. Be polite, even if it killed you. Voorus blew on the surface of the tea and took another swallow. It was as bitter as the first taste. His tongue felt dry. "Do you have any sugar?" he asked Hadre.

Hadre shook his head. "I expected this meeting to b– " He made an apologetic face. "I'm sorry, Lady QuiTai. I told you I'd make a terrible spy."

"You two meet here often?" Voorus asked. The gossips would love this.

"No. Our last meeting was accidental, and we had planned to meet tonight to finish some business, but after this we will not come back here again," QuiTai said.

"The Zul clan does business with the Devil?" Voorus asked Hadre.

"It was an entirely personal matter between Lady QuiTai and myself. Not business." Hadre seemed offended.

Voorus pointed to QuiTai. "She said business." He set the tea cup on the floor and crossed his arms over his chest.

"I delivered a personal message for Hadre, in exchange for which he promised me some information. It is a perfectly legal transaction," QuiTai told him.

"What was the message?"

"Listen here, Voorus – "

QuiTai held up her hand to silence Hadre. "I told Kyam Zul to leave Ponong."

She sounded so convincing, but that couldn't be the truth. "That's it? I told him as much myself a few days ago."

"So did I," Hadre said. He nodded, his expression reflecting something like regret.

QuiTai turned to Hadre. "I did my best, but it wasn't enough. My apologies."

Voorus snorted. "Of course Kyam didn't listen! He hates you."

Voorus couldn't read the glance they exchanged. Apparently, they knew something he didn't. He didn't like being the only one in a room that didn't understand what was going on.

It was as if he'd peered into a window, but instead of seeing the room behind it, an alternate world was revealed.

"I only asked that you try, Lady QuiTai. Success was never part of our arrangement," Hadre said.

"I told him that I could get him onto a smuggler's ship bound for a free port. He didn't turn my offer down, but he hasn't taken me up on it either."

Why was he here if they were going to talk over his head? "But he has signed articles of transport! Both Chief Justice Cuulon and Governor Turyat signed the papers. Why does he need to take a smugglers' ship?"

Voorus felt like shrinking back as QuiTai's strange eyes turned to him again. It was as if she peered into his brain, and the way his head felt, that was a little frightening.

"That's a good question, Captain Voorus. A very good question. I think Hadre has the answer, and it's part of the picture I need to see if we're to unravel the mysteries of the past few weeks. So, Hadre, why *is* Kyam still in Levapur?"

Hadre sucked in a long breath. He rubbed his thighs. "Grandfather isn't going to like this."

"I have a feeling Grandfather Zul isn't going to like anything we say tonight."

Hadre gazed at QuiTai with admiration Voorus couldn't understand. He'd heard every word she said, but didn't understand why Hadre acted as if it were a revelation.

"You've figured it out," Hadre said.

QuiTai's thin shoulders rose in a jaded shrug. "As your cousin is fond of pointing out, I'm quick to form a theory before I have proof. This time, I must be certain of my facts. Matters have come to a rather delicate juncture, and one false move could be disastrous."

Voorus glanced from Hadre to QuiTai and back again. "What has she figured out?"

"Information first," QuiTai said. "Then I'm going to tell you gentlemen a story."

CHAPTER 17: STRANGE ALLIES

"Who goes first?" Hadre asked. "I'm not sure of the protocol."

He wasn't sure he could tell them everything. It was one thing to rebel against Grandfather; quite another to allow strangers a glimpse inside the family's hold, so to speak. He felt he could confide in QuiTai. Despite her protestations, he was sure she had some feelings for Kyam. Besides, he'd promised her the information. But then she'd shown up for their meeting with those thugs of hers and the limp body of Captain Voorus. They could have talked after her people put Voorus on the bed in the servants' quarters, but she'd stalled him.

He was a bit ashamed that he'd thought she was responsible for Voorus' state. The fear dispelled as he'd watched her bustle around Voorus, checking his vital signs and looking quite grim. Finally, she'd stepped back and announced that Voorus would probably sleep for an hour and that he'd be in pain when he woke, but she didn't think he was in immediate danger.

"I'm most interested in hearing about the soldiers your grandfather brought here on the *Winged Dragon*," QuiTai said.

"I – " She smiled as if gently berating herself. "It would be unwise of me to state my perceptions now. Please, Hadre. Tell us about them."

Voorus leaned forward. "There isn't much to tell. After we took everyone to Cay Rhi, we were told to sail back to the harbor and await instructions."

"Who did the orders come from?" QuiTai asked.

Family was all the mattered. A man who betrayed his family was nothing, not even dirt.

"Hadre, lives are at stake."

He reluctantly admitted, "Grandfather."

She nodded. "Go on."

"The next day, the *Winged Dragon* sailed into port. To my surprise, Grandfather was on board. He rarely sails anymore. And even more surprising..."

Hadre turned pleading eyes to QuiTai. Did she really need to know this? She gestured for him to continue.

"He stayed on board. He wouldn't let me tell anyone he'd come, even Kyam."

"Why not?"

Voorus also seemed interested in an answer.

Hadre shook his head. "I have no idea why he refuses to talk to Kyam. He always has these convoluted reasons for everything he does, and in the long run, I always wonder why he bothers, but that's Grandfather for you."

"But he came here for a reason. I can only assume he wanted to talk to someone and didn't trust that a farwriter message would be private enough. It must have been a very important message for him to deliver it personally."

She had a way of cutting to the heart of the matter. It was as if she'd been there. If she knew so much, though, why did she need to hear it from him?

Despair was an unaccustomed emotion for Hadre, and he didn't like it one bit. He glanced at QuiTai. She didn't smile or try to make it any easier for him. He'd seen that expression on her face before when she'd been aboard the *Golden Barracuda*. At the time, he'd been glad he hadn't been the one squirming under her gaze.

"The soldiers, Hadre."

Maybe she was going to let him keep one secret. Relief poured over him.

"They came with Grandfather. They aren't military, despite their uniforms. They're Grandfather's private army."

He'd expected some reaction from QuiTai, but she only nodded as if she already knew that. Voorus, however, worked himself into a state of outrage.

"Private army! That's illegal."

"In Thampur, maybe – but as you're well aware, Voorus, there's a second set of books when it comes to the law here," QuiTai said.

Voorus' head snapped in her direction. "How do you know about that?"

"That you're studying the law? If you were trying to keep that secret, you failed."

It looked as if Voorus might lunge off the cot at any moment. Hadre motioned for him to calm down.

"Since Grandfather Zul set down most of the colonial law, I'm going to assume that he's well aware that he can get away with many things on Ponong that would cost him his life in Thampur." QuiTai raised a finger. "Private army." She raised another. "Attacks on innocent civilians." A third finger rose beside the other two. "Slavery."

"Slavery!" The stool flipped over as Hadre jumped to his feet. How dare she suggest a Zul kept slaves!

Voorus had also risen. "Shut up! Not another word! That's a military secret!" He advanced on QuiTai. "Oh, I have you now. You're going to hang."

"What are you talking about?" Hadre looked from Voorus to QuiTai. Voorus shook, but he couldn't tell if it was from rage or fear.

QuiTai calmly brushed her braid over her shoulder. "Shall I tell him, Captain Voorus, or do you want to? Tread carefully here, because if you try to make it sound pretty and reasonable, if you dare breathe a word of justification, I will correct your version."

It dawned on Hadre that this wasn't a baseless attack. QuiTai and Voorus knew something. They were simply fighting over how to explain it. He had to give QuiTai grudging respect. She'd delivered a devastating blow, and there was no way to ignore it now. His stomach lurched as he leaned over to right the stool. He took his time settling into it as he tried to calm the horrible sense of doom hanging over his head.

Voorus turned to him. The shame in his eyes wasn't faked. "When we went to Cay Rhi, we discovered that the Ravidians had enslaved the Ponongese natives. We killed the Ravidians and secured the compound."

"As well you should have," Hadre said. He didn't understand why Voorus had such a hard time telling his tale.

Voorus' throat bobbed as he swallowed something that obviously left a bad taste in his mouth.

Relentless, QuiTai growled, "Tell Hadre what 'secured' means"

"We were under orders. I personally didn't agree with it. None of my men do."

"How terribly uncomfortable for you, Voorus. How do you sleep at night?" QuiTai snapped.

Voorus seemed to be pleading with her, but from the look on her face, she wasn't in a merciful mood.

"We let you go. I'll bet you didn't know that. My men called off the search." Voorus sounded like a plaintive child.

QuiTai made it clear she wouldn't let him get away with that. "And yet, if I were to step out on the streets, would I be arrested?"

Voorus' lips quivered as he seemed to struggle with himself. "Yes."

"For what?" she asked.

He sank onto the cot. His voice was a rough whisper Hadre barely heard over the rain. "For knowing."

"And I'd be executed. For knowing the truth."

Voorus nodded. He seemed to shrink and age before Hadre's eyes.

"What are you two talking about?"

QuiTai turned to Hadre. "The colonial militia was under orders from the Thampurian military to capture a secret Ravidian bioweapon project hidden on Cay Rhi. That much you gathered from our conversations on the *Golden Barracuda*, or probably guessed once Captain Voorus and his men ordered your men to take us to the island. What you didn't know about was the plan to keep any Ponongese slaves in captivity. I liberated around twenty, but had to leave the rest behind. They are still in chains, Hadre."

"That's against the law!"

Her eyes narrowed. "Thampurian law. It's probably legal here, where it won't offend the delicate sensibilities of Thampurians who like to pretend they're the most civilized people on the planet."

Hadre had never been so offended. "That's going too far, Lady QuiTai. It goes against everything we believe in. It's one of our earliest laws, over a thousand years old. We freed our slaves hundreds of years before anyone else on the continent, and yes, we're very proud of that. The Thampurian people would be outraged if they heard about this."

"That's rather the point of the Thampurian military's order, isn't it?"

Hadre groaned. He assumed QuiTai knew who controlled Thampur's military as well as he did. The King's cousin and trusted confidant. The rudder hidden under the waves. Grandfather.

Maybe QuiTai and Hadre could understand what was being left unsaid, but Voorus couldn't follow it. He caught glimpses of something big but none of it made sense to him. "You're going to hang," he told QuiTai.

She waved her hand, dismissing his threat. "So you keep telling me. And oh yes, I quite believe that you'd like to, but wouldn't it be uncivilized to hang someone just for saying something you don't want to hear? Or worse, knowing about something that goes against every principle you believe in?"

"You don't know what I believe in, snake."

"Panic isn't becoming in a soldier. Gather your balls, Captain."

"This isn't getting us anywhere. Captain Voorus, please, just answer her questions. If you're going to hang her anyway, what does it hurt to tell her what you know?" Hadre asked.

"Well said, Hadre." QuiTai pressed her palms together and bowed to him.

Thunderclaps made it impossible to speak for a moment. Voorus almost pulled the blanket over his shoulders, but then remembered that would expose his legs. He wanted to go to sleep. He was still a bit dizzy, and the cot's leather strips pressed against his bruised legs.

"All I've heard are insults, not questions." Voorus didn't like feeling stupid. Every moment he passed in QuiTai's presence made him feel dimwitted. Was it possible that this woman was really that intelligent? He'd seen her come up with some good solutions on Cay Rhi. Of course, she'd tricked them into leaving her unattended while she helped some of the slaves escape, but everything else she'd told them had been useful. She'd probably saved the lives of a few of his men. He bet that galled her.

"Who decided to ban the Ponongese from the marketplace?" QuiTai asked him.

"I've been trying to figure that out since it happened! I've been trying to reach the governor and chief justice, but they've gone into hiding."

"I know about your efforts."

Of course she did, so why did she bother to ask?

"The colonial militia wasn't involved, was it? The other soldiers carried out the orders." Her voice was soft, almost as if she wanted to absolve him of responsibility.

"I demanded to know who gave them their orders, but they refused to tell me. I know that they were summoned to the government building to explain their actions." Voorus felt like a failure.

She looked concerned. "Those soldiers laughed at the governor. Didn't they, Voorus?"

"How do you know — "

"Governor Turyat told me. Or perhaps it was Chief Justice Cuulon. It was a bit muddled at that point. I would have pried further but ran out of time."

Voorus laughed. "They told you? The governor and the chief justice? They told you? I'm the captain of the colonial militia, and I can't get anyone to tell me anything — but you, the Devil's whore, they tell you about a secret meeting? I'm supposed to believe that?"

QuiTai said nothing. The look on her face chilled him. Did her power extend high enough that she could command a private audience with Turyat and Cuulon, when he couldn't even get into the front courtyard of their compounds? What the hell was going on in Levapur?

"Moving on, who decided to close the schools?" she asked.

"What? Close the schools?" He was really beginning to hate this conversation.

"So you didn't know. I suspected as much. And, of course, you had no part in the attack on the new Ponongese marketplace in Old Levapur. I have many witnesses who will swear you stopped the other soldiers. I'm also aware that you apologized."

Voorus' mouth dropped open. He turned to Hadre. "I never — "

"Why in the name of the Goddess of Mercy would you deny apologizing?" Hadre asked. "Only right thing to do, given the circumstances."

"Thampurians should never break ranks. It gives the natives the wrong impression." It sounded stupid to Voorus when he said it out loud; but at the time, it had seemed so reasonable. "And why, why did they pretend they didn't speak Thampurian? Hmm?" He crossed his arms over his chest and dared QuiTai to explain that.

"That woman wasn't pretending. She only speaks Ponongese, as do most people in Old Levapur."

"They should learn to speak the language," Voorus grumbled.

"Yes, you should." QuiTai's jaw clenched. She took a deep breath. "You should be glad someone in Old Levapur does speak Thampurian and told the others about your apology. Otherwise, Captain, you and your men might not have been allowed to live."

QuiTai took a glass of rum from Hadre. He offered one to Voorus, but she grabbed it before Voorus could. She didn't care if it upset him. Against her better judgment, she would protect Voorus even from himself.

When QuiTai bent down to examine his eyes, Voorus flinched. She fought the urge to slap him. "Your pupils are almost the same size now, but you should wait until the ship's doctor has examined you before imbibing."

"You had no problem giving me a dose of black lotus earlier."

"We had to move quickly. Someone else could have heard your whistle. You were in a great deal of pain and carrying you here was bound to hurt more. It seemed safest for everyone involved if you were in dream."

"Aren't those barbs usually tipped with venom?"

"Yes. But we weren't hunting food, and none of us particularly wanted to be connected to the mob that attacked you."

"Connected?" Voorus' already suspicious expression deepened.

She would not show how annoyed she was with Voorus. "For a man who has lived on this island as long as you have, you know very little about my people."

"Didn't seem important."

"I hope you're rethinking that willful ignorance. Or maybe I don't. Keep living in your little world, Captain. The isolation must be so comforting."

Hadre cleared his throat. "Do we have time for this?"

QuiTai knew Hadre was right. She didn't need Voorus on her side now that he'd confirmed her suspicions, but it was stupid and careless to make an enemy of a man who could be on the verge of a moral revelation.

She leaned against the table and sipped the rum Hadre had meant for Voorus. There was less of a chance that it would be poisoned.

"I promised a story. Get comfortable, gentlemen."

Hadre watched her with quiet expectation. Voorus leaned back against the wall. He motioned for her to continue. She almost spoke, but then glanced between the men. Something familiar about them opened a new avenue of thought. While she didn't think all Thampurians looked the same, the similarities between Kyam and Voorus had struck her before. Now she saw a resemblance between Hadre and Voorus.

Before she could stop herself from veering off her plan, she asked, "Voorus, why were you exiled to Ponong?"

"Lady QuiTai! That isn't a question one asks," Hadre said.

"It isn't a question a Thampurian asks, but I'm not worried about your precious pride. Voorus?"

He shrugged. "I wouldn't tell you if I knew. What does that have to do with anything?"

Hadre looked uncomfortable. He wouldn't look at her.

"Does it have anything to do with the current situation, Hadre?"

Voorus sat up. "Wait! He knows? How could he know?"

Hadre took intense interest in the drink in his hand. "No," he finally said.

"Tell me!" Voorus' face grew pink.

QuiTai watched them. She was even more convinced of the connection now. Something was unfolding, but if Hadre said it had no bearing, she'd believe him.

"Leave it, Voorus." Hadre gestured to QuiTai. "She has something she wants to tell us."

"I have a right to know."

She swore she could sense Grandfather Zul's hand in this.

Who else could put Hadre into such a wrestling match with his conscience?

QuiTai organized her thoughts. She'd allowed this interesting thread to lead her off her path. It was probably nothing more than one of those prickly matters of Thampurian face-saving. They worked themselves into such a state over silly secrets. Sinking into their little domestic intrigues was like getting mud on your sandals. It only slowed you down. Greater danger deserved her full attention.

"The story, gentlemen, as promised. After the last great war between the Ravidians and Thampurians, an ambitious Thampurian looked at a map of the Sea of Erykoli and realized that even with the Ravidians beaten back to their southern harbor and their Erykoli fleet utterly destroyed, the continental market offered limited opportunities. Vast, yes, and rich, but it wasn't enough for him. And even though the Ravidian's sea power had been curbed, they had harbors on the Te'Am Ocean , giving them access to the rest of the world, while the Thampurians were limited to the Sea of Erykoli. He wanted to beat the Ravidians to those markets across the Te'Am. All he needed was a portal to reach them. An ocean portal, since sea dragons don't care to march across dirt."

"The Ponong Fangs," Hadre said, as if the thought had just occurred to him.

"He could have sailed around the Ponong archipelago, but it took a long time and there were few outer islands with fresh water or food, and fewer places where an ocean-going junk could harbor. So he explored the archipelago until he found his portal, the Ponong Fangs." She inclined her head to Hadre. "The only deep water passage through the archipelago to the Te'Am Ocean. The only problem was that it was seemingly impassable. The currents are strong and can shift in seconds. The monolith stones a captain can see are nothing compared to the ones lurking under the waves. None of that stopped him. He lost three ships – "

"Four," Hadre said. "But how did you – "

"I have sources of information beyond this island." She didn't want to get into that. "So, he lost four ships in his quest to chart a safe passage through the Fangs. Such tenacity. If his success hadn't been so disastrous for my people, I'd admire him."

Voorus looked bored.

"Stay with us, Captain. I'm not relating this history for my amusement," QuiTai said.

"Or for mine," Voorus said.

She smiled weakly at him before continuing. "He charted the passage, and suddenly he alone had the key to the portal. The outside world and all its markets were his to trade with. The problem, of course, was that he'd wrecked four ships, and the partners in his joint venture demanded he make good on those losses, especially since he refused to share the chart of the Fangs with them. The harbor in Ponong was perfect for ocean-crossing vessels, but unless one were sailing through the Ponong Fangs, there was no reason to come to it. His charts were for Zul ships only – proprietary information – so only Zul ships came to Ponong, and he couldn't very well charge his family to use the harbor. Not to mention that he didn't own it."

Her temper rose as it always did when she thought about the theft of her home, but it was of no use now.

"Other than fresh water and food, there wasn't much he found worth trading for on Ponong. Worse, he was buying goods from the natives, not selling to them. He tried exporting fruits and cloth back to Thampur, but the fruit spoiled during the trip, and Thampur is too cold for our thin sarongs. Then he saw a jellylantern. Inexpensive lighting was valuable. Even though he'd cut the sailing time to and from the Li Islands by a month or more, juam nut oil was still pricy. Worse, it was dangerous, especially on board a wooden ship. Imagine the market potential on Thampurian vessels alone for jellylanterns, much less every dark hovel across the continent! So he brought a private army to Ponong, took over, and magnificently handed the charter to the king to make sure no jealousies arose. That's how Ponong became a royal colony."

"Everyone knows this. I mean, not that a Zul did it. I thought the king was behind it. But why does it matter?" Voorus asked.

"Just to remind you of the very personal interest Grandfather Zul takes in Ponong. He got his first taste of real power here, and I'm sure he liked it. For the first years of the colony, he was the governor. No Thampurian really wanted to come here, but there were business opportunities, so the thirteen families got into the habit of shipping over their embarrassments to get them out of the way while still establishing their interests. That in turn got embarrassing for Grandfather Zul, as he was no remittance man. He'd made the Zul clan the most powerful and richest clan among the thirteen families. Rumor has it that his personal fortune exceeds the king's. So over fifty-five years ago he turned over control of the island to Governor Turyat and went back home to take his place at the head of the Zul clan – and, more importantly, as the right hand of the king. He couldn't sit on the throne, but he could have the nearest thing to royal power."

"Lady QuiTai! Please!"

"If you find the truth offensive, Hadre, think for a moment how terrible it is for the Ponongese. Your patriarch is a man of business who epitomizes the Thampurian ideal. My people lost sovereignty, land, and justice in the deal. Don't expect me to admire your grandfather's accomplishments without mentioning the cost."

"It cost him four ships."

"Four ships that were joint ventures. Not Zul family ships. His investors lost money. The Zul clan got all the reward and let everyone else pay for it." She dared Hadre to protest those facts.

"Typical Ponongese whining over the past," Voorus snapped. "Get to the part that matters."

"This all matters, Voorus. Maybe not to you, but it does matter."

Despite her admonishments to herself, she let her temper take the story down side paths. She took a deep breath. Then she sipped her rum. The bite of the alcohol was nothing compared to how sharp her tongue felt.

"So Grandfather Zul sails back home and into the history books as the greatest merchant of all time. He's ensured a steady flow of income and spurred the king to colonize the Li Islands as well, so they have a monopoly on jellylanterns and juam nut oil. All very well and good. He now has position, power, and incalculable wealth. What he doesn't have that he once owned and was forced, to his mind, to abandon, is control over Ponong. That rankles, I'm sure. And this, Captain Voorus, is where things get interesting."

"About time."

"His grandson, Kyam, is forced into exile. Or at least, it looks that way. Something about the Oin Affair, Hadre?"

"That's supposed to be top secret."

"So of course, everyone knows. Maybe not the details, but knowing there was a scandal is enough. Ponongese aren't the only people who like a good story. There isn't much to do on this island except gossip." She fixed her gaze on Voorus. "Nothing goes beyond this room. You have my word on it, Hadre. How about you, Captain? Can you keep confidence?"

"Who would care? You're talking about things everyone already knows."

"Not as seen from this angle. Give us your oath, Voorus," QuiTai said.

The center of the storm had moved, but loud thunderclaps still shook the kitchen building. The rain still poured. Chances were that anyone would wait until it was safe to ford the flooded streets, so she had some time left, but as soon as the rain let up, she would have to flee. She didn't think anyone was after her, but this was no time to get careless.

"All right. I won't breathe a word of it," Voorus grumbled.

Hadre sighed. "It shouldn't have been such fuss. Kyam made a mistake, yes, but his superiors in intelligence were willing to censure him and let it go, but Grandfather insisted on exile."

She already knew that. Poor Hadre. He really would have made a terrible spy. He'd spoken freely at the Red Happiness, and every word of that conversation had been reported to her. Still, it was nice to know he was being honest.

"Then a few Ravidians show up in Levapur, and Kyam works himself into a froth over their activities. I have no proof of it, but I suspect Grandfather Zul goaded him into it. After all, up until that point, Kyam had been content to drink away his days and dabble at painting. Suddenly, he's a man of action again. He sees the potential to escape exile. I wonder if Grandfather Zul also hinted that he should get my help."

Voorus leaned forward, his face contorted as he tried to figure it out. "Wait. You were working with Kyam?"

She missed Kyam. At least he could keep up with the twists and turns of a conspiracy. Whichever branch of the Zul family Voorus was descended from, it wasn't the brightest one. "You knew we were working together, Voorus. It wasn't as if we hid that from you, from anyone, which is why I suspect you were told to take me to the fortress and hang me before I helped Kyam uncover the full truth about the Ravidians."

He sputtered outrage. "Any patriotic Thampurian would have helped you against the Ravidians."

"Patriotic? Yes. But one taking money from them? No. Don't look so shocked, Voorus. Oh, and you too, Hadre? Really? Neither one of you see it?"

Kyam would have. Certainly, he'd dismissed her hints, but deep down, she knew he'd believed her. She looked up at the ceiling so they wouldn't see her roll her eyes. It was excruciating to lead people through every tiny detail.

"Governor Turyat and probably Chief Justice Cuulon are corrupt. You know that. You just don't want to admit how corrupt they are. They were, and maybe still are, taking payments from the Ravidians. They probably picked the plantation on Cay Rhi for the Ravidians to set up their secret bioweapons project since they knew this area marginally better than the Ravidians. The one they picked was remote and rarely visited by Thampurians. I'm sure the fact that the plantation owner had married a Ponongese woman had some influence on their decision to doom him. They, and the harbor master, were in it up to their ears."

"They'll hang for that," Voorus growled.

"I hope so, Captain. I genuinely hope so. But I wish they'd hang for allowing the Ravidians to enslave the Ponongese on Cay Rhi. Oh, I realize that we're splitting legal hairs here. Execution tends to have the same result despite the charges. But of all the people on this island, Voorus, you should appreciate the application of law."

He almost blushed. "I've really just started my studies."

"I'll see to it that you get better instruction."

Voorus frowned. "I don't want the Devil's help."

"Help from Thampurian legal scholars, Voorus, with no strings attached. No favors, no tricks, no special treatment expected. In fact, I prefer as much neutrality as you can muster. Believe me. I genuinely want you to succeed in the study of law."

His eyes narrowed. "Why? I thought you didn't like me."

"I don't, but that's personal. I'm looking at the bigger picture."

That was too much for Voorus. He laughed bitterly. "You expect me to believe that you won't ask for favors?"

"That which is good for society is often disastrous for the individual."

Voorus looked confused. She bit back a sigh.

"I have a deep interest in justice. Sometimes the law is applied in such a manner that justice prevails, but not often, and certainly not here in Levapur. But let's not get into that right now."

He stared at her for a long time. "You are the strangest woman I've ever met." Then he sighed. "So why didn't you just parade the escaped slaves in the town square and denounce Governor Turyat? You said turning the Thampurians here against him was the point of taking the slaves."

She felt like patting Voorus on the head. He had been paying attention. "I didn't want to give the other plantation owners any ideas. Plenty of countries on the continent proudly talk of their anti-slavery laws, but still allow it in their colonies. Shifter races feel superior to any race that's shift-less, which is probably why the Thampurians and Ravidians hate each other so much. Slipping into the mindset of enslaving the Ponongese isn't that far of a step for a Thampurian who already feels that Ponongese are a lower form of life."

Shifting uncomfortably, Hadre wisely chose not to argue that with her. "What about Kyam?"

He certainly looked after his cousin. He hadn't been joking when he mentioned that he often came to Kyam's rescue. She hoped Kyam appreciated it, but suspected he didn't.

"Kyam was beautifully set up to be the hero of the hour on Cay Rhi, but even that wasn't enough insurance. So the colonial militia received orders to keep the enslaved Ponongese in chains when they seized control of the compound. The colonial militia didn't all agree with the order, but they're so desperate to return to Thampur that they'll sacrifice almost any personal honor to win forgiveness for their prior sins. To a point. That was the biggest risk he took."

"He who?" Voorus asked.

"Grandfather Zul, of course."

"Of course? Nothing is 'of course' in this, this..." Voorus looked to Hadre for support but didn't get any.

"Grandfather Zul gambled that ultimately, the colonial militia would turn against Governor Turyat over the matter of the slaves. Oh, not open rebellion, but you wouldn't sacrifice yourselves to protect him when the Ponongese found out about the slaves and all hell broke loose."

"But that didn't happen," Hadre said.

"Not yet." She held up a hand. "Let me show you the big picture. It really is a marvel how quickly Grandfather Zul adapted. I admire him, although I'd surely rejoice if he fell dead. No offense, Hadre."

He looked confused. "None taken. I'm feeling the same way right now."

"What?" Voorus asked. "What's going on?"

QuiTai handed him a glass of rum. "On second thought,

enjoy." His slow mind exhausted her.

"So I escape from the island with some of the slaves. If I'd been caught, we all would have been executed immediately. Voorus already admitted as much. I have no idea how Grandfather Zul planned to forge ahead under that scenario, but I survived and the slaves escaped, and as far as he's concerned, I just put gale force winds in his sails. It was so perfect from his perspective because I'd be an independent instigator of the scandal. It would never be traced back to him. How he must have rubbed his hands together in glee at that development. Only I don't do anything. I don't stir up a rebellion. I don't publically denounce the governor or colonial militia for keeping slaves. I don't even write an angry letter to the editors of Thampurian newspapers to protest this atrocity."

Voorus snapped his fingers. "Yes! That's it. You didn't do anything. I kept expecting a huge battle to wage across Levapur, but *pffft*. Not a thing."

"Then Governor Turyat, and Chief Justice Cuulon for good measure, quickly signed articles of transport and invited Kyam to make a triumphant return to Thampur. Only he can't, because his grandfather warned every captain of every Thampurian ship that he'd have them keelhauled if they honored those papers. Right, Hadre? Kyam is stuck here. Why? You know, don't you?"

Tugging on his collar, Hadre nodded.

"I offered him transport on a smuggler's ship, but honestly, I knew he was already doomed." As soon as she said it, QuiTai gasped. The Oracle was never wrong, but if she was her own Oracle, where had that vision come from? She thought back. Who had been the conduit when she heard the vision? Chief Justice Cuulon. And now that she thought about it, she'd plucked that vision from his dream, from his fears, not from his memory.

The Oracle is never wrong? QuiTai almost chuckled. '*The Oracle has been known to make mistakes' is closer to the truth.* Except that this time, she had it right.

"What do you mean by doomed?" Hadre asked.

Voorus drank his rum in one gulp. "Why didn't you do anything about the slaves, Lady QuiTai?" He stumbled a bit over the honorific, but the first time would be the hardest for him. "If you mean it when you say you don't want to start a bloody rebellion, I'll believe you, maybe, but why didn't you do that other stuff? You do want the other slaves to be freed, don't you?"

Of the two men, Voorus was the easiest one to face.

"I was ill. One of the werewolves bit my ankle when I escaped from the fortress, and it got infected. So I wasted a few days in bed fighting a fever. That, apparently, was not acceptable. So Grandfather Zul decided to provoke me."

"That's easy to do. You're always angry about something," Voorus said.

"The marketplace." Hadre looked like a man awaking from a dream.

"It wasn't us, the colonial militia, I mean. It was those other soldiers," Voorus snapped.

"Acting under Grandfather Zul's orders, not the governor's. When Governor Turyat begged them to stop, he warned them that it would only anger me. The soldier smiled. I should have paid closer attention to that detail," QuiTai admitted.

"I still wish I knew when the governor told you about that meeting."

"Never mind that right now, Voorus. The important part is that I didn't react when the Ponongese were ejected from the marketplace and forbidden to take out the fishing fleet." She would never tell them she had reacted, but not in a way anyone suspected. Kyam would have figured out she was the one behind the sudden rise in the price of rice. She didn't feel like helping anyone else reach that conclusion. "So Grandfather Zul upped the ante. He closed the Thampurian school. That's when I knew for sure this plot was tailored to get my attention and not just to sow general unrest. Ask almost anyone, and they'll tell you I pay the tuition for half the students. It's my pet project, one with no discernible profit. It's obviously personal, so that's where he made his move. At that point I knew he wanted my undivided attention, but I had no idea what he wanted from me, so he got nothing for his efforts. I wonder if the old man began to panic.

He certainly got mean. And he decided enough with the finesse. So he sent his soldiers to the new Ponongese marketplace to attack innocent Ponongese in broad daylight so there would be plenty of witnesses. He couldn't trust me to overthrow the governor any more. He took the matter directly to my people and dared them to fight back."

"So what happened? Why didn't they?" Hadre asked. Swept up in the story, he leaned forward, eyes bright with interest.

QuiTai pointed at Voorus. "He apologized."

Hadre leaned back. "That's it?"

"You'd be amazed at the power of a true apology. My people knew he meant it. He didn't just apologize though. He displayed deep personal distress. He cried."

"I did not."

"Quit being so Thampurian."

Voorus winced as he stretched out on the cot. "That's only going to work for so long, you know. We have these tiny victories – you don't incite a rebellion and I make a gesture that might have been interpreted as tears – but eventually we're merely little sailboats facing a typhoon. From what you're saying, Zul can keep upping the stakes. Have you felt the tension in town? It's simmering and ready to boil over."

He'd understood the important part of this conversation. She had to be grateful for that.

"It's been steadily building over the past few months. Kyam felt it. So did I. We couldn't figure out the source." They hadn't tried. Would it have made any difference?

"What good does it do to know who is behind it or how long this course has been charted? As Captain Voorus points out, Grandfather's next move might ignite the oil. How do we stop it?" Hadre asked.

She'd given him time to accept the truth, but she wouldn't let him get away with keeping his secret. Hadre had to confess.

"You know very well what this is leading up to, Hadre. If we give him what he wants, maybe he won't make that next move."

"Never!"

QuiTai shook her head. She didn't see any way out of it. Kyam would have understood. He wouldn't be happy about it, but he'd offer to make the sacrifice. She closed her eyes for a moment. "There are worse things, Hadre."

"Worse what?" Voorus asked. "What does he want?" He looked from Hadre to QuiTai.

"The message Grandfather Zul traveled all those miles to deliver personally to Hadre. The message he couldn't trust to a farwriter." Her gaze met Hadre's and held it. She knew she had the right answer. Kyam could laugh all he wanted to at her guesses, but she was right much more often than she was wrong.

"Would you stop talking in riddles and meaningful glances? Just tell me," Voorus said.

"Grandfather Zul wants Governor Turyat to be forced out of office so the king will name his grandson Kyam Zul as the next governor of Ponong. He ordered Hadre not to interfere."

"If only Kyam had listened to me, or Voorus, or you, Lady QuiTai," Hadre whispered.

Voorus snorted. "That's it? A rich, privileged member of the thirteen families gets a cushy position with a fat salary? Where's the tragedy in that? Why are you trying to stop it? Let the old man have what he wants, for the love of the Goddess of Mercy, before blood runs in the street."

CHAPTER 18: GRANDFATHER ZUL DEMANDS AN AUDIENCE

ell me what happened today. TtZ

This was more like it. A simple request for information.

The price of rice doubled. Rumor has it there was a fight in the marketplace when a mob of Thampurians attacked a merchant's stall. No verification, but there's another rumor that a group of Thampurians broke the windows of a rice merchant's shop on the edge of the Quarter of Delights, beat him, and looted the store. Colonial militia is keeping a lid on rumors, but of course there's talk.

Thampurians rioted? TtZ

He smirked. Yes, you old bastard. Thampurians. The farwriter's bell rang before he could compose a reply.

Why did it happen? Why did the price go up? TtZ

People panicked on a rumor. The rice merchants took advantage. People got angry and fought back.

He envisioned Zul pacing an elegant room with high ceilings. The floor would be a rare wood or expensive stone.

The furniture would be delicate and graceful.

Bring me QuiTai. TtZ

Bring?

To this farwriter. TtZ

He gulped.

It's raining heavily. The streets are flooded.

Then get wet! Bring me QuiTai tonight! TtZ

His hands shook as he picked out the letters.

She'll kill me when she finds out I've been spying on her for you.

Do you think I can't have you killed tonight? TtZ

He sank into his desk chair. At least Zul would let him die quickly. QuiTai wasn't the kind to dabble in mercy.

I'm not sure where to find her.

Then you'd better start looking. TtZ

Are you sure you wouldn't rather talk to the Devil?

It took him a long time to decipher the reply. When he did, he dropped the scrolling paper and backed away from it. Zul was laughing.

The Dragon Pearl was uncomfortably quiet. Many employees hadn't come for the evening shift. LiHoun knew it wasn't the rain. Addicts would drag themselves through waist-high water to get to a pipe, but even the dens upstairs were deserted. Fear had settled over Levapur. It had him in its grip too.

He sat on the back veranda near the street and rolled a kur with trembling hands. QuiTai's meeting with her local lieutenants earlier in the evening had been contentious. One of them had been attacked by Thampurians when they caught him with a bag of rice, despite his bodyguard. She'd told them to stop selling rice to Thampurians. They'd countered that most of their business was with Thampurians. A few bags of coins had quieted most of their grumbling, but he could tell QuiTai was still worried. So was he.

He inhaled the floral smoke from the kur. Instantly his blood heated and he felt the rush of energy. He held it in his lungs until it felt as if they would burst. As he exhaled, deep coughs shook his shoulders.

He watched the water flow through the street while he took another puff. What should he do? He didn't know. He blinked as he thought he saw a ghostly shape move toward him, but then he heard the splashes and cursing and knew it was no spirit. He braced himself.

Kyam Zul came up the steps.

"Good evening, uncle. Have you eaten?" Kyam asked.

LiHoun watched him warily. "Yes. And you?"

He nodded to LiHoun as he wiped rain out of his eyes. "I need to talk to QuiTai."

LiHoun put his finger to his lips and shifted his gaze to the open shutters behind him.

Kyam squatted next to LiHoun. He ran his hand over his hair, pushing his straight black bangs out of his eyes. He bowed his head and winced before speaking. "I'm taking her offer." He finally looked up. "You'll pass on my message?"

LiHoun exhaled relief. "Yes."

Kyam nodded again. He turned to watch the rain pour down, sighed deeply before rising, and headed back out into the rain.

Hadre and Voorus stumbled into Hadre's cabin aboard the *Winged Dragon* like two drunks. Hadre sent for the doctor as they crossed the deck.

"We should have stayed at the compound," Hadre said.

Voorus plopped into a chair and pulled off his boots. "You would have gotten just as wet, and I didn't fancy staying there alone."

"You don't trust Lady QuiTai?"

Voorus' gaze sharpened. "You do?"

Hadre nodded. "In this, yes." The farwriter's bell dinged. He ignored it.

"Why?" Voorus unbuttoned his uniform jacket and pulled it off. Bruises mottled his arms.

Hadre tried to think of an explanation. Finally, he shrugged. "I admire her."

The bell rang again. He swore it sounded impatient. Once a message had been received, it would keep dinging until he acknowledged he'd received it.

Voorus gestured to the farwriter's cabinet. "Are you going to get your message?"

"It's from Grandfather, so no. Not yet. I'm too angry with him right now."

Voorus shed his trousers. "Sorry, but I want to crawl into bed. Where's your ship's doctor?"

"He should be here soon."

"Speaking of QuiTai, she never referred to the Devil tonight. Does he allow her that much freedom? I thought she was completely his creature," Voorus said. "And can you imagine that woman working for you? The Devil must be brilliant if she bows to him."

Hadre hadn't noticed, but now that Voorus mentioned it, it struck him as odd. Not that QuiTai had talked about the Devil much when she was on board the *Golden Barracuda*.

Voorus yawned loudly. "Maybe she doesn't hate your cousin as much as I thought. She didn't say anything bad about him. I kept expecting her to, because – well, if you'd ever seen one of their disagreements, you'd know how she usually speaks to him."

"That's not how they were when they were on the *Golden Barracuda*. She was much the same as she was tonight. All business."

He wasn't the kind to delude himself, but maybe Voorus was right. Maybe she had left the Devil. She wouldn't talk about something like that with men she barely knew, she wasn't the type, but she had been in that cabin with Kyam. They certainly fit together well. If she cared for Kyam more than she admitted, she'd help him escape the island. Wouldn't she?

The farwriter bell clanged again.

Hadre spun around. "All right! I hear you." He gave Voorus an apologetic glance. "One of these days, I'm going to stuff that bell with cloth."

He unlatched the door and folded down the shelf. Hadre ripped off the paper and waved it.

"Grandfather asks for a report. 'Tell me what happened today,' he says. Good luck with that, sir."

"Caught between QuiTai and your grandfather. That can't be comfortable."

"I'd rather face plague and pirates, but no one ever asks me." Hadre winked at Voorus.

Another message was already appearing on the page. It was time-stamped two hours after the first message. Hadre read it. Dread settled in the pit of his stomach. He turned to Voorus.

Voorus sat up, eyes wide. "What is it? Bad news?"

"He says to bring him QuiTai. Now."

LiHoun jumped when Lizzriat ran out onto the veranda. "Sorry, sir. I didn't think customers would see me here tonight."

"Never mind that." Lizzriat knelt next to him and gripped his forearm. "I must see QuiTai tonight. Now!"

"QuiTai?"

"Don't play stupid with me. I know you're one of her favorite informants."

He'd never seen Lizzriat upset, worried, or angry before. Now his curly red hair was in disarray, as if he'd gripped it tightly, and his eyes were hollowed with fear. His lacy shirt hung open at his throat.

"Tomorrow, I can arrange a meeting."

"Tonight! Don't you hear me? It must be tonight!"

LiHoun tensed from the rising panic rolling off him. "I

don't know where she sleeps. She's very secretive." He tried to pull his arm away and long, curved fingernails dug under his skin.

"You don't understand, LiHoun. Zul will kill me if I don't bring her here tonight to talk to him!"

"Zul? Kyam Zul?"

"No. The grandfather."

"He's here in Levapur?"

"No!" Lizzriat covered his face with his hands. At first, LiHoun thought he cried, but when his hands dropped, LiHoun saw it was fatalistic laughter. "By farwriter." He took a shaky breath. "I'm dead. I'm dead. That's all there is to it. I'm dead."

"Grandfather Zul told you that he wants to speak to QuiTai." He wanted to make sure he had the message right.

"Yes."

LiHoun mulled over that for a while. Tonight, everyone wanted to talk to QuiTai, even he. There was no putting it off any longer. He rose. "No promises, but I will do what I can."

Lizzriat pressed his hands together and bowed until his forehead touched his fingertips.

"She'll be very angry with you if she comes here in this rain only to find you dead. I suggest you don't disappoint her in that manner."

"You sound like her." Lizzriat managed a wan smile, but it had no staying power.

LiHoun honestly didn't know where QuiTai might be. Her paranoia wasn't unreasonable, given her history with the Devil and the colonial militia, but it was damned inconvenient right now. She probably hadn't left Levapur after her meeting with her lieutenants. Not in this rain. But even in Levapur, she could be anywhere.

He knew of seven of her safe houses. At least that was a start. He didn't want to lead anyone to her, though, in case he were followed, or to show them where to look for her in the future.

He scratched his head. If only he could think like her. She'd been disguising herself as a Thampurian lady since she'd left RhiLan's apartment. Where could a single Thampurian lady rent a room without sparking gossip? Where would she be left alone?

The corner of QuiTai's mouth curved up as she gestured to LiHoun to enter her room. "Am I this predictable, uncle?"

Water dripped off him. His legs ached and he couldn't stop coughing. Her smile turned to concern. She took his arm and led him to the small bed in the sparsely furnished room.

"Lie down." She went to the chest at the end of the bed. "Here's a blanket. If you want something dry to wear, there are a couple of sarongs in the wardrobe. And, you'll be glad to hear, I don't have tiuhon tea, so you'll just have to make do with a bottle of rum and cold rice."

He shook his head.

"Something has happened. Tell me."

"Lizzriat says Grandfather Zul wants to talk to you. Tonight. If you don't come, Lizzriat will be killed."

"Trap?"

"Possibly, but he looked truly frightened."

"How did he know to tell you?"

"I wondered that myself. It means he knows I worked for the Devil when he hired me."

"Hmm." That would be something to puzzle over later. She had priorities. "I wanted to speak to Grandfather Zul tonight anyway, so I suppose I should answer this rude summons, although I'd hate for him to think he can snap his fingers and make me jump. Still, my pride is the least of our concerns, isn't it?"

He swallowed hard. The sharp lump in his throat wouldn't

be moved. "Grandmother, forgive me. I understand if this means an end to our friendship, but Grandfather Zul also ordered me to bring you to my farwriter, on pain of death."

She staggered back a single step, but that was enough. Her face was unreadable. At such times, he feared her most. While he'd searched for her, he'd thought about leaving his betrayal out of it. Even when he found QuiTai, the temptation to hide the truth had been overwhelming. He saw what she'd done to Petrof. He'd seen the bloody remains of the werewolves in the marketplace. He couldn't have explained what changed his mind.

"You always said I could sell my information to anyone as long as I gave it to you first." His excuses sounded weak even to him. LiHoun shuffled to the door. "I'm going. In case I was followed, I don't want them to know I found you, so I will go to several other random places about town. If you're going to kill me, at least let me perform this one last service. Tomorrow is as good a day to die as any."

She blinked. He could tell she was furious. He knew before she even spoke that her voice would be quiet and that each word would be enunciated with great care lest he misinterpret her message.

"Don't let Grandfather Zul know you confessed to me."

He shook his head. "I won't."

"We will speak of this later. I have business to attend to right now."

"I think Grandfather Zul knows you're the Devil. I didn't tell him."

"Later, LiHoun." Her voice was terse.

He bowed with great reverence. "Be careful, grandmother. This town is full of treachery and spies."

"You too, uncle. Don't lead them on too merry of a chase. After all, they might not exist, and I'd hate for you to fall ill."

He wasn't sure if that was a threat. In a way, it made him feel better. If she decided to forgive him, there would be no more secrets. If she didn't, he'd bought his own death with Zul coin.

As soon as LiHoun was gone, QuiTai ran to her wardrobe. She cursed her Thampurian clothes. Even though she'd given up on the corset and a few of the underskirts, there were still so many layers. She unbraided her hair, combed her fingers through it, and gathered it into a bun. Her hands shook as she jabbed pins to hold it into place.

She winced as she thought of LiHoun's betrayal. It pained her almost as deeply as Jezereet's death. He'd called her daughter. She wiped away an angry tear. There was no time for such nonsense.

On her hands and knees, she dug through the dusty boxes hidden in the false bottom of the wardrobe until she found one she hadn't used for a long time. It didn't matter that the wig inside was messy. After five minutes in the rain, it would simply look like wet, bedraggled hair.

She took a length of white silk and bound her chest tightly. Unlike the Thampurian corsets, which emphasized her assets, this breath-taking constriction flattened her chest. She pulled a shirt over the binding and raised her arms to make sure she could move. She hoped she wouldn't have to climb tonight.

LiHoun. She closed her eyes. Of course she'd told him to sell his information wherever he wanted to. She heard it first, and if she wanted to keep it secret, she paid him more. It was a simple arrangement, much as when he'd run errands for her back when she worked in PhaJut's brothel. He'd never been her employee. He'd always been strictly for hire. But what had he told Grandfather Zul about her? Why did Grandfather Zul even know her name?

Her fury focused unfairly on Lizzriat. Another Zul spy.

But hadn't she always warned everyone in the Devil's syndicate that the town was full of spies? Why was she suddenly angry about it? She was fair game, like anyone else. After all, she was the face of the Devil.

LiHoun and Lizzriat. No doubt there were a few other

spies desperately searching for her right now. It was a beautiful move, she had to admit. Grandfather Zul had turned the ground beneath her feet to quicksand at a crucial moment. Knowing it was part of his plan didn't stop the fog of rage and uncertainty growing in her gut, because this could only be the beginning. She had no idea where the next blow would land. All she knew was that she had to let them come as they may and not waste time trying to protect herself. She had to focus. Anger wasn't useful. Neither was moping around like a scorned lover. The past was past and the future was unfolding before her. If she didn't hurry, it would spin out of her control. Tomorrow was the third day. Time was up, unless she could stop it.

Still fuming, she turned her attention back to the wardrobe.

The sarong she picked was well-worn. The pattern was classic Pha-style batik, a touch that most Thampurians wouldn't consciously notice, but the brown, tan, and orange design seemed more masculine. She reached for the back hem, pulled it between her legs, and pinned it at her waist. The billowing gathered sides would disguise the feminine shape of her thighs, but she couldn't do much about her calves now that they were exposed.

After slipping into plain sandals, she turned and twisted in front of the small mirror inside the wardrobe door. Nothing was out of place. She stopped and faced the mirror.

Teenage boy, she thought. I'm a teenage boy. Her posture subtly shifted. As soon as she saw an awkward mix of cockiness and self-consciousness, she grinned at her reflection. It, too, said teenage boy.

She covered the jellylantern and went to the window. She saw no one in the alleyway. She climbed onto the sill and dropped down into the mud and weeds that choked the narrow lane. A flock of jungle fowl grumbled as she walked past their perch under the thick leaves of a low plant, but they were the only ones who noticed her turn into the next alleyway.

QuiTai raised her hand to knock on the door, but hesitated. Perhaps this wasn't a good idea. She knocked anyway.

She heard the groan of bed springs and decisive footsteps across the floor. Before she could dart down the stairs, the door opened.

Kyam took a second to recognize her.

"Are you alone?" she asked.

He nodded and backed away from the door so she could enter. After he shut the door and locked it, he turned to her. "LiHoun gave you my message?"

She shook her head. If she'd known, she wouldn't have come here. It only made it worse to see him again.

"I've decided to take a smuggler's ship. Can you arrange it for me?" Kyam asked.

Maybe this is what it felt like when LiHoun betrayed her. She never expected it would feel as bad from this side, as if her heart were brittle glass fracturing under the lightest touch.

"What's wrong? QuiTai." Her name was a sigh on his lips. She couldn't bear it.

Kyam tried to hug her.

She wanted to close her eyes and rest her head on his chest. She wanted a lot of things she could never have. She stepped back. Maybe there was a way out of this. Maybe this was the story with the happy ending – evil vanquished and good rewarded – but then she remembered that to most people, she was evil.

"I have to talk to Grandfather Zul. Could you unpack your farwriter and tune it to the right frequency for me?" She didn't like the way her voice sounded. It was thick with grief. She wiped the back of her hand across her mouth, as if that would wipe away the lies she would surely have to tell.

"You're shaking. You're soaked. Sit down. I'll make some tea."

"No, Kyam. The farwriter. Now. People's lives depend on it."

His eyes narrowed. "What kind of trouble are you in? Is it

the Devil?"

She laughed. It sounded a bit hysterical to her ears.

Why do I care so much about his fate? As Voorus pointed out, it isn't exactly a tragedy to become governor.

Why am I making it happen?

Because she knew already that she'd be the one. She'd foreseen it on the *Golden Barracuda*. It had seemed funny to her then. Now it was another horrible thing she had to do.

"Do you want a drink instead of tea?" He was still watching her with such concern in his eyes.

She shook her head. "I need my wits for this conversation. I'm sure you know. Talking to Grandfather Zul..."

"Sweetheart, I can set up the farwriter. I can put you on the right frequency. But he never answers my messages."

"He'll answer mine."

Kyam opened his trunk's biolock and set the contents in piles on the floor. He leaned into the trunk to open the farwriter's hidden compartment.

QuiTai sank into a chair. She shoved a lock of the wig's hair out of her eyes. Water dripped down her back. Misery suited her. No one should feel comfortable doing what she was about to.

"So, if I may ask, how do you know my grandfather wants to talk to you?"

"He sent a message to me."

"He sent a message to you." Kyam spoke slowly, as if the words were foreign and he was trying to translate them. "What message?"

"He said he'd kill the messenger if I didn't respond."

Kyam stared at her.

There was never an easy solution, never a good answer. She could barely meet his gaze.

"I don't know about you, but I think I need that drink. Maybe two." He rose from the floor and went to his cooking fire.

"You believe me."

He nodded as he poured a generous drink into a glass.

"I know my grandfather, so yes, I believe he said that to you, even though it was just an empty threat. I'm curious why he's interested in you. What have you been up to since we parted ways on Cay Rhi, my dear?"

She had to stop being so afraid. She had to get into the right mindset to face Grandfather Zul. He might be able to sense her fear, and she didn't want him to have that edge. There still might be a way to give him something without giving him everything.

For Kyam, she summoned up a ghost of her usual smile. "Oh, you know. The usual. No good."

His smile brightened. He leaned against the cabinet, facing her, his long legs crossed at the ankles. "That's my g– Almost forgot. Must not call you my girl."

"Kyam, I'd love to banter with you, but there are lives at stake."

"So you believe. I guess I am being a poor host." He set down his glass and picked up the farwriter.

She bit her bottom lip as he charged the field battery. What would she say to Grandfather Zul? 'What the hell do you want, you evil old dirt Thampurian' probably wasn't the right tone to set. 'You wanted to talk to me?' could come across as too angry. 'I've looked forward to meeting you' was almost too ingratiating, like the men who came backstage after a performance expecting to meet the character, not the actress. Although that wasn't too far off the mark. She was playing a part. She wasn't scared, worried, and furious QuiTai. He expected the Devil's Concubine. No. He expected the woman who became the Devil. She had to step into the role and play it to the hilt.

Kyam flipped open a book and ran his finger down to a line. He turned the frequency dials. "Just in case you get any ideas about memorizing this setting, we change it every day."

"Sensible."

He turned to her, his face a picture of exasperation. "Okay, I'm dying of curiosity. Why the hel– the heck are you suddenly mixed up with my grandfather? Did I miss something?"

"Where have you been all day?"

"Packing. Why?"

He didn't know about the rice riots. No wonder he hadn't slammed the door in her face.

"Kyam, now that you've decided to leave Ponong, are you going to stop this silly feud with Hadre?"

He shrugged.

"It would make me... You will need... He's always had your best interests at heart. He's the only person you can ever trust to do that."

"You two have become friends?"

Co-conspirators was closer to the truth, but she was about to betray Hadre too. He and Kyam could re-bond over their hatred of her.

She pointed to the farwriter. "Is it ready?"

Kyam bowed in the Thampurian manner with a flourish of his hand toward the machine.

She walked to the farwriter, still uncertain of what she might say to Grandfather Zul. "This is horribly rude of me, Kyam, but please leave."

"I wouldn't miss this for the world. You and Grandfather? I'm dying of curiosity."

"I need to concentrate."

Kyam chuckled. "It's as if you already know him."

"I know enough about him. Really, Kyam, this is important. I have to focus."

He put a hand on her shoulder. "You find me distracting?"

She glared at him until he removed his hand.

"I promise I'll sit over here and won't say a word." Kyam stretched out on his bed and cupped his hands behind his head.

QuiTai wanted to wipe the smirk off his face. If he only knew, he'd take this as seriously as she did.

She turned the farwriter around so she wouldn't have to look at him while she typed her message. He wouldn't be able to read the incoming messages from across the room. As a precaution, she'd burn them after reading them. That was all she could do.

Her fingers stretched toward the keyboard.

CHAPTER 19: THE STAKES OF THE GAME

*S*he sent the message and hoped it was the right one. Every minute that passed with no reply made her feel ...like an unwanted visitor forced to sit in the hallway while newer arrivals were shown into an office. Was Grandfather Zul trying to put her into her place? He'd obviously forgotten how patient the Ponongese were.

Kyam's bed creaked as he rose. She watched him over her shoulder. He took a kettle off the cooking fire and poured steaming water into a teapot.

"I finally received my remittance, so I can afford oil now." He opened canisters and sniffed their contents before choosing one. "Like I said, he never answers my messages. Even when he did, it took a while to get a reply."

He poured out the water and put tea leaves into the pot. "I'll make a cup for you too."

"No thank you."

"I'm not going to poison you."

The bell on the farwriter dinged.

"Never trust anyone on this island, Kyam. Anyone." QuiTai turned her attention to the line of text appearing on the paper scroll.

It's a pleasure to finally speak with you, Lady QuiTai. TtZ

He'd chosen the form of Thampurian etiquette. She wondered if she should reply in a Ponongese manner or follow his lead. He'd lived on Ponong and would understand the gesture. She bit her bottom lip. Was she over-thinking a simple exchange?

"Kyam, is Grandfather Zul one to play mind games?"

From the look on Kyam's face, that question offended him. She should have remembered Hadre's warning. Having to tiptoe around one Zul was bad enough, but juggling two at the same time was going to be impossible.

"Poorly worded. Let me try again. Is he known for his wit?"

"He's the terror of the salons in Surrayya. Mother won't even invite him anymore, although he shows up when he wants to. It's not as if she could have him barred from his own parlor."

"No. Of course not."

"You sound distracted."

"I am. I'm trying to talk to your grandfather and you keep — " She gestured a blabbing mouth with her hand as she leaned closer to the farwriter. That didn't help her decide how to reply to the message.

Kyam checked the color of the tea and poured a cup. "Is there a problem?"

"Just clarifying the rules of the game at this point."

She stared at the words. 'To finally speak with her.' What did that mean? He addressed her as Lady QuiTai. What meaning was hidden behind that show of manners?

"He's really not that bad of a man. You just bring out the worst in people. Sure you don't want tea?"

"Hmm? If you're going to pester me until I say yes, then yes. Now hush."

I regret that we can't meet in person, Grandfather Zul. Q

If he was going to be polite, two could play at that game. She almost laughed. Only a Thampurian would think of manners as a weapon. Well, a Thampurian and her. She had a mental image of them circling each other. She wondered what he looked like.

Kyam set a cup of tea on the table. She quickly ripped the scroll and carried it over to the cooking fire. He chuckled as she burned the papers. "Always so secretive."

Conversation with Kyam would be too distracting, so she didn't encourage him with a response. He spun a chair around and straddled it, his arms resting on the back as he stared at her. He had to know that was annoying, but she wouldn't let him draw her into conversation that way either.

This time when the bell rang, she ripped the paper as soon as the message finished typing and carried it to the fire.

I, too, wish we could have spent some time together when I was in Ponong. I would have expressed my great admiration for your manipulation of the rice market. Although, of course, you hadn't implemented that plan yet. You surprised me. That doesn't often happen. Oh, not that I didn't think you were capable of it. Call it a lack of imagination on my part. It never would have occurred to me to do such a thing. Well played. Except that rice shipments are on their way to Ponong already and within two days, you'll no longer have control of the supply. TtZ

Good luck getting those shipments up to Levapur from the harbor, old man, she thought as she touched the corner to the flame. It blazed yellow with a blue heart and then turned to a creeping line of brilliant orange that slowly ate the words. QuiTai crumbled the blackened paper between her fingers and rubbed it into ash. It annoyed her that she felt flattered by his message. She wasn't used to respect from Thampurians, although the Zul clan had always been different.

She smoothed her sarong.

"Now he's really in trouble," Kyam said.

Her head snapped up as her eyes narrowed.

He gestured to her hands. "You always do that just before you rip someone's heart out and feed it to them. Verbally, of course, although I have no doubt you could do it in the literal sense too. It took me a few times to catch onto that gesture, but I learned to watch for it." He watched her far too intently.

She walked around the far side of the desk to avoid walking too close to him. He'd pushed up his sleeves and run his fingers through his hair. They had enough history that she knew exactly what was on his mind when he made his voice rumble softly and turned those big, dark eyes on her. She wouldn't let him distract her. Time to get down to business.

A rebellion is a messy thing. No matter how many troops you bring in to squash it, like a forest fire, it will burn deep, unseen, until it flares up again where you least expect it. It's an ugly cycle. The only way to stop it is to make sure it never starts. Q

Typical Ponongese. Never fight back. They gave me this colony. They let me take over without so much as a squawk of protest. TtZ

Unbidden, QuiTai's fangs lowered. Her chest rose and fell with rapid breaths. She turned so Kyam couldn't see her heated face. She ripped off the paper and wadded it in her tightly clenched fist.

In a flash, Grandfather Zul's strategy unfolded before her. The clarity washed away her anger as quickly as his words provoked it. She leaned back in the chair and inclined her head toward the farwriter as a nod of respect, although the old man would never see the gesture.

"If Grandfather could see your face, he'd be a little frightened."

"He's toying with me. Never mind. Drink your tea and do try to be quiet."

Shame on her for being so easily provoked, not on Grandfather Zul for doing it. She'd do the same to him if she could.

Before she could type a reply, the bell rang again.

I didn't realize you were so close to Kyam, although I suppose it was inevitable. He wants nothing more than to be loved by someone with an unobtainable heart. I raised him that way. I find it interesting that you turned to him tonight though. Has he told you about his wife? TtZ

Kyam stood. "What's wrong?"

She waved him away as she read the massage again. Another bell clanged, but it was an alarm in her mind this time, not the farwriter. "It's not what he said, it's what he's trying to do. He just mentioned your wife, but that's not – "

Kyam swore. He raised his hands as if to calm her. "I can explain – "

She talked as she scanned the message again. "Quit being so Thampurian, Kyam. I was a sex worker and an actress. If I hadn't bedded married men I would have starved to death. If they hadn't lied about their marital status, I would have died from shock. He's trying to get under my skin. He's distracting me from more important matters so I won't figure out – " Panic shot through her. The real message was suddenly clear. "Slow! I'm so slow! Damn it!" She glanced at the door. "He knows where I am. He knows which farwriter my message is coming from."

"Of course he does. I thought you knew. He has separate machines for everyone, all tuned to different frequencies. That's why I warned you that he didn't usually answer my messages."

She was so angry with herself. "I heard what you said; I didn't listen to what you meant. You don't talk just to hear your voice. I knew that!" She slammed her palm against the desk.

The farwriter's bell rang again.

"Oh, just lovely. What now?" she asked through clenched teeth.

Do you hear footsteps outside his door, Lady QuiTai? Those are my men. Oh, don't worry. They aren't there for you. You, my dearest Devil, have a starring role in the next act.

As promised, she heard footsteps in the stairwell. Thirty soldiers were under Grandfather Zul's command. Had he sent them all? And for whom? Not Kyam. He was the real star of the final act of this grotesque play.

"Kyam, there are men coming up the stairs. Go play hero and stop them."

"How do you know that?"

She flung out her arm and pointed to his door. "Just go! Now!" She didn't think they'd hurt him since they were there to make sure Kyam became governor. That would change the odds in a fight.

Kyam threw the door open and rushed out on the landing.

He leaned over the railing to look at the lower flights of stairs. "They aren't colonial militia."

She stood over the farwriter now, desperately reading each letter as it appeared.

My men have come for Kyam's Ponongese neighbors. I don't know if you've met them, but that hardly matters. What does matter is that if you refuse to do exactly what I tell you to, they will be executed. I've heard they have three children. I've heard children are your weakness. TtZ

QuiTai couldn't breathe. The children! RhiHanya, RhiLan. They'd been so kind to her. But they weren't going to die for that. They were going to die because she'd been too clever to go to the Dragon Pearl or LiHoun's place. She'd brought death with her.

She wanted to run to their door and bar it with her body. She should fight to the death to save them. It took every ounce of control not to do it. Her breath came in short gasps as tears brimmed in her eyes.

Damn you, Zul!

She heard many boots running up the stairs. The smack of a fist against flesh rang out. She had to figure out how to make them stop before they hurt RhiLan's family. Fighting wouldn't do any good. The way to stop the death squad was to convince Grandfather Zul to call them off.

Think, damn it, QuiTai. Think!

She buried her head in her hands as she heard the door across the landing bang open as if it had been kicked in. They'd fought past Kyam.

QuiTai typed quickly.

Why do you want Kyam to be the colonial governor? Q

Grandfather Zul couldn't see her face. He couldn't sense her trembling fingers. He couldn't hear Kyam fighting the soldiers outside the apartment. All he knew were her words. She hoped they'd shocked him. She hoped he'd wonder how she'd figured out his end game.

"Answer me, you old bastard," she muttered at the machine as she wrung her hands. She glanced out the door, torn. She couldn't breathe. "Come on. Prove to me this is worth all the misery and your stupid schemes. Make me believe this isn't just about your ego. Because if it is only that, I will hunt you down and I will kill you."

War is coming. TtZ

QuiTai's eyes widened. She slowly sank into the chair. She knew there was a desperate fight not ten feet from her, but it seemed much further away. The world collapsed into the space between her and those words. Time suspended.

Do you want a governor who collaborates with the Ravidians, or do you agree that my grandson is a better choice? TtZ

She might not have believed Grandfather Zul if it hadn't been for the rumors she'd heard from friends back on the continent. They didn't realize what their gossip meant, but with so many similar stories coming from disparate countries, she'd had a feeling conflict would soon break out.

War was coming. That changed everything. This wasn't merely the ego of an old man. As much as she hated Grandfather Zul, she couldn't disagree with his thinking.

A plan flashed into her mind. The details weren't perfect, but saving RhiLan's children was the priority. She hated the adrenaline pumping through her blood, her trembling hands, her desperately fumbling mind.

Kyam will be governor by tomorrow. Call off your men and undo the damage they've caused. Q

You don't expect me to give up my advantage on a vague promise, do you? How do you propose to make my grandson the governor in one day? TtZ

If he wanted specifics, he should have given her a moment to think.

"Ahmni!" RhiLiet screamed from across the landing.

QuiTai's heart ripped. Memories of the night of the Full Moon Massacre overwhelmed her in all its chaotic gore. She swore she could smell the blood and entrails, hear echoes of QuiZhun screaming *Ahmni* just as RhiLiet had, panic and fear making the child's cry so shrill she knew she'd never forget it. Her mind reeled back from her memories as it sought somewhere safe to flee, but she couldn't allow herself to freeze as she had that night. This time she wouldn't fall to the floor, helpless and paralyzed.

She couldn't type the letters fast enough.

Rice. Q

She could tell him that much. Details of the plan came to her in flashes. It would work, but she needed time to fine tune it. Rice was leverage. She'd already shown him it could mobilize mobs.

QuiTai leaned forward and typed another message.

I'll need your private army. Call them off. Q

It seemed like an eternity before an answer came. She glanced through Kyam's door to the landing. Why did he have to send so many men? Why were the children begging and screaming? What had they done?

So you do have a real plan. My men are at your service. TtZ

The screaming next door stopped a minute later. Men's footsteps clattered down the steps. She heard the children crying, RhiLan wailing, and RhiHanya shouting out curses at the departing men. Finally, she was able to take a deep breath. Not too late, this time.

Will contact you later tonight with details. Q

Her hands shook as she ripped the long scroll from the farwriter and took it to the cooking fire. When it was ash, she mixed it into her cup of tea and tossed it out the window.

That had been too close. She'd have nightmares for days. How could she have been so stupid? She'd played right into Grandfather Zul's hands. If he'd just told her what was at stake, she would have helped him.

The shivers spreading through her body her partially rage, partially fear. She'd put children in danger. She'd never forgive herself. She'd never forgive Grandfather Zul.

Kyam stumbled into his apartment. His hair was a mess and he'd lost a few jacket buttons. It took a few huffs to catch his breath. "They weren't here for us. I wonder why they were after RhiLan's family."

Puzzled, she glared at him. Her fear and anger focused on

Kyam. "You can't honestly... How blind are you, Kyam? Those men are your grandfather's soldiers. They attacked RhiLan's family to force me to agree to do something for him."

Kyam shook his head. "He wouldn't do that."

"Did you hear what I said when I came to you tonight? He was going to kill people if I didn't contact him."

Kyam's dark eyes filled with anger. His fists clenched. She'd forgotten that she was dealing with a true believer.

She sighed and shook her head. Maybe he deserved his fate. If only she hadn't burned the proof. Exhaustion hit her in a nauseating wave. She smelled her own sweat.

Oh, Kyam, if you were only the lover I need right now! But you're too much of Grandfather Zul's possession for me to endure, and I still have so much to do tonight.

"Good evening, Colonel Zul. Thank you for your assistance."

"Are you ever going to tell me what you two talked about?" he asked.

"Ask him. Apparently, he's feeling quite chatty tonight. You might get lucky and get an answer for once."

RhiHanya stood by the broken door across the landing. When she left Kyam's apartment, QuiTai pressed her hands together and bowed. RhiHanya's eyes narrowed, but QuiTai realized she didn't recognize her in her disguise.

Past RhiHanya, she saw RhiLan kneeling with her arms around her three children. They looked scared, but unhurt. RhiLan's man was on the couch, his head wrapped in bandages and his arm in a sling.

They'd probably never feel safe in their home again. The children would hate and fear Thampurians all their lives. This was a game for grown-ups, she reminded herself. People got hurt. Most of them survive, and that was the best she could do for them.

She approached RhiHanya. "You gave me three days, auntie. I beg patience of you."

RhiHanya jerked back, recognition spreading over her face.

"You know her?" Kyam asked. "How do you know my

neighbors?"

QuiTai could have strangled him. He was smarter than this. Much smarter. "Welcome to the party, Colonel Zul. You're fashionably late."

"What about the smuggler's boat?" Kyam called out as she walked down the stairs.

She was too frustrated with him to bother answering. He'd missed the boat in more ways than one, but she was too much of a coward to spell it out to him. He'd find out tomorrow.

CHAPTER 20: LI HOUN

QuiTai hated this ugly, rotting apartment building on the edge of the Jupoli Gorge, hated that it still stood despite the neglect, hated that she couldn't bring herself to burn it down. Every time she'd walked past it on her way to Petrof's house, she'd averted her eyes and held her breath. The blood and gore had long since washed away; the bodies had been buried. That didn't stop the memories of the night of the Full Moon Massacre from flooding her senses. The horror of that night would never dim. Even now, it echoed through her life. Sometimes it felt as if all she had were vengeance, loss, and guilt.

For the first time in two years, she walked up the bowed steps. From dark rooms behind carved window screens, cats' eyes watched her. Some blinked slowly, as if about to drift into sleep. Others were wide open. Inside, she heard the hushed padding of feet across the creaking floor.

The sheet in the doorway pulled back. A woman with alert ears held it aside as she bowed low.

QuiTai heard herself swallow as she stepped into the

shadowy foyer. The building smelled like whiskey, of old wood and dust.

A night spirit moth fluttered against an aged green light jellylantern on the wall. Like the Li, she could see well in its dim light. The wallpaper peeling from the walls hadn't changed. The balusters on the narrow staircase's banister were as crooked as LiHoun's teeth. There was the doorway that had led to her parent's apartment. Here was where QuiZhun used to dance. This was where her neighbor had sunk his fangs into her so she wouldn't open the door to the werewolves. She felt as if the building had been waiting like a jilted lover for her return, whispering, 'See what memories you made me hold for you?'

Li women and children crept out of doorways and down the hall toward her.

QuiTai turned to the woman who showed her in. "Friends may fight, but they also forgive," she said in Li. It was a favorite saying of LiHoun's, although he often used it sarcastically. His women probably heard it often enough that even if she mispronounced any of the words they'd understand what she meant. She jutted her chin toward the stairs. "Is LiHoun up there?"

The woman bowed lower. "He has been waiting for you, grandmother," she said in uncertain Ponongese.

QuiTai pressed her hands together and bowed.

She climbed the stairs.

This is the step where I realized my mother was dead. This is the step where I heard QuiZhun scream for me. This is the step where I went mad.

"Have you eaten, grandmother?" LiHoun called out when she reached the top step.

She followed his voice into the front apartment.

He sat on a mussed bed with no mosquito nets. His blankets were so exhausted by years of laundering that they couldn't summon up enough energy to have a color. The weathered wood floor had turned gray. Now that the rain had passed, moonlight seeped through the shutters. Kur smoke rose from an overflowing try of butts.

"You have reached your decision," LiHoun said.

She entered the room. "Yes."

He waved a hand toward boxes on the floor. Curled farwriter paper sat in heaps. "I saved every message from Grandfather Zul. It wasn't until tonight that I realized there was no record of my replies. At least you will know the kinds of questions he asked."

"I have too much left to do tonight to read through them. Tell me how it began."

"I've been selling him information for years, mostly about Governor Turyat. When you returned to Levapur with Jezereet and your daughter, it was at the beginning of monsoon season. The brothels were slow, as they always are the first month of the rains. I passed on old information, but soon ran out. So I mentioned how you were a great favorite of Chief Justice Cuulon before you left Levapur and you might renew your acquaintance. Grandfather Zul also wanted information about him."

LiHoun's hands shook as he rolled another kur.

"Go on."

LiHoun struck a match. He talked around the kur pinched between his lips. "Over time, he took an interest in you. He liked your spirit, he said. I tried to remember things you said, because they amused him. He expressed admiration for your business skills."

"How very flattering. A secret admirer."

Deep coughs shook LiHoun's shoulders. "He seemed relieved, genuinely relieved, that you survived the Full Moon Massacre. He had reservations about your alliance with the Devil, but it seemed to offer you protection and there were no further attempts on your life."

"Until Petrof came after me."

"I haven't told him anything about that."

"Did he ever ask about the Devil?"

"Not that I recall." LiHoun's gaze rose to hers. "During that time, you also came to me for information. I rarely mentioned what you were up to. I started holding back things. Forgive this old fool, grandmother. If I betrayed you, it wasn't deliberate."

She wasn't ready to have that conversation with him. "Do your legs still hurt from your hours in the rain tonight, uncle?"

He rubbed his thigh.

It had to be done. Order had to be maintained. She hardened her heart.

"Get up. Gather your women and older children. You have penance to pay and not many hours to complete it."

He grinned. She realized he might welcome punishment. So many men who worshipped her did. They hoped it would bring forgiveness.

"Bring about half the sacks of rice stored in the Devil's old den here. Do it quickly. Oh, and have someone find me fresh clothes. Then tell them to leave me alone. I must think about my next moves."

On her walk upslope from Levapur, a plan had been revealed to her, but every nuance had to be examined. So much rode on her understanding of Kyam. Would he react the right way? She had more conviction in the predictability of the Thampurian mob, but they too were a risk.

LiHoun limped to the doorway. "It will take us more than an hour."

"Not much more, I hope. I will be very angry if this entire operation isn't completed by sunrise, and this is only step one."

LiHoun watched amazement dawn on QuiTai's face as he showed her the stacks of rice sacks he and his women had piled in the foyer. She'd never gone to the Devil's old den and seen how much rice she'd bought. The stacks came to her chin.

"There is enough left in the Devil's den to feed non-Thampurians who need rice?" she asked LiHoun.

"For a day, maybe two. Your lieutenants urged people to buy more than they normally do. As soon as word got out about the rice riots, they sold as much as they could carry, but there's still much more left."

"In a couple days, things will be back to normal. Once the price falls and people trust the supply again, we can resume our regular black market business."

LiHoun felt as if he'd aged ten years over the course of the night. He hoped she didn't have further plans for him. "Was it worth it?"

"In coin? We'll see. Probably not. But I'm glad I did it. Otherwise, I wouldn't have had a tile in my hand to play against Grandfather Zul."

She sat on the staircase. LiHoun squatted at her feet. His women hovered in doorways and on the upstairs landing as they anxiously awaited a sign. He wished he could comfort them, but QuiTai was at times unpredictable. She could seem perfectly sociable one moment and then lash out the next. He's seen what she'd done to others who failed her. He wondered if she toyed with him on purpose. The tension was a seething knot in his stomach.

"I never had a personal stake in this game. That's what irritates me the most. Enslave the Ponongese on Cay Rhi?" She shrugged. "I wasn't the one in chains. Close the marketplace? I can buy everything I want from smugglers. Close the school? I have no children. Make Kyam Zul the colonial governor? As Voorus said, 'Where's the tragedy in that?' Spark a rebellion? I could have bought my way on board a smuggler's ship and gone to live on the continent. You see? Not a single good reason why I should be dragged into this game. He could have found a simpler way to put Kyam in that post. But no. It had to be convoluted and put people in danger, and worst of all, he involved me. No! Worst of all, I did his bidding. I knew I should just walk away, but I bowed to his wishes. Hadre warned me. I didn't listen."

LiHoun's phlegmy chuckle brought a frown to her face.

"You find it amusing, uncle?"

He wondered if he believed her own words or if they were merely part of her act. She always jumped into the thick of things. "Grandfather Zul should watch his back from now on."

Her expression went blank. Every hair on his body stood at end. She relaxed, but he could tell she'd forced it.

"Did you know Kyam Zul is married?" she asked.

He knew his shock showed on his face. Thampurians took mistresses, but he'd sensed Kyam had a deeper interest in QuiTai. Perhaps he'd been wrong.

"Grandfather Zul tried to use that to turn me against Kyam. That shows he doesn't know me as well as he thinks he does."

"Kyam Zul would have made a good concubine for you."

Speechless for a moment, she raised an eyebrow. "Concubine?"

"You're the Devil. The Devil needs a second in command. A companion."

"I am quite content to be without a regular lover, thank you. Besides, I doubt Colonel Zul would wear a green sarong."

Despite his caution, LiHoun laughed. "No. I think not. Besides, he's leaving the island as soon as we find a smuggler who will take him to the continent."

She made a face. He suspected something had changed in her plans, but she rarely shared details with him.

"Tomorrow, it would be convenient if Governor Turyat and Chief Justice Cuulon continued to cower in their compounds," she said.

"I'll see that they get their black lotus earlier than usual. That should keep Governor Turyat busy. Chief Justice Cuulon is a bit trickier. Perhaps if I escorted SuYan to his bedroom, he'd find a reason to stay."

"SuYan?"

"One of PhaJut's workers. She tries to fill the role you left behind." LiHoun didn't think QuiTai needed to hear that there would never be a woman her equal, even from her days in PhaJut's brothel, but it didn't hurt to flatter her a bit. "SuYan goes through the motions, but her heart isn't in it. Her customers put up with it but they still ask if you'll ever return."

"Not unless I grow very bored, and I doubt that will happen." She tapped her bottom lip. "Did you tell Grandfather Zul about my estate, or that I had you steal the sea wasps from the Ravidian's bioweapons breeding grounds?"

"Never. Never." LiHoun shook his head vehemently. He hoped she believed him. He tensed again and saw his women react with despairing looks. He signaled for them to be patient. There was still hope. There was always hope. QuiTai was probably weighing the ramifications of killing him. He'd give her as much time to mull it over as she needed.

QuiTai let the silence stretch. She covered her mouth when she yawned. "It's late."

"The sun will rise in several hours."

She stood.

He wanted to plead with her, but his dignity wouldn't allow it. One of his women keened as she realized QuiTai had reached her decision.

"We're going upstairs to have a little chat with Grandfather Zul. He's going to send his soldiers here so I can make good on my oath to him."

That wasn't what he'd expected. He groaned as he rose. He was too old for this. "I will, of course, do anything you ask, but may I ask a favor, grandmother? I accept my death, but please, just tell me my fate. The uncertainty is torture for my wives and children."

She seemed to consider his regret before speaking. "This is the crux of my problem. The Devil would execute you as a matter of principle. QuiTai would weigh intent and the value of the relationship against the resulting harm. I am both. You understand my difficulty. If word gets out that the Devil allowed someone to betray him and live, it sets a bad precedent. But we have history, uncle. You called me daughter. You're my right hand." Her voice filled with sorrow. "I've thought about this quite a bit. The only way to reconcile the Devil's needs with QuiTai's is to get your solemn oath that no one will ever know you sold information to Grandfather Zul. This stays between us. You never betrayed me, so I have no reason to kill you. Understand? We will never speak of it again. And from now on, you are completely mine."

Relief sent him staggering back a few steps. He couldn't believe his luck. Overwhelmed, tears welled in his eyes. He would have killed for her at that moment. He would have erected shrines and offered sacrifices to thank her, but he knew she'd hate such a display. Sometimes QuiTai was more Thampurian than Ponongese. It wounded him to show only a little of his gratitude, but he bowed until his forehead touched his clasped hands because he knew it was the only thanks she'd accept.

"Tell your women my word is good. Tell them I choose to forgive, but that they, too, must keep our quarrel private. Tell them and set their hearts at ease."

Before LiHoun said a word, his wives seemed to sense the verdict. They hugged each other then bowed and shyly smiled at QuiTai. She, as usual, bristled at the adoration.

Her expression hardened as she quietly spoke for his ears only, "Forgiven, little brother, but never forgotten."

Chills stabbed his heart, even though he admired her now more than ever. He barely nodded.

"Let's send that message to Grandfather Zul. I'm running out of darkness," she said curtly as she headed up the stairs.

"You don't need to wait with me, uncle. I know you're in pain," QuiTai told LiHoun. They sat on the steps of his home. Levapur stretched below them.

"Cats suffer from curiosity. I'd rather you know I'm eavesdropping."

QuiTai wrapped her arms around her knees. She smiled at him. "You want a story, uncle. I'll tell you tomorrow. I promise it's a suckling pig to go with your rice."

"I've had enough rice this week to last me many months."

She chuckled. When she was this weary and fate seemed to have all the tiles, what could she do but laugh?

LiHoun looked around the front of the building as if seeing it for the first time. "I always wondered why you didn't burn this place to the ground. Your ghosts live here."

"My ghosts live inside my head. They have no need of

verandas and steps to haunt me." She stretched her arms as she looked up at the sky. "I never realized you could hear the Pha River from here. It was never quiet enough to hear it when... before." She sniffed. The scent of the jungle filled the air. "I wanted to get them out of Old Levapur, so as soon as the Red Happiness turned a profit, I moved them to this place. It wasn't much nicer then, but at least the roof didn't leak."

"I remember when you did that. The roof leaks now."

"For the past few years, I let guilt eat at me because I thought it was my fault that they were here, right in the path of the werewolves for the Full Moon Massacre. But Petrof told me he was paid to kill my family, so he would have gotten to them no matter where they were. It doesn't make me feel any better, though."

"Did he say who paid him?"

"I didn't give him a chance." She rested her cheek on her knees. "Whoever it was, they also paid him to kill me. When I came back to Levapur last week, my goal was to find out who it was and put an end to this."

"Did you?"

"I have a good idea. Governor Turyat and Chief Justice Cuulon were afraid the Oracle would tell me they'd sold out to the Ravidians. Or, at least, I think that's why they wanted all the Qui on Ponong killed."

"Are you going to kill them?"

That seemed like such a distant concern to her now. "I gave Captain Voorus of the colonial militia enough information that he might take care of them for me. If not, I'm not in any great hurry. Knowing your enemy is half the battle sometimes."

"You're going to give them a chance to hire another killer to come after you?"

She laughed. "Who would they go to if they wanted to hire an assassin?"

"The Devil," they said in unison as they grinned at each other.

QuiTai met Grandfather Zul's men in the street before they reached LiHoun's place. They weren't in their uniforms, as she'd requested. "Which of you is the leader?" she asked.

The tall one in front took a step forward.

She didn't care to know his name, and he didn't offer it. "You have your orders from Grandfather Zul?"

"Yes." He obviously wasn't happy about it, but his little ego didn't concern her.

"Just so we are clear, you will do as I say without question. Do your men understand?"

He nodded. She met the gaze of each of the men so she could see their agreement.

"There are sacks of rice in the house over there." She pointed to LiHoun's. "You will carry them downslope. It will take a few trips." The work she planned for them was hard, but they had many sins to atone for.

The leader fought to control his sneer. "Where are we taking them, snake?"

Perversely, his rudeness pleased her. The corner of her mouth curved up as she ran her hands over the front of her sarong. "To the governor's office in the government building on the town square."

He clearly thought she'd lost her mind. "But it's the middle of the night! It's closed."

"Then you will have to break in. And please, don't be sloppy about it. No breaking down doors or anything as crude as that. I also suggest you make your trips as stealthy as possible. If anyone sees you with rice, they'll probably kill you for it."

QuiTai passed between them as she headed down the road to town. She paused to look over her shoulder at them. As she'd expected, to a man, they watched her. From anger to undisguised loathing, their feelings for her were clear. "Once the rice is delivered, I'll give you the rest of your orders. Be quick about it. The dawn of a new day approaches for Levapur, gentlemen. I'm sure your master wants you to witness it."

CHAPTER 21: THE HERO OF LEVAPUR

QuiTai thought about sitting behind the governor's desk but decided that perching on the stacks of rice sent a better message. They were the fulcrum on the balance of power. She arranged the sacks of rice directly across from the governor's desk into a throne of sorts. From that elevated position, she could look down at even the tallest Thampurian. Satisfied with her effort, she climbed into place and waited for the rest of the players to arrive.

She'd dressed in deep Thampurian velvets for the coming interview. The embellishments on her cropped jacket and waist scarf were subdued and matched the velvet. Her heavy mourning veil pulled back over her hat to reveal her face, but her outfit would still inspire somber thoughts. Costuming was so important when setting the tone of a scene.

The governor's office was spacious and quite opulent, although it smelled faintly of stale water and black lotus. Some of Grandfather Zul's men slouched on chairs with delicately turned legs; the others leaned against book shelves full of tomes that had never been opened. Their muddy boots streaked the inlaid wood floor.

On the large map behind the governor's desk, sea dragons coiled around Ravidian ships and pulled them under waves. The Thampurians had the nerve to paint the king's chop on every island in the Ponong archipelago when no Thampurian had ever set foot further than the boundaries of Levapur. Such arrogance would play into her hands.

QuiTai stifled a yawn. It had been a long week, but the end was in sight. Before Kyam had intruded in her life, she'd always woken refreshed. She promised herself a respite from Thampurian matters as soon as this bit of business concluded – and an even longer break from Kyam.

The sun had just risen and brought heat with it. Suffocating humidity pressed against her chest. A sea breeze could have flowed through the typhoon shutters leading to the veranda overlooking the town square to cool the room, but she didn't order Grandfather Zul's men to open them. She could survive the heat far better than they, and she liked watching them sweat.

Although she'd expected a crowd to gather outside the building eventually, she was a bit surprised to hear so many Thampurians had come to the town square already. Their punctuality did them credit.

Another angry voice carried up to her from inside the building. She pictured Kyam and his escort in the building's middle courtyard, where jewel fish swam in placid circles around a floral sea dragon. The soldiers who'd been sent for him had been warned not to say anything to him beyond the summons. That didn't stop Kyam from bellowing questions at them as they drew closer to the governor's office.

The door banged open.

"You!" Kyam said when his gaze found QuiTai.

"Really, Colonel Zul, have you no other way of greeting me?"

"What's the meaning of this?"

"We should wait for the other guests. I suspect the growing

mob outside is making it difficult for them to enter the building. They should have come around to the back entrance as you did."

The voices in the town square rose.

"Ah, I believe that's Captain Voorus and his men arriving now."

"Do you have a death wish?" Kyam asked.

"I am flattered beyond words that you care for my safety, Colonel Zul, but believe me, I am well protected."

He glanced at his grandfather's private army. "Them? You're working with Grandfather now?"

"Very much against my wishes, I assure you. I should have listened more carefully when Captain Hadre warned me that no matter how hard a person resists Grandfather Zul, somehow one ends up doing exactly what he wants you to. Words I advise you to take to heart."

In another part of the building, big brass doors slammed shut. The footsteps of men running up the stairs to the governor's office echoed in the courtyard. Moments later, someone knocked on the door.

QuiTai gestured to Kyam, but he said nothing. "Come in, Captain Voorus."

Voorus didn't have the entire colonial militia with him, but he'd taken her message seriously enough to bring most of them. Between his men, Grandfather Zul's private army, Kyam, QuiTai, and the stacks of rice, the governor's office was now quite crowded. The stifling air made it worse.

Voorus' lieutenant lost his patience with the confused silence. He rushed across the room. "Arrest her!"

Her gaze slowly moved from his face to his boots and up again. She took a deep breath as if preparing to sigh. A hint of a sneer pulled at her upper lip.

He lost his nerve and looked to Voorus for guidance. "Sir?"

Voorus moved though the crowd to draw closer to her. His grim face gave away his thoughts. He didn't want to trust her, but he sensed something important was going on. "Not yet."

"Wise choice, Captain Voorus," she said.

"What are you playing at?" Kyam asked her.

"Playing is such an excellent choice of words, Colonel Zul. Only this is no game. Think of it as the final act of a rather complicated – I suppose you'd call it a tragedy. In my eyes, it's a dark comedy, although I'm not inclined to laugh. For everyone else here, this is the conclusion of a rather dull morality play."

"Listen to that crowd outside! Let's arrest her and go," the lieutenant said.

"Silence, little brother." She spoke in careful Ponongese so he'd be sure to understand.

Humiliation flashed across his face before anger returned. "I don't – "

"You know very well what I said," she told him in Thampurian. "You're only a bit player in this, so stand there and pretend to be a concerned onlooker while the principals say their lines."

Fully enraged, he pointed in her direction. "Look at what she's sitting on! Rice! Let's take it!"

"Get your boy under control, Voorus."

Voorus' pained expression showed how exhausted he was. He carried on his duties, however. Her estimation of him rose a bit more.

"He has a point," Voorus said.

She tsked. "This is the Devil's rice. You would steal it? How very Thampurian of you. I'm afraid that I can't let that happen, though." She crooked her finger at the leader of Grandfather Zul's men.

They grumbled, but they shoved their way through the colonial militia. They stood in front of her, arms crossed over their chests.

"Let's see. I have thirty. You have" – she craned over the heads in front of her and took a quick count of the militia – "twenty-two. Outnumbered." Her bottom lip almost pushed out in a mock pout, but there was no need to overplay the scene. Kyam's mood, she noticed, had gone from loud anger to quiet seething.

"Surely – But you're Thampurians," Voorus said to the men protecting the rice.

"You'd be surprised what a Thampurian is willing to let happen for the sake of expediency, Captain."

From the way Kyam and Voorus flinched, she knew they'd both read layers of meaning into her statement.

"Why are you here? Why is the rice here? Don't go on like you always do. Just tell me what's happening," Voorus demanded.

Kyam's dark eyes narrowed as he looked between Voorus and QuiTai. He slammed his palm against the governor's desk. "Damn it, QuiTai. Stop with the games or the play or whatever elaborate stunt you're trying to pull and tell us what's going on here."

The rabble outside chose that moment to begin a chant. They had, she thought, a rather good sense of timing.

"As a concerned citizen, albeit one without full rights..."

Kyam's thick brows drew together. She swore he growled. This was no time for him to flirt with her.

"I'm here to alleviate the suffering of the Thampurian people; which, you'll have to admit, is rather generous of me."

She held back a wince. She'd meant to say it was generous of the Devil. The other men in the room didn't worry her, but she had to be careful to evoke the Devil as a distinct person from herself or Kyam might catch onto her slips. Maybe he wouldn't now, because he was too angry to think straight, but later he would probably reflect on this conversation many times and the pattern would become clear.

"And out of character. What's the catch?" Kyam asked.

Voorus also watched her. The rest of the men cast nervous glances at the typhoon shutters as the crowd outside grew louder.

QuiTai batted her eyelashes at Kyam. "None." She waited until his shoulders slightly relaxed to add, "Well, maybe one."

"Of course there is." The muscles along his jaw clenched.

"I don't like being forced to do this, but at least I know the ramifications of my actions. Because of our history, I'm going to extend that courtesy to you. Your grandfather would not be as kind." Oh, how he glared at her! "When you give this rice to the mob out there, you will be signing your fate, Colonel Zul."

Grandfather Zul's men turned to watch her. They were suspicious, but didn't seem to know if they should stop her.

"And what fate is that?" Kyam asked.

"You'll become the next Governor of Ponong."

Kyam laughed, but stopped when he saw she was serious. "Assume I'll never put the pieces of the bigger picture together and tell me why you think that will happen."

"Word will reach Thampur that you stopped a rice riot and acted decisively in the absence of leadership by the current governor. The groundwork has been laid for this decision. The right words have been whispered into your king's ear. All that needs happen is for you to play your role, to be the hero in the hour of need."

"What if I refuse?"

He was listening. That was a relief.

QuiTai gestured to the men in front of her. "They won't let you. If they have to, they will drag you out in front of the crowd and tell them you were the one who brought them rice. Won't you, gentlemen?"

Grandfather Zul's men obviously didn't like where the conversation headed, but they didn't know if they should stop her. She'd tricked them into leaving their field farwriter at LiHoun's, so they couldn't ask Grandfather Zul for advice. They didn't strike her as the sort who would remember there was a room full of farwriters on the first floor of this building. There was probably even one in the governor's office, but like the one in Hadre's cabin on the *Golden Barracuda*, it was hidden behind a panel. Without guidance, they were hers to manipulate.

"What if I drag Governor Turyat here and tell him to give the rice to the mob?" Kyam asked.

Poor Kyam. He hadn't had the benefit of a long night to mull over every aspect of her plan. If there was a way out for him she hadn't thought of, he wouldn't figure it out until too late either. Why did he fight her? He knew she would always be steps ahead of him.

"These men won't let you. But suppose you could talk

Captain Voorus and his men into attacking your Grandfather's thugs, and suppose you won. Suppose you were able to drag Governor Turyat out of his compound and through the mob to this building. What next? He would likely sell the rice to them and pocket the proceeds."

Kyam and the colonial militia harrumphed and grumbled, but not one defended Governor Turyat's character.

"Then word will get back to Thampur that he profited from a momentary spike in rice prices – "

"That you caused!" Kyam said.

"Oh, how very clever of you, Colonel Zul. Yes, the Devil is behind the current false shortage, although one must thank the rice merchants of Levapur for exploiting the situation and exacerbating it. There is no shortage of rice, as you can well see." She patted the sack of rice under her hand. "And the Devil only changed his price to match the legal price. Thampurian greed caused that." She pointed to the typhoon shutters.

The sounds of the mob outside grew louder with the passing moments. A group sang the Thampurian anthem, while another chanted for rice.

"You said, 'momentary spike in prices.'"

QuiTai clutched her hands to her heart. "Colonel Zul! You've learned to pay such close attention. I'm flattered. Yes, temporary price spike. Within two days, the regular rice shipments will reach this island. News travels fast, so already I assume smugglers have loaded their vessels with rice and are flying here under full sail to take advantage of the market. I predict within a week we'll be inundated with rice and the prices will drop; but that won't save you, because the Thampurians here will be so outraged by Governor Turyat's behavior that they'll demand he be replaced."

Kyam yanked the chair from behind the governor's desk and plopped into it. He was so desperate. He could probably feel the net tightening around him, but no matter how he struggled, he was ensnared.

"What if I force the governor to give away the rice?"

"Ah. Excellent point. A good solution. For you."

If only they were alone, she could remind him of his sense of honor. She would drop to her knees and plead if she had to. With so many witnesses, she could only hope he was the man she thought he was.

She jabbed her finger into the sack of rice under her hand. "If this doesn't end the way Grandfather Zul wants it to, he will use these men to continue to provoke my people until they rebel against Thampurian rule – and frankly, I've already done everything I can to stop it. This is my last play, Kyam. And I'm sorry that it doesn't have a happy ending for you, but that's a damn sight better than Ponongese and Thampurians dead in the streets."

"You love a good story, but where's the proof?"

"That was his original plan: start a rebellion, then have you quash it with the help of his men. Ask them." She gestured to Grandfather Zul's men.

The chair banged against the floor as Kyam got to his feet. He strode over to her. "Take that back! You lie. My grandfather would never do such a thing!"

"Gentlemen, did you attack Colonel Zul's neighbors last night on the orders of Grandfather Zul?"

They looked anywhere but at Kyam.

"Were your orders to kill them unless I agreed to obey Grandfather Zul?"

They still would not answer her.

"Did you attack innocent Ponongese in Old Levapur on the orders of Grandfather Zul? Did you shut down the schools and force the Ponongese out of the marketplace on the orders of Grandfather Zul and on his orders alone?"

"All lies!" Kyam shouted.

Voorus stepped forward. "I can vouch that what she says about the marketplace is true. Those orders never came from Governor Turyat. He even pleaded with them to stop. This man smirked when Governor Turyat warned him that the Ponongese might rebel. And even though I haven't been able to reach the governor for several days, I witnessed the attack on the Ponongese in Old Levapur, and I can tell you that the colonial militia wasn't involved. We stopped it. We were sickened by it."

"No!" Kyam looked stricken.

She knew how he felt. It wasn't easy to find out your gods were false. It was for his good, though. Kindness looked like cruelty sometimes.

"Walk away, Kyam. Leave this building right now. Get on a smugglers' ship and leave Ponong. I dare you to try."

Rhythmic pounding boomed through the building.

"The doors!" Voorus said. "The mob is attacking!"

"I suggest you dump the rice over the veranda railing into the mob, Kyam, because if they get into this building, they'll probably rip every one of you apart," QuiTai said.

Voorus paled as he no doubt recalled the aftermath of the Ponongese attack on the werewolves in the marketplace. "Listen to her. For the love of the Goddess of Mercy, listen to her." When Kyam didn't move, he signaled for his men to move forward.

Grandfather Zul's men pushed the militia back.

"When you stop being stubborn and decide that this is the only solution, do one thing for me, Mister Zul. Hold back some of this rice. West Levapur has been effectively cut off for over three days. I should think they've run out of food by now," QuiTai said.

Voorus went from pale to a shade close to death. "I forgot about them!"

"I'll bet you enjoyed imagining this," Kyam said to QuiTai.

"Oh, I am a complete villain, Colonel Zul. Evil incarnate. Your Grandfather could have simply exposed Governor Turyat and Chief Justice Cuulon's deal with the Ravidians to start a scandal that would have done the job; but no, he wanted extra insurance. He had to involve every living person in Levapur in his grand scheme and risk their lives. I may have sacrificed you, but he built the altar."

"Deal with her later, Zul! Help us get this rice to the mob!" Voorus and his men tried to get at the rice but couldn't break through Grandfather Zul's men.

The leader of Grandfather Zul's men said, "Colonel Zul, we're only allowed to let you take the rice. We have our orders."

It didn't matter that Kyam looked at her with such hate. All that mattered was that he knew now she'd told him the truth, even if he didn't want to believe it.

"I loathe you," he told QuiTai.

"Yes." It was done. He'd accepted his fate.

QuiTai slid off her perch. She tapped the arm of the man nearest her. "Gentlemen, please report to Grandfather Zul that I've upheld my end of the bargain. Tell him that I expect the slaves on Cay Rhi to be released immediately. Tell him I said, 'Well played.'"

Kyam grabbed a sack of rice. No one stopped him as he opened the typhoon shutters and headed out onto the veranda. "Calm down! We will get rice for you!" he shouted to the people below. A unified roar rose from them.

Voorus ran to the railing. "You better dump the rice over like she said. They'll kill us if we try to make them wait in lines. We don't have enough men to control them, even with your Grandfather's troops."

Kyam shot QuiTai a poisonous look before tossing the sack over the railing. A cry went up from the mob. Then the screaming began.

Kyam yelled, "Is that enough?" at his grandfather's men. "Can we have the rice now?"

Their leader nodded. They stepped aside.

That was victory enough for QuiTai. They'd never realized they confirmed everything she'd told Kyam about Grandfather Zul's part in this matter, but she could tell from Kyam's face that he saw the truth.

A vein throbbed at Kyam's temple, but now his anger split between her and his grandfather. "Then help us with the rice, or I swear I will kill every last one of you," he told his grandfather's men. "Come on, Voorus, let's get this over with."

The soldiers and Kyam grabbed as many sacks as they could carry and threw them over the railing.

It was, QuiTai decided, a very good time to exit the scene. She'd done what she'd promised. And if the mob overran the government building, she'd have a head start on them.

Kyam grabbed QuiTai's arm and dragged her out on the veranda. He gestured below. "Look at this! Look at them!"

Everywhere a rice sack fell, battles broke out over control of it. People who staggered away with a handful of rice were attacked as soon as they moved into the mob. Women and men knelt to pluck grains of rice out of the mud, their faces contorted in fear and desperation. The mob made sounds so primitive that the hairs stood up on her arms.

As the mob surged toward the plummeting sacks, people fell under the rush. She thought for a moment she recognized the school teacher Ma'am Thun below. It was hard enough to watch without making it personal. She lost track of the woman before she could verify who it was. Kyam was so very wrong thinking that she enjoyed any of this. It was horrible. Dread crept through her blood, which already pulsed with the urge to run as far away from here as she could.

QuiTai tried to pull away from Kyam as her stomach lurched. He shoved her against the wall and glowered down at her. Every deep breath pushed his chest against hers.

"Is this the Devil's plot or are you really working for my grandfather? The truth, or I swear I'll – "

"Working with your grandfather, but not for him."

He shook her hard. "Parsing words, as usual."

"Don't press so close, Colonel Zul. People will talk."

He snarled at her.

"We made an agreement on Cay Rhi. From now on, you work for your people, and I work for mine. There's no profit in this day's work. I'm giving your people rice. Remember that." She wrenched out of his bruising grip, but she suspected he let her go. "Remember who started this, and who brought it to an end."

"QuiTai! Grandfather Zul said to give you this message," the leader of Grandfather Zul's men shouted as she headed for the office door. "Governor Turyat and Chief Justice Cuulon hired Petrof. He said you'd know what that means."

Grandfather Zul ordered them to tell her that in front of witnesses? How stupid did he think she was?

"It means, gentlemen, that he wants me to clean up all loose ends for him so he won't get his hands dirty in this filthy affair. It's also a rather inelegant attempt to set me up for a murder charge. It seems he considers me one of those loose ends too. Tell him I give him thanks for the information, but I already knew; and no, I will not assassinate Governor Turyat and Chief Justice Cuulon for him. I leave them to the courts and Thampurian justice." She nodded sharply at Voorus. "My word on it."

She wouldn't look at Kyam. Regrets were the only things they might share now.

She walked out of the governor's office. Her footsteps echoed as she made her way to the back offices where she hoped to climb down to the street. The shouts of the mob were muffled but still frightening. The building's brass door held, but there were deep cracks in the wood around the hinges. That had been closer than she liked. It was such an ugly world sometimes.

Trembling, she rubbed her arms. It wasn't fear of the mob or what she'd seen in the town square that made her shake. She wasn't worried about the colonial militia or grandfather Zul's men. It was far more annoying than that. She'd always suffered from stage fright, and it had always been worse after she'd performed.

Jezereet had always laughed and held her face between her hands before kissing her. "You were wonderful! What are you so afraid of, *krith amaci*?"

"Nothing," QuiTai told Jezereet's ghost. "Not anymore."

She stepped into an office. Rows of desks piled high with files sat waiting for the workers who would return when peace was restored. It seemed so ordinary that the scene struck her as surreal. Was life really that normal for other people? They had no idea how lucky they were.

No more, she promised herself. No more adventures, no more grand schemes. Just a quiet, profitable, predictable life of crime. She'd stay as far away from the Zul clan as possible. She hoped once they realized what happened when they played high-stakes games with the Devil that they'd steer clear of her too.

She shook off her mood and lifted her chin.

Several hours from now, you will know that I kept my end of the bargain and created a hero for you, Grandfather Zul. As we agreed, I got everything I wanted too. But while you were distracted by my theatrical flourishes, I stole something precious from you. Maybe not today, but very soon, you'll find out I destroyed Kyam's faith in you. And now he's beginning to hate you as much as he hates me.

I win.

THE END